FACING EAST

A Novel

Stepheny Forgue Houghtlin

Also by Stepheny Houghtlin

Greening of a Heart

Sanibel Press
ISBN-13: 978-0692406748
ISBN-10: 0692406743

For My Parents

Madeline Thompson Forgue

Norman William Forgue

You wandered down the lane and far away

leaving me a song that will not die

Stardust

Hoagy Carmichael

Facing East

1

Our childhoods finally come to an end when there is no one left who dreams of us as children. This thought occurred to Katherine White when she awakened from a dream of her grown daughter in pink cotton underpants running through the sprinkler on a hot summer afternoon. In the dream, Louisa appeared exactly as she had looked on that day, soaking wet and laughing. Katherine wondered if these childhood memories, archived in a parent's dreams, added to the length of time it takes to grow up.

When Katherine became a widow, she said it felt like someone placed two strong hands on her back and gave her a hard shove across the "growing up" finish line. Breaking through the tape, tears streaming, there was no one to catch her as she stumbled to the ground. Sitting there in her ashes, she was afraid. Did widowhood mean that once and for all, she must leave behind the carefree and irresponsible girl she had once been; the girl slathered in baby oil and iodine, sitting on a towel at one of Evanston's beaches, while waiting to be discovered?

Katherine wouldn't have found it necessary to move to Chicago if on the morning Timothy died, she had pinned a note on his lapel that said, *Return to Me.* He would have come home on this ordinary Saturday morning that was woven into the fabric of their lives. Saturday, the day when Timothy headed to the hospital to check on his surgical patients, and spend an extra hour catching up on paper work. Thinking back, Katherine could recall the sun shining through the glass in the French doors, which cast sun blocks on the carpet, but she couldn't remember if either of them had said goodbye.

That morning, unbeknownst to Katherine, a woman, part of the cleaning staff at UNC Hospital, was making her way through the small offices that belonged to the doctors in the cardiology department. She was in the old wing of the hospital where the florescent lights buzzed behind plastic ceiling panels. Whatever the age of the linoleum floors, they looked like glass, a buffered sheen that was wearing the surface away a millimeter at a time. The cleaner reached Timothy's door, and rapped lightly. When there was no response, she used her master key to let herself in. She took several steps into the room before she looked up and found the doctor who occupied this office, slumped over his desk. His thermos was tipped over and coffee soaked the papers spread before him.

"Jesus, Mary and Joseph," she gasped and crossed herself, a motion that looked more like chicken scratching than the slow, deliberate tracing of the cross the man sprawled before her would have observed. Backing out of the office, she turned, and ran down the corridor calling for help.

Two nurses and a doctor tried resuscitation, but finally the doctor in attendance quietly pronounced their colleague dead. An hour had elapsed. A nurse went to find Douglas Raider, who was Dr. White's friend and neighbor, but was told he was still in emergency surgery. If they could reach Dr. Raider's wife, they would ask her to go next door with this shocking news. The nurse later said that it was a phone call she would never forget having to make. Others told Katherine where they were, and what they were doing when they heard Timothy had died. It reminded her of the day Kennedy was shot.

Johanna Raider was at home having a leisurely morning on the couch while her husband was at the hospital. She was still in her blue seersucker bathrobe that bore her monogram, her long narrow feet slipped into soft scuffs. Immersed in the deep Cornish setting of a Robert Goddard mystery, she begrudged the ringing telephone. For a moment she thought of ignoring the call, but a doctor's wife knows better; she picked up the receiver.

2

It was a one-sided conversation; the nurse delivering the news while Johanna listened in disbelief. When the call ended, she tried to struggle from the soft down-couch cushions, but her legs would not cooperate. It was several minutes before she tried again to go upstairs to dress.

Minutes later, Johanna cut through the holly hedge that separated their property from the Whites. Katherine had already exchanged her work gloves and pruners for a glass of ice tea. She was sitting on one of the heavy wrought iron patio chairs that Johanna had long ago labeled passive-aggressive menaces. "You try and move one of these suckers without getting black and blue marks on your legs!"

Katherine looked up from her book and waved. "Come have a glass of tea. I'm waiting for Timothy to get back from the hospital." Johanna's face crumbled.

Alarmed, Katherine rose from the chair. "What's the matter?"

"Oh, Lord, Katherine."

❖

When Louisa, Katherine's daughter, received the phone call about her father, she was at her office on Northwestern University's campus in Evanston, Illinois. She'd agreed to meet a grad student she was supervising. Her reward for coming in on Saturday, and for being patient with excuses for further delay in the student's work, was a blinding headache and the beginning of a scratchy sore throat. Avoiding both the flu and colds all winter, she emphatically told herself that she had no time to be sick in these last few weeks of school. Answering the phone, it was Johanna Raider, in a barely audible voice.

"There is no easy way to say this, Louisa." There was a pause. "They found your Dad at his hospital desk this morning. He had a heart attack."

"But he's going to be okay?"

"I'm sorry, honey, he's gone."

Louisa sat silent trying to understand what she was being told. When she began to cry, she kept repeating, "No, no, no."

Louisa, Clay, her husband, and her daughter, Beatrice in New York, coordinated airline tickets. They met in the baggage claim area at the Raleigh-Durham airport.

Johanna, trying to help Katherine pull herself together, encouraged her to focus on her family as a way of coping. "Being together will help all of you." And so far it had.

With Katherine's capricious turn of mind, she'd long personified the yellow Queen Anne house she'd lived in for thirty years. Located in the historic district of Chapel Hill, she often observed the house holding court for its neighbors. This evening, after Timothy's service, the beautiful, regal dwelling sat pale and stricken. The palpable sorrow behind its facade had caused Her Majesty to withdraw from all courtly responsibilities.

Close friends and family came back to the house, spilling onto the porch; the older folks were accorded seats on the wicker porch furniture. Anyone driving by might think the scene was staged, as if an artist had been commissioned to paint a canvas entitled, Americana. The American flag that hung from the front porch column lent itself to this old-fashion setting. After several hours, people began to leave.

Johanna remained behind. She stood with Katherine on the wraparound porch looking out on the front garden. "It's nice when the campus is quiet like this," she said.

"I love this reprieve between graduation and summer school. I found a parking space yesterday in front of University Florist on the first try."

"It always feels like the University is trying to find its center again with a yoga exercise, taking in, and slowly letting out a deep breath." Katherine smiled in appreciation for the thought.

"There's something reverential in the quiet this evening don't you think?" Johanna wiped away the moisture at the edges of her eyes with the back of her hand. "I'm sure it's out of respect for Timothy."

"I like the thought of that." Katherine turned towards Johanna. "He enjoyed siting out here this time of year with less traffic and more quiet."

"I'm sure people told you they were glad you'd hung Timothy's flag." Johanna didn't ask if Katherine would continue Timothy's ritual, displaying the American Flag between Memorial Day and Veterans Day.

"I thought of it before I left for the funeral and found it in the garage. I didn't realize it was this faded." Katherine dabbed the end of her nose with a Kleenex. "You know how it is when you make a European phone call, and there is that delay between speaking and hearing?" Johanna nodded yes. "One second, I thought, I'll buy Timothy a new flag for his birthday, and in the next second, I remembered what has happened."

Katherine left the railing of the porch and walked over to one of the wicker rocking chairs. "Come on, sit a minute more." Johanna pulled another rocker closer.

They sat in silence for several minutes and rocked. Johanna said, "I love the front garden in shadow like this. Can you smell the honeysuckle?"

Katherine put her hands over her face and let out a slight moan. It was several minutes before she looked up again. "I still can't believe this. To think in early March we were sitting here enjoying the forsythias and all the bulbs, blooming throughout the garden."

Katherine thought about Chapel Hill's last estimated frost date in April that had come and gone without incident. "It was such a spectacular spring. The early Star Magnolia blossoms had their full run."

Johanna motioned with her hand towards the back garden. "Those plum trees you planted in the back that I love; their magenta flowers must have lasted a month."

"Even the Bradford Pears were an extravaganza." Katherine didn't agree with the tree's detractors, who believe them to be over-planted. At least not while they bloomed.

She pointed out into the fading light. "Timothy declared a moratorium on planting bulbs last Thanksgiving. "Enough is enough," were his exact words. Once the bulb catalogues started arriving, I knew he'd change his mind."

"You could plant more." Johanna was counting on the fact that the day would come when Katherine would put aside her grief and resume her gardening.

"Not on your life. There's a reason why you leave the bulbs to someone else, anything over a couple of dozen is back breaking." They both laughed, though Johanna, who didn't like to get her hands dirty, didn't ever plant anything in the ground.

"We'll see what you think about that in November," Johanna said. The screen door squeaked, and they looked up to see Beatrice, Katherine's granddaughter, standing silhouetted in the light. A petite young woman, she was standing in her bare feet, dressed in a sleeveless black dress. She looked like the child Johanna had watched grow up, who would occasionally awaken from a bad dream, and come looking for her grandmother.

Katherine called to her. "I see you gave up on those killer stiletto high heels." Beatrice's hair was now pulled back off her face in an elastic band, mascara smudged beneath her eyes. She crossed the porch and settled into another rocker beside the women.

"Mom sent me to check on you."

"How long have we been out here?" Katherine tried to read her watch in the dim light.

.   "Are you okay, Gran?" Beatrice asked.

"We've been talking about your Granddad's relentless bulb planting program."

Johanna stood. "Douglas will send the high sheriff out looking for me if I don't get home." Katherine clung to her friend while they said goodbye.

"I wouldn't have had this happen for the world."

"Nor I" was all Katherine could manage to reply.

2

The next morning Beatrice woke up on her back, the buttons of her cotton nightshirt undone and her arms thrown back on either side of the pillow. She heard the grandfather clock in the library strike fifteen minutes past some unknown hour; it felt early. She did not move, but listened to the fan whirring in the air conditioning system. She was in her grandparent's king-sized bed in the big house she'd visited every summer as long as she could remember. The chintz polished cotton fabrics were still the same, a Waverley pattern called, Spring Meadow. The name conjured images of tender new grasses and spring ephemerals where Beatrice could imagine the warmth of the sun on her face and bare arms.

In fact, her Grandmother's fabric and matching wallpaper had nothing to do with a spring meadow. On a white background a green vine repeated itself. Every few inches there were pink and yellow flowers tied on the vine with blue ribbons. Beatrice thought the entire space, filled with light, was romantic, still fresh and welcoming, the French doors across one wall its best feature. Her grandfather once told her all the flowers were a bit much for him, but she'd promised never to tell.

As a child, she'd slept many times here in her Grandparent's room, most often on a down quilt that was placed on the floor at the foot of the bed. Her Gran covered her late at night with a clean white sheet with an eyelet border. She'd always preferred to sleep in this room, rather than upstairs in the grandchildren's bedroom, with its twin beds and single window. Here, if not too hot, the door to the screen porch was left open and the ceiling fan, reversed for the summer, pushed gentle and soothing air over her, the night sounds entering the room to sing her to sleep. This morning, the day after her Grandfather's funeral, Beatrice was thankful little about the room had changed.

The house was quiet except for shower water running in the bathroom. Beatrice had stirred when her grandmother, a creature of habit, first crept from bed and left her to sleep. She was going outside in her nightgown, knowing she wouldn't be seen, to water the glazed pots on the patio. Beatrice admired her maternal grandmother's energy and enthusiasm for the many things in her life she was interested in. Beatrice thought about, and then dismissed the idea, that her Gran might not be able to take care of the garden without her grandfather's help. It was true that in recent photographs she looked a little older, but as Beatrice's mother, Louisa, had observed after a strenuous family trip, "She had no trouble staying the course."

Beatrice was pulling the sheets and blankets straight to make the bed when her Grandmother came out of the bathroom dressed, her hair still damp. She smiled and said, "I'm glad we had a slumber party. It's been a long time." She joined Beatrice to help, giving her own pillow a couple of shakes to redistribute the down feathers.

Beatrice repeated the ritual with her pillow and added a punch. "I dreamt about Granddad."

"Did he come to tell you goodbye?" Katherine stood straight after finishing her side of the bed.

"Yes, perhaps he did." Beatrice did not want to start the morning off making her grandmother sad, but took a chance and asked, "Do you remember when you and Granddad brought me that handkerchief from Italy? I called and asked you what I was supposed to do with it?"

"I think I said, 'Save it for a special occasion and tuck it in your purse.'"

"I brought it with me." They walked onto the screen porch and sat together on the wicker couch, the same couch Beatrice, as a child, watched TV on in her PJ's. This morning she sat in her nightgown.

"I remember I picked the hanky for you because it had the Lily of-the valley embroidered on a corner. It was lovely."

9

Beatrice leaned her head over on her grandmother's shoulder. "You said you hoped I wouldn't forget the words to the song we used to sing when we traveled in the car."

Katherine began to sing, (*"White coral bells upon a slender stalk, lily of the valley deck my garden walk, oh don't you wish that you could hear them ring, that will only happen when the faeries sing."*) Beatrice joined in and they sang several more rounds of the song. This made them laugh, something they hadn't been able to do much of in several days.

Sitting for several more minutes, they held hands. Katherine finally said, "Let's go join your Mom and Dad. I think I smell coffee."

Beatrice was the first to ask the question that would need answering. "Your whole life revolves around this place, Gran, will you stay on in this big house by yourself?"

❁

Louisa sat at her father's desk in the library situated off the entry hall. She heard her mother opening the door off the family room leading onto the deck. She was going out to water the pots that had been newly planted at the beginning of April. There were half a dozen garden magazines lying around that contained articles and photographs that her mother had submitted. The latest issue of the Carolina Gardener magazine featured, The Joy of Container Planting by Katherine White.

Louisa wondered if her mother could manage the garden without her father's help. She thought of Victor, who through the years had worked for her parents, and made a mental note to ask about him.

This morning Louisa looked around the room through blurry eyes. Sentimental and family oriented, she'd spent many an hour in this room looking at the old photograph albums and listening to the stories about the black and white photographed faces that hung on one wall. The bookshelves were crammed full, favorite coffee table sized books lay piled on the library table situated in front of a large window that

10

looked out on the side garden. Two Windsor chairs were pulled haphazardly up to the table; a book her father must have been reading was left open displaying a French vegetable garden.

Both her parents encouraged Louisa's reading when she was growing up. It was a legacy they'd given her that she now faced without her father, who forever e-mailed book recommendations to her. Still in shock, Louisa felt sick. She got up from the desk chair and walked the few steps to the library table where she picked up her father's book, and held it against her chest.

This library was her father's domain, the place they called his hidey-hole. In this room he watched sports and movies that were too violent for her mother's taste. Here he managed the financial side of their lives, which he'd always done proficiently. To insure his claim on this room, he had additional bookshelves built in the family room where he encouraged Louisa's mother to shelve a large collection of garden books. It proved to be a great idea. The books, arranged by subject, were crowned with post-a-notes sticking up like an Anglican choirboy's ruffled collar.

Since the phone call Louisa received about her father's death, she had been on automatic pilot. The long day of the funeral the day before had finally gotten the best of her. She'd run out of resistance to fight a full-fledged cold. After yesterday's experience, Louisa now realized that the funerals she attended in the past, however regrettable and sad the occasions might have been, had touched her in a once removed sort of way. Never before had she been enveloped in this pall of sorrow and shock as she was now.

This time the pews were filled with friends and colleagues, who were there to say goodbye to her father. He was the one who had selected the hymns that were played, and the scriptures that were read, because he had previously left his wishes on record in the church office for the burial service that would one day be his own.

Louisa grew up worshiping at Chapel of the Cross, but her father's service had transformed the sanctuary from something familiar to a place of unrecognizable dimness. There seemed to be only a feeble light coming through the stained glass windows to light her way. It was incomprehensible that she followed her father's cremated ashes from the nave of the church outside to the columbarium. She stood there shivering in spite of the beautiful May day.

She had never fully appreciated the comfort that friends bring, with their laughter and stories, when stopping by the house after the reception at the church. Even if they never finished the food that was sitting in the refrigerator or wrapped in plastic on the counter tops, it was indeed a time-honored way to help the bereaved. It had helped her. Clay was eating a plate of cold fried chicken and potato salad when she'd taken her cold and gone to bed last night after an endless day.

Louisa moved to a chair next to the fireplace and gazed at the paintings on the library wall, for the most part watercolors by local artists. There were pieces of art throughout the house that her parents had collected on their occasional travels; art they bought to remind them of their adventures. These trips were hard to plan between her father's patients, and her mother's volunteer world. Staring into the empty space between herself and the art, she began to massage the back of her neck while tears slipped down her checks.

After the service people kept saying, "Your Dad was a wonderful guy, Louisa." Father Williams said in his homily, "Timothy White was a complex man, extroverted, with a keen sense of humor, and a brilliant mind. So many of you have mentioned how unfair it seems that one of the top cardiac specialists in the country should die of a cardiac infarction." Louisa agreed; it was unfair!

While she listened to Father Williams talk about her father's attributes, she'd thought of her own certainties about him. He'd always been there for her, loved her, and cheered her on. People say 'that time heals.' Here in her father's chair, smelling faintly of his aftershave cologne, she hoped this was true.

3

Three days after the funeral Katherine drove her family to the airport. It was a hasty parting, grabbing luggage out of the back of the car and kissing one last time. Weeping, Katherine got back in her car to drive back home. She knew she was driving too slowly for interstate traffic, but crying made it a dangerous way to travel, even in the right hand lane. A man in a black Suburban sent her a loud and clear message when she reached Exit 273 by waving goodbye with one finger.

In the dusk of this first evening on her own, only Willie Nelson would do. In the family room, Katherine found the Stardust CD near the top of a stack next to the CD player. She put the disc in and turned up the volume. Nelson's plaintive voice drifted out the French doors and followed Katherine across the patio where she stood swaying with the music. (*Sometimes I wonder why I spend the lonely night, dreaming of a song, the melody haunts my reverie, and I am once again with you.*)

Stardust had been one of her father's favorite songs. Whenever she listened to this music, it transported her to the back seat of her parents car, where she could listen to them sing. Her mother often said, "Before you could read or write, Katie, you knew all the words to songs like *Sunny Side of the Street* and *Georgia on my Mind.*"

One of Katherine's favorite family stories occurred when years later Louisa called to ask what Beatrice was talking about. "She keeps saying, "Sing comfy heart." Katherine broke the code when she remembered the opening lines to *Melancholy Baby*, a song she sang to her granddaughter. ("*Come sweetheart mine, don't sit and pine...*").

Tonight, as she swayed to the music, she wondered if in the mystery of things, her parents could look back from where they had slipped off, and recognize her voice singing along with Willie? Perhaps they would begin to sway too. Now would Timothy sing along?

Katherine could not imagine her life without this music that had helped to shape her life. She once told Timothy, "I feel sorry for the kids today with the kind of music they listen to. Hardly romantic is it? I bet none of the boys sing in a girls ear these days, not like the boys I danced with."

"Like me!" Timothy had waltzed her around the kitchen and whispered something in her ear to make her laugh.

Tonight, if not for this music on the Stardust CD, she was in danger of fading away like the final scene in a black and white movie when the heroine walks into the fog and disappears. *(when our love was new and each kiss an inspiration, but that was long ago, and now my consolation is in the stardust of a song.)*

When the song ended, Katherine remembered a Southern colloquialism she'd heard over the years: *'dead before he hit the floor.'* It was as if she jammed her foot on a gas pedal in a car, and in a matter of seconds, she'd accelerated from sweet nostalgia to outrage. "No!" she cried out. Timothy, who had saved so many lives, should not be dead.

Moaning, she crossed over and sat on a patio chair. She held her head in her hands for several minutes before she could look up and out upon the garden again. The cool late May evening kept watch over her until she was able to rise and go into the bed she had shared for the last forty years. On her bedside table lay a book by Thomas Merton, Trappist monk, whom Katherine read and admired. It was Merton that said solitude was necessary for *"the recovery of one's deep self."* Before Timothy's death this lovely phrase, so typical of Merton, sounded like a holy necessity. Now the notion of solitude had little to do with creating space in her life for prayer, but had everything to do with being alone.

❦

In the months that followed, Katherine began to feel that she'd been captured by people's fixed notions of who she was, which didn't allow for the fact that she might have changed, and was capable of new ideas and a shift in opinion. Even mere acquaintances felt they knew her because they'd heard her speak on a variety of topics. A few months prior to Timothy's death, Katherine received a phone call from a woman who was organizing a women's retreat.

"I appreciate the invite," Katherine said, " but I'm not sure I have anything new to say that would be of interest."

"You mustn't feel that way. When people hear you will be with us, they will sign up in droves."

With this kind of flattery, Katherine wound up agreeing to lead one of the morning meditations. She was still concerned that over-exposure had strapped her into a straight jacket, for which she had only herself to blame. She'd shared her spiritual journey with church people, her gardening passions with garden clubs, and her love of historical gardens with preservation groups. She'd done a lot of talking, perhaps too much. Katherine asked herself, *how am I ever going to catch up with who I've become?*

The morning of the retreat Katherine spoke about wisdom. Standing at the podium she said, "I once believed wisdom was something you could pull up along side of and take on board, like a container that sits on a shipping dock, but I've changed my mind. Now I compare wisdom to the standard equipment package that comes with our cars." People in the room were amused and chuckled.

"We've all been given an allotment of wisdom. The imperative is to learn how to access what's deep within our hearts." Katherine hoped the people taking notes would underline the idea that they were already wise.

"I realize now that I don't possess all the gifts God has to give, but, I know I have been given enough of them to live a full, rich, and interesting life."

After the lecture, a group of ladies stood round Katherine telling her how much they appreciated her words. "We want you to know we think of you as a wise woman."

Thinking back on the retreat after Timothy's death, she understood why people felt she was equipped to handle whatever came her way, including the death of her husband, even if that wasn't true.

Her close friends said, "You'll be just fine. You're the only woman we know who can reset the clocks on the electronics in the house." Even the clock in Katherine's car displayed the correct time.

On the May morning of Timothy's death, Katherine worried if she had enough of anything that would remotely equip her to deal with this loss. During the funeral she tried to imagine her own internal pipeline reaching the reservoir of still waters that Father Williams was praying about in the Twenty-Third Psalm. All she could reach was a well of sadness that seemed bottomless. In the days that followed, Katherine guessed that neither her family nor friends who had been sitting in the pews around her, were prepared when her normal exuberance lapsed into a persistent feeling that she'd lost an election by a vote of no confidence.

The only thing of solace was the maintenance of her garden where she invested what available energy she possessed. For the better part of a year her friends acted as cheerleaders in her life, but Katherine intuitively knew they were keeping a calendar having already decided among themselves an appropriate expiration date for her grief.

Katherine resumed her monthly spiritual direction visits with Father Williams at Chapel of the Cross. In the comfort of his study in the church offices, they would begin by sitting side by side in silence for a few minutes.

"How are you feeling Katherine?"

"I'm still having trouble concentrating. When I can't read, you know I'm in trouble."

"Let's have a prayer and then I have a question for you." Father Williams bowed his head. When he was finished, he said, "Tell me about your heart's desires, Katherine." He paused and let the request take hold. "Because these desires are what you have to be going on with."

It took a moment before Katherine could think of what to say. "I've never separated myself from my life with Timothy. There has never been Plan B. It was all of a piece, the seamless garment, which could not be divided." She knew Father Williams was amused by her biblical reference because he grinned at her.

"You need a Plan B now, Katherine. It's the only way this malaise you're feeling will shift."   Take a look into your heart and find what's worth noting."

"What if nothing comes readily to mind?"

"It will. Come back and see me when you have something to report."

Katherine felt that if she were asked the right questions, she could find her answers. The question of what desires she might have to be going on with, helped her to put her shoulder against a closed door and give it a nudge. An opening occurred, the door ajar. There was no other way Katherine could explain the idea of moving, which came to her one morning while she was making herself a pot of tea. Groggy after a bad night's sleep, tired of feeling tired, she thought, *I can wake up in any city, and be this unhappy, why not be unhappy in Chicago, its such a great place.* The fact that the area had once been home, and that Louisa lived close by, made this a reasonable possibility.

She told Father Williams during one of her subsequent visits, "There was a strategy in the school system called, 'best guess spelling,' which encouraged young children to write regardless of how they spelled. I have precious letters from Beatrice as proof of this encouragement."

"Then think of this decision to move as your 'best guess.' You will know if you have done the right thing after you get where you are going." Katherine liked this approach. She consulted no one else, but continued to pray and write down further options in her journal.

Over lunch one day at the drug store on Franklin Street, Katherine asked Johanna, "Notice anything different about me?" It took a minute, but Johanna said, "Have you lost your sunglasses?"

"Not lost. I saw my reflection in a plate glass window the other day. Why didn't you tell me those dark glasses made me look old?"

"That's not true."

"I got home and pitched them in the trash. Since then I've been wondering how much of what I've looked at all these years became altered because of those dark glasses?" Johanna didn't comment, but Katherine registered her puzzled look.

4

When the first anniversary of Timothy's death passed, Katherine was ready to talk. One night, riding home from the symphony, she turned to Johanna who was driving the car. "There is no easy way to tell you this, but I've made up my mind that I am going to sell the house and move to Chicago."

Pulling into Katherine's driveway, Johanna was at first speechless, but then she laughed. "You can't be serious."

"But, I am."

"Why haven't you said something?"

"I needed to sort this out myself."

"Without me? Have you forgotten I'm the friend who will take your part even if you rob a bank?"

Katherine grinned. "And, drive the get away car?"

"That too, I guess." Johanna sat silent for a moment. "I'm stunned, Katherine." You do realize you're running away. A geographical change is not the answer." Her reaction sounded sharp and critical.

Katherine snapped back. "My, don't we sound like an AA meeting," but then she answered Johanna's accusation with a story.

"I did run away once when I was eight years old from the summer cottage my parents owned in Michigan."

Johanna, who normally enjoyed Katherine's reminiscences, relented and asked, "How come?"

"I have no idea, but before slipping out the back screen door, I helped myself to a handful of plums from a bowl on the kitchen counter and put them in a brown paper bag. I headed into the cornfield behind the cottage." Katherine paused and savored the recollection.

"I've never forgotten the hot summer sun or the sound of flies buzzing in the heat, the uneven ground between the corn rows where I walked. By the time I reached the end of the field, I'd eaten all the fruit. It didn't take long to decide my running away was over. I turned around and went back to the cottage. No one noticed I'd been gone." Katherine finished her tale. "To this day, when I buy plums, I think of that long ago summer."

Johanna was not moved. "Chicago isn't exactly out the back door, my friend. How about a few weeks at the beach, it's a heck of a lot closer?"

"You'd help me pack my bags to have a free place to stay if I told you, I was moving to London."

Johanna managed a laugh. "Impractical, however. Being unhappy in London will cost you twice as much."

"You're right. No, Chicago it is. I'm going home."

"Look, I know we all have moments when running away seems a good idea. I've driven to the mall to shop in order to avoid a fall out with Douglas." She smiled. Katherine didn't feel like humoring her.

Johanna went on. "If you like, call it a flight into Egypt until all manner of things are right again, but moving? I can't fathom why you feel this is necessary, your life is here."

"I had a profound dream."

"And a Godlike voice said, 'Sell your home, leave your friends, and move back to snow and ice in Chicago?"

Katherine ignored the sarcasm. "I was sitting in a small theater that looked like the Chelsea. On the screen it seemed there was a scaled down Technicolor movie playing. A young man appeared and presented me with an infant. He stood and watched me hold the baby for some length of time. Finally he asked, 'What are you going to name the baby?' I had no answer. In a moment he said, 'You could call it Holy.'"

Johanna stared back. "I'm sorry, but what does this have to do with Chicago?"

"Over the next few weeks I tried to figure that out." Katherine did not explain that through the years she dreamed of babies or young children when something new was emerging in her life.

"Think about it, Johanna, do we dare proclaim anything about our lives holy, knowing everything we have done and left undone? It made me fidgety just thinking about it."

"I still don't see what this has to do with your decision."

"After Timothy died, Father Williams asked me if there were any desires left in my heart to be going on with? I felt sure there were not. I've been walking around this year in a haze, in shock, I suppose. No matter how hard I have tried to deny it, Timothy is gone. This dream suggests I can call a new life, *holy*." Katherine reached over and took Johanna's hand.

"It would mean a lot to me to have your support in this. Try and understand."

After a moment of silence, Johanna relented. "I want you to be happy."

In spite of saying this, in the weeks ahead, Katherine heard Johanna repeat in one form or another, "This is a fool hearty decision. Your life is here." Her attitude remained frosty. Katherine thought of it like ice on a windshield that takes a long time to defrost.

One afternoon after a cup of tea they stood together, Katherine washing the cups and Johanna drying. Looking out the window into the formal garden beyond the house, Johanna gave Katherine a little jab with her elbow. "I'm sorry I have been so difficult about all this. I have no right to make your decision harder than it must already be. If this were reversed, I know you would have cheered me on." She paused. "I have abandonment issues."

"You do not." They laughed at last.

Johanna took Katherine's hand for a split second before walking towards the back door. "I'm still not sure if you're courageous or a coward."

With the closing door, Johanna didn't hear Katherine call after her, "I prefer the courageous bit."

Katherine watched through the kitchen window as Johanna walked through the back garden towards the break in the hedge between their houses. Most of the time Katherine was able to forgive the fact that she hadn't been able to offer much consolation. She felt guilty. The two couples had talked many times about their plans together in retirement. If their roles were reversed, Katherine was sure she would feel guilty too.

Johanna's intractability wasn't surprising. She depended on Katherine. Even their mutual friends felt if they invited one of the women, they must invite both. Katherine never acknowledged the problem, deciding it was best to let her friends work it out.

Katherine had supported Johanna through breast cancer, the death of both her parents, and a failed first marriage. The summer evening the Whites invited Johanna to come along for hamburgers and music on the porch at The Carolina Inn was a night Johanna said she would be forever grateful. Douglas Raider was there too. She'd known Douglas over the years, but not well. Timothy was always saying, "He's the next door neighbor and friend everyone wishes they had."

Katherine was sure Johanna noticed the sudden increase in Douglas chatter. She kept dropping one-liners. "He's generous to a fault, he gives vast sums of money to worthy causes, he mentors young professional men and women, he serves on all these boards, and still has time to inquire about people's children, their aging parents, and offer them other kindnesses." Katherine's final comment was far from subtle. "Best of all, he has no discernible baggage that men of a certain age bring to a new relationship."

This night, the Carolina Inn porch was full of young college students and professionals having dinner. Over the years, people came and went, the faces of those who dined changed, but there was a sameness about them all. The same button down shirts with the sleeves cuffed back, the same khaki shorts or pants, the short hair, the girls in sundresses and flats, gold hoops hanging from their ears. Katherine found the exuberance of the young invigorating, and she liked to make plans on a Friday night because it seemed to make the weekend longer. That night Katherine and Johanna noticed that none of the young men were wearing socks with their loafers. "Perhaps you boys should do the same." Timothy and Douglas scoffed at the idea.

Douglas, who had never married, had let medicine take precedence over the women he'd been paired with. His actions this particular night indicated he might be ready to be captured by a beautiful woman. Six months later at The Fearington Inn, a wedding took place. Johanna sold her house in the Hope Valley area of-Durham the second day it went on the market, and moved into Douglas's home.

In the years that followed, the four friends made plans to grow old together with time to travel and pursue mutual interests. Since Timothy's death, Katherine could hardly help herself, and she was unable to help Johanna this time. They would both have to figure it out after Katherine moved.

5

Several meetings with Timothy's financial planner assured Katherine that she could face the future without concern. Her gratitude for Timothy's financial expertise left her tearful for the better part of a week. Grateful as she was with this news, in the months that followed, she made up her mind that she wanted to go back to work. One of her heart's desires, that did not seem splintered to pieces without Timothy, was returning to the book publishing business. Jacqueline Kennedy had done it, and so could she.

It was not in Katherine's nature to think it was too late to resume a career. She began a diligent search for current information on publishers in the Chicago area. Her out of date knowledge dated back to 1957. She'd finished her freshman year at Duke University, and applied for a summer job at Kroch's & Brentano's bookstore at 29 S. Wabash in Chicago. Forever after she declared, "I have had better paying and more prestigious opportunities, but Kroch's was the best job I ever had."

Through the years Katherine had occasion to tell her story about working at Kroch's. One evening she and Timothy were entertaining a few neighbors. Everyone was talking about books; not an uncommon subject in a University setting like Chapel Hill. Timothy was saying, "She's never met a bookstore she does not like, although why she bothers, I can't explain." He was referring to the large library of first editions of classic literature she'd inherited from her parents. Included in this windfall were a number of best sellers of the era. Timothy offered an obscure example of one of the titles. "She's got *Kon-Tiki* for God's sake."

"Thor Heyerdahl!" Katherine said proudly. "I read him in high school. Six men cross the Pacific on a raft, it's great."

Refilling wine glasses, Timothy, in high humor, said, "You have to understand, just entering a bookstore sends Katherine into some sort of nirvana with a look of sheer bliss on her face." Timothy got a laugh when he added, "I'm not sure I get a look like that on my best day."

It was then that the subject of Kroch's came up. These avid readers wanted to know more about what she'd done while working at the store. "I have Carl Kroch to thank for my summer jobs for three years. He took over the business his father started and merged what became Kroch & Brentano's."

"Working there must have been an education in and of itself," one of the friends commented.

"I learned a lot about art. There were paintings and photography displayed around the store. Kroch's was credited with the finest selection of art books in the region."

"They had her doing a bit of everything," Timothy added.

"I stocked shelves, checked people out at the cash register, helped set up the regular book signings with the major authors of the time. It was great fun."

One of the neighbors chimed in that he worked in Chicago after college and remembered the store. "The booksellers were famous for their knowledge. Different ages and personalities."

"They talked about every imaginable category of books. Unpacking boxes in the back of the store was an introduction to subjects I'd never thought about. Not even Duke could provide the kind of education I was given."

"Tell them about Alice." Timothy liked stories about little known people who made an impact in their fields.

Katherine explained, "One summer I worked under Alice Morimoto Goda, whose job it was to track down obscure out-of-print titles for customers around the world."

"Katherine became a depository of information that guarantees her a spot on a Trivial Pursuit team." Timothy grinned at her. Several of their friends promptly quizzed her and proved Timothy's point.

"My parents bragged to their friends that I was getting a great education that for once they did not have to pay for."

The same neighbor who'd lived in Chicago said, "I couldn't believe it when they finally closed. I'm pretty sure it was 1995. Kroch's was a destination in Chicago."

"You're right. I was visiting Louisa and her family when Kroch's & Brentano's closed its doors. I made a special pilgrimage downtown to attend the final book signing they were having. The author was heavyweight-boxing champion George Foreman who was promoting his autobiography, *By George.* I even remember the name of the employee, Hans Summers, who is credited with waiting on the final customer."

"Why remember that name?" Everyone was still seated around the dining room table enjoying a second bottle of wine.

"I always thought he would make a great premise for a short story."

One of the neighbors asked, "Why in the world did they close the bookstore if it was so touted?"

"Believe it or not, the 'full service' that Kroch's prided themselves on could no longer compete with discount bookstores like Crown books that opened a few blocks north. That last night, I stood with a small group of people outside on the street. We looked like a group of mourners. There was an older woman who talked to us in a quiet, refined voice. She reminded me of Barbara Bush with her white hair and a double strand of pearls. I've never forgotten the scene or her, though I never saw her again."

Katherine tried to make her voice sound wispy. "My dears, we're saying goodnight to a piece of Chicago history." Of course, we all nodded in agreement and murmured things like, "It's such a shame."

"She mentioned S.C. Griggs, a Chicagoan, who became the nation's largest domestic book publisher, and A.C. McClurg who followed him, for what evolved into Kroch & Brentano's."

"There was a Brooks-Brothers-type young man who spoke up. Gesturing towards the tall woman he was standing with, he told us that they lived in one of the twin story towers at McClurg Court Center. New to the city they had no idea who McClurg was. I dare say most people today don't know McClurg's story."

"The woman who was talking with us asked him if he was familiar with *Tarzan of the Apes*?" She smiled at her small audience. We smiled back because we all knew where she was going with the question.

"Edgar Rice Burroughs, the Oak Park native, brought McClurg's firm their most lucrative publishing deal with that book."

"Wonder what the old Tarzan comics are worth these days?" Timothy asked.

"Eventually we all shook hands, and wished each other well before walking away. We said our goodbyes to this privately owned bookstore. It was a sad ending for a place that pioneered ideas of store design and book displays." Katherine added a final pronouncement on Kroch's. "They will remain an important chapter in the Chicago book world."

❋

Nearly two years after Timothy's death, the closing date for the sale of their home was set. Katherine was confident there would be no last minute problems with the sale; she made her plans accordingly. It was time to place a call to Robert Davis, the son of her parents' oldest friends. He'd been several grades ahead of her in school, but they'd spent hours together reading and playing board games while their parents remained at the dinner table talking or once a month playing poker. Katherine followed Robert to Duke.

Though her research was invaluable in regards to the current state of affairs in the Chicago publishing world, Robert remained the logical person to approach about a job. He'd taken over his parents' business and had been running Davis Publishing for years. When she placed the call, a receptionist informed her that Mr. Davis was away at a conference, and could be reached the following week. Eight days later she was put through to him.

"Katherine, is this really you?"

"It is indeed."

"Are you in town?"

"I will be shortly."

"Bring a warm coat. It's April 9th and we're having snow flurries this morning." He laughed. "Don't tell the Chamber of Commerce I told you that."

After fifteen minutes of genial conversation, Katherine finally asked, "Any chance you have a spot in the firm for an up and coming editor with prospects?"

"You're looking for a job?"

"I want to go to work, Robert." They talked further, and though he graciously acknowledged her talent, and was sorry, he had nothing to offer.

"Let me ask around and see if there is anything out there you might be interested in. After you are settled, call me."

That night Louisa phoned. "I'm checking on you, Mom. Did you reach your friend, Robert Davis?"

"Staying in touch seems to have meant as much to him, as it has to me. We've always managed Christmas cards if nothing else." Katherine had often told Louisa the story of Robert's parents, Ruth and William Davis. They were both academics at Northwestern University when they first became friends with Katherine's parents.

"I think of them sometimes when I walk across campus. That would surprise Robert."

"Most of their friends, when they were not at their day jobs, were aspiring writers and artists."

"Wasn't it the mid 1940's, when some of those friends financially backed them?"

"None of them had any real background in the publishing business, but the Davis' began what they envisioned as an old-fashioned publishing house. They wanted to bring back worthwhile, out-of-print books, and to introduce new writers who had been rejected by big publishers."

"What I could never get over was the fact that in the beginning, they edited and designed the books themselves. You told me they stored and packed them for mailing from the basement of their home on Sheridan Road in Kenilworth."

"Not only that, but they hand delivered books in Chicago and area suburbs in the early years of their business. Hard to believe when you think about it." Continuing to talk, Katherine began to wander through the empty rooms of her home. Only the furniture remained in place. There were boxes piled in neat stacks waiting to be put on the moving van.

"When I was packing books last week, I found a piece of ephemera tucked in one of their books."

"One of their books you gave me has an obit in it. I've walked over and taken it off the bookshelf. It says, 'Ruth and William Davis continued to select and publish what was dear to their hearts. Children's books, feminist books, and new editions of hard to come by literary treasures from the past.' It says here that in an early interview, Ruth Davis said, 'We will be publishing exciting, new and well-crafted fiction and nonfiction.'"

"It was an ambitious and naive undertaking for two people with zero background in the publishing business. Legends like Leonard and Virginia Woolf cast long shadows over people like the Davises."

"1917 was a far simpler time when The Hogarth Press started in London."

"Which was filled with independent bookshops, but William Davis believed a good book could make its own way, and that if they could sell quality reprints and new fiction, which was their core vision for this undertaking, they would succeed."

"I still find the whole thing implausible," Louisa interjected. "Neither of them knew how difficult it would be for a new publisher to get books into bookstores or libraries. Imagine finding out the hard way that librarians depend on reviews when selecting books for the library. Novice writers garner few of those."

"They also discovered that booksellers rely on publisher representatives, salespeople around the country who act as liaisons providing a publisher's catalogue that the salesperson can sit down with a bookstore owner or the acquisition person at the library, and encourage selections. It took them several years to finally realize that peddling their own books was frowned upon."

"As I said, it's a wonder they survived."

"In later years they admitted that if they'd known about the difficulty of finding good sales people, mostly men then, they might not have gone forward. They found out the hard way that Davis Publishing, with no representative to urge payment, got sent to the back of the line to wait for their money."

Katherine went on. "Somehow, they continued to issue neglected classics by women and eventually offered their first original mystery, which was well received. They later sold the paperback rights to that book to Bantam in New York. It took time, but they found and hired a regional sales force. Robert and I talked this morning about the fact that after he graduated he headed up the Midwest Sales. He said they kept sending notices to John Collier, who wrote for the New York Times Book Review, who finally recognized Davis Publishing in an article."

"I doubt he could have learned the business from two more dedicated and hard working people. I bet no one ever questioned where his future lay."

"I took some ribbing from him when I went to work for the University of North Carolina Press after graduation. I paid him no attention. It was the Carolina-Duke thing. Duke grad or not, I was proud to be a part of a publishing house that thirteen faculty members

31

and trustees chartered. They became the first university press in the South. I worked while your Dad was finishing up his training. and after you were born."

"It sounds like the two of you had a nice time reminiscing."

"I'll get back in touch with him once I'm settled."

That night laying awake in the dark, Katherine resigned herself to the fact that she was moving to Chicago without employment. Oddly enough, she felt encouraged because Robert had not laughed at her. At least he did not say out loud, "You're too old to get hired." The phone conversation felt like the Bartlett Tree Company had been called in to make an opening in the tree canopy. Robert had allowed light to shine on her new path. Turning on her side, Katherine would continue to say her prayers, cross her fingers, and hope that something turned up.

She attended a final round of parties a week prior to the move. It was exhausting from an emotional standpoint. Friends were still aghast. "We can't believe you're going back to all that cold and snow?"

"Ah, but you forget about global warming," her intentionally glib reply. One thing she would not miss about Chapel Hill was the academic liberals and their latest rants. Saying goodbye to the things she and Timothy had shared was the worst part of this time. They'd raised a daughter, created a history that defined over forty years of knowing each other. Leaving their home, the garden that she had poured her soul into with Timothy's help, was gut wrenching. The last few days she couldn't face her daily stroll through the garden to check on things. She'd developed a persistent headache from weeping over every little thing. The packing men kept asking her if she was okay? Moving day she left the house for several hours and hid next door while Johanna came and supervised. Somehow she got through it.

When it came time to close the door and walk to her packed car sitting in the driveway, she was all but hyperventilating. Certain as she could be of this decision to move, she would never be able to explain what it was costing her to execute. She must try and handle these changes in the best possible fashion, best foot forward and all that. She reminded herself that Jesus was waiting on this new road beckoning to her. She wouldn't look back as she pulled onto Franklin Street; she already felt like a pillar of salt as she licked her lips, tears running down her face.

6

When Katherine returned to the 'Windy City' in June, the familiar
scenes along Lake Michigan greeted her as if she'd never been away.
The views of the lake and lovely parks that she'd loved as a child
seemed unaltered. Even the Lincoln Park Totem Pole that James Kraft
had given the city had been replicated.

Tourists were still selecting and mailing beautiful boat marina post
cards. Best of all, she found in good weather, people of all ages still
walked along the lakefront paths with children in their strollers and
leashed dogs in tow. These paths were the closest thing Chicagoans
had to a lovely Italian piazza where in the evening people make their
passeggiata. She could hardly wait to join them for an evening stroll.

Important to this lake front scene are the elegant apartment
buildings that line the West Side of Lake Shore Drive. Katherine grew
up wondering about the people who lived in these expensive
properties, always enthralled with the exquisite interior photographs in
a magazine like Architectural Digest. She imagined an urban and
sophisticated couple saying good evening to their doorman before
asking him to hail a taxi to take them to some smart and expensive
restaurant. Given Katherine's disposition, she believed the occupants of
these lovely buildings were living rich and interesting lives in a
beautiful and fascinating city. Now Katherine owned one of these
amazing apartments. She selected the historic Gold Coast area to move
to, part
of Chicago's Near North Side community, roughly bounded by North
Avenue, Lake Shore Drive, Oak and Clark Streets.

In the late 1980s, the Gold Coast and neighboring Streeterville had
been the second most-affluent neighborhood in the United States. She
suspected that Louisa and Clay questioned what a woman of her age,
and widowed at that, could be thinking when she bought an apartment
in one of these high-rise buildings in the mixed neighborhood of

mansions and row houses. They did not verbalize their concerns in front of her, but she'd caught several looks pass between them.

She didn't try to explain that she was ready to embrace a new and meaningful life that was still in front of her. She was afraid it would appear insensitive to Louisa, who was still grieving the loss of her father. Even with no doorman, and hailing her own cabs, she'd made up her mind to find out how 'beautiful and interesting' life might be as seen from her east facing windows that provided views of the lake.

It did not bother Katherine that the city might have a reputation for political corruption. The city's arts and architecture, diversity of population, cleanliness, and excellent public transportation was what mattered to her. It all contributed to Chicago's personality. Mayor Daley dubbed it the "city that works." It worked for Katherine.

She stood at the sink in her new kitchen arranging flowers a month later. She was celebrating the final departure of the workmen who'd finished their painting, replacing carpet and drapery installations. The momentum of her move, the obsession with getting the details right had taken up most of this time since her arrival. With the workmen out of her life, the enormity of everything that had taken place hit Katherine with the magnitude of cold water pouring from her new Rain-Forest showerhead. The intensity of purpose that had driven her since making the decision to leave Chapel Hill evaporated. Setting the flower arrangement on the coffee table, she made it no further than the living room couch. There she wrapped herself in the pale yellow cashmere throw that was draped over the arm of the couch, and cried herself to sleep.

❁

On the last Saturday in August, Katherine grabbed a book and headed for the Lincoln Park Zoo. Chicagoans were luxuriating in perfect lakefront weather. A cloudless blue sky greeted her as she left the building to begin a walk up Lake Shore Drive. The occasional breeze ruffled her hair. Now and then she took her hand to smooth the blowing strands back in place. The humidity of August was lifting, which made this mild exercise all the more pleasurable. Entering the zoo, she walked along one of the many paths that were bordered by ample perennial plants. She took her camera out several times to photograph the salvia and phlox, white and fragrant. There were butterfly bushes and hydrangeas, black eyed Susan's, sedum and grasses. She was not sure how many people took the time to notice, but these gardens were an additional incentive to spend time at the zoo when she was in need of a garden fix.

She kept her eye out for a bench where she could claim an empty spot. She had to out pace a woman who looked like she was headed for the same vacant seat. Plopping down, Katherine's facial expression was one of innocent winner, engrossed in the scores of people milling around, including the lady that missed her chance. If not for a valuable lesson Katherine had learned, she would have lost out on this seat. When she first started using Chicago public transportation after moving back to the city, she was waiting at a CTA station with packages in each hand. Thinking she would let the other passengers on the platform get on first, she hung back as the riders rushed around her. When the doors closed in her face, and she was left standing on the platform with her mouth open, she realized her southern manners weren't going to help her catch a train, or in this case, find a bench to sit on.

Katherine settled in to watch the zoo enthusiasts. She envied the toddlers strapped into their strollers, heads back, mouths open, having their afternoon naps. How wonderful it would be to hitch a ride with one of them, and take a quick nap herself. Katherine hoped every child had someone to push them in a stroller, to push them on a swing, and someone to read to them. The brigade of strollers on parade indicated that at least one of these needs was being fulfilled.

When the people who walked by all began to look the same, she reached into her purse for the book she'd brought, and flipped it open. Her bookmark was a sales receipt from a shirt she'd bought on sale at Lord and Taylor. She read several chapters before her head began to nod, each time awakening her with a jerk. She finally deposited the book back in her bag and stood to find something cold to drink.

Walking among the crowd Katherine was sure she was having a Pentecostal experience. She lost count of the number of languages she was hearing. She was a strong proponent that people who come to the United States must learn English to insure their assimilation into the American way of life. Nonetheless, watching the number of Hispanic people enjoying an outing, she regretted she had not made better grades in Spanish class.

While growing up, Katherine had visited the zoo many times. Sipping the icy lemonade she'd bought, she wished her mother were here to walk beside her. Together, they could watch the zoo animals roam free, while the inhabitants looked out from their enclosures.

Countless times she'd walked by herself along the lake path from the Lincoln Park Gun Club, through a tunnel under the drive, and into the zoo. She shuttered to think in this day and time what could have happened to her. Now it seemed an unnecessary risk, but back when people did not lock their doors, children walked by themselves to and from school, and rode their bicycles everywhere; no one worried. Kids must have disappeared, bad things must have happened, but protected in a cocoon of innocence that growing up in the 1940s and 1950s provided, she had no memory of terrible things happening to either her or friends.

In these times, Katherine would not allow the little girl that remained within her, to slip off alone to see the monkeys. Like everyone else, she figuratively held tight to that little girl's hand and walked on among the fit and the unfit, the tattooed and face painted, alongside photographers strapped to cameras and beside young couples, hand in hand, wearing shorts and sandals. She had to pull her sunglasses from the top of her head to hide the tears that for some explicable reason welled up in her eyes.

Hopefully, the seals and elephants, the tigers and bears, would still be here after she was long gone. That in itself helped her through this unexpected sadness over the passing of time, loved ones gone, and the changes and losses of her life. She fell in behind several power-walking mothers who were pushing strollers as if they were on a mission. Katherine left the zoo to join friends at RJ Grunts for an early supper.

"Are you settling in?" A question her friends, who had remained in the Chicago area after graduation from Evanston Township High School, genuinely wanted to know.

"I keep waiting to recognize someone on the local TV news or read about a friend in the newspaper. How come all of you," she pointed around the table, "are not on the 6:00PM news?"

Katherine loved being back in Chicago, but at the same time she felt like a newly retired CEO who without work to define her, no longer knew who she was. She was surprised to find her identity in question. No longer a wife, no longer responsible for the myriad organizations she belonged to, no longer giving lectures or writing for *The Carolina Gardener*, she was adrift.

She'd worked as hard as any paid professional to earn respect, making a contribution that became a valuable asset to the organizations she was involved with. She was only now realizing how hard all of this was to lose considering the years it had taken her to build a reputation. It was an awkward time when she no longer belonged to where she'd come from, nor belonged to the place she'd arrived.

Katherine was determined to persevere. She was grateful for ensuing invitations from old friends. She enjoyed sitting around their dining room tables late into the night catching up on old times. They invited her to several philanthropic events where afterward, she became a member of The Art Institute, and bought season tickets for the Chicago Symphony and the Joffrey Ballet.

On the phone one day, Louisa said, "You hit the deck running, Mom. You won't have time to work, you realize that."

"It's not entirely clear how I'm going to create a new life now that I'm here, but I'm positive becoming a Volunteer Par Excellence all over again is not the answer.

"You still want to find a job?"

"I'm ready to call Robert Davis again. I hope he has a lead, but I'm prepared if this takes awhile."

The next morning, Katherine called Robert who sounded pleased. "Good morning. Are you all unpacked?"

"I am indeed. Though how I've managed it I don't know. I keep running to the windows to look at the lake. It changes color all the time. It's fantastic."

"I hope you'll invite me to have a look for myself."

"That's why I'm calling. I know it's short notice, but I wondered if you'd like to stop by after work? I can toss a salad and poach some salmon." Katherine heard a voice in the background.

"Excuse me a minute, will you?" While waiting, she glanced at the Tribune newspaper spread on the table next to her morning cup of tea. Robert came back on the phone. "Are you still there?"

"You must be busy, I won't keep you."

"I can't come tonight, Katherine, but would you invite me tomorrow night? I have some ideas I'd like to run past you." They agreed on seven o'clock the following evening.

Robert Davis arrived more handsome than Katherine remembered, though his hairline had receded, and he appeared a bit retro in his Madras plaid jacket. There was a weariness about him, a rather cautious step that seemed slower than need be. The minute he began to talk, however, still quick and funny, the changes she first noticed, disappeared. Katherine need not have worried over an awkward reunion, which only lasted the time it took to give each other a hug. They picked up where their telephone conversation from Chapel Hill had left off, the familiarity of a shared history taking over.

Over the light supper Katherine prepared, they agreed to a short recap of what they'd been doing since they'd seen each other last. Katherine sensed Robert was reticent about his personal life, so she offered to go first.

"Did you know that Louisa and her husband bought the house on Asbury?"

"I drive past there all the time on the way to visit friends in South Evanston. I always think of you and your parents." He smiled at Katherine. "They were always kind to me when we were growing up. I've wondered who owns the house."

"My only granddaughter has the room and bath that were once mine. Whenever I visit them I expect to find my mother in the breakfast room waiting to read to me as she did when I came home from school for lunch."

Robert, who grew up in Kenilworth Illinois, settled there with his bride after college. His routine mirrored his fathers' who commuted to the city on the Northwestern Railroad to the offices of Davis Publishing.

While Katherine experienced a loving marriage, Robert had been divorced for years. "I'm afraid the pressure I have always placed on myself, I inadvertently placed on her as well. It was too much on my easy going wife."

"I'm a bit of a perfectionist myself," Katherine admitted.

They continued to talk in the living room while dusk descended and the lake turned steel gray. Robert accepted a cookie from the plate he was offered and a refill on his after-dinner coffee. He went on to explain what had happened to his marriage.

"I like to think there were some good years, but with no children, Deborah had enough of my one track life. She left me the house, the dogs, some furniture, and moved back to Nashville and her Vanderbilt connections. A year later she remarried, and as far as I know, she is living happily ever after."

"I'm sorry, Robert, really I am." How lucky she had been to have a happy life with Timothy. A life she probably took for granted often enough.

Robert shifted in his chair to place his coffee cup on the little table beside him. "On to business, Katherine."

Katherine put her cup down as well and turned to give him her full attention.

" I have a job to offer you."

"You mean it? What happened after I called you from Chapel Hill?"

"I got smart." Robert grinned at her.

"This is stupendous, Robert. I'm thrilled." She clapped her hands.

"One of my senior editors, Vanessa Bolton, is leaving. If you want the job, you will be taking over some of her acquisitions. She began her career as an assistant manager in a bookstore." Robert knew of Katherine's experience at Kroch & Brentano's.

"Smart girl, I look forward to meeting her, but I'm sure you're sorry to lose her."

"She was working in sales and marketing at Scott Foresman when I hired her away ten years ago. She acquires adult fiction and nonfiction including autobiography and current events. Her passion has been women and girls fiction. She's moving to New York to join a recently acquired husband." Robert grinned.

"Will she be around long enough to show me the ropes?"

"If you can start right away, she will give you two weeks. You can decide what part of her work you would like to take on and I will move the rest to the other senior editors. Your title will be an editor with prospects. Isn't that what you called yourself when we talked over the phone?"

When Katherine phoned Louisa later that evening, she was giddy. "It has come to pass that like the shepherds abiding in the fields, I have been visited by an angel who has brought me news of great tidings." She paused for full effect, and then said, "Drum roll, please."

"How much wine have you had tonight?"

"Robert Davis offered me a job with a generous beginning salary, my own office, and a shared secretary. There is some flexibility in work hours if needed. I start right away."

"I'm happy for you, Mom. Wow, you must live right, you know that?"

"Evidently."

"Everything else okay?"

"Today turns out to be one of my good days."

❊

The welcome Katherine received on her first day lacked the warmth and enthusiasm of a North Carolina gathering. Instead it was a restrained and formal, *how do you do.* The disdain from one of the women in particular was obvious when Sandra Dune, an unmarried woman in her early forties, offered Katherine only the fingertips of her outstretched hand. "So you're the new protégé." She smirked and slipped into a chair at the conference room table where everyone else was now sitting.

Chapel Hill might have insulated Katherine from the competitive big city world, but she knew in an instant that Robert had slept with this plain looking woman with her aggressive and caustic manner, and not that long ago.

Robert motioned Katherine to the chair beside him with obvious pleasure, which left the staff wondering what she'd done to garner this invitation to sit, so to speak, at his right hand. Robert cleared his throat and got their attention. "Thank you for welcoming Katherine. We're fortunate to have her as I'm sure you will all agree once you get to know her."

Katherine smiled at the group around the table wondering if they had already guessed she had not been employed for a long time. Did

42

she appear as an aging woman whose friendship with their boss gave her a free pass around go? Certainly Sandra Dune, who sat frowning at her, thought this was the case. It was going to be up to Katherine to correct their miscalculations.

Robert started them all with a recap. "Katherine and I grew up together because our parents were best friends. Of course, neither of us were around when my parents outgrew their basement office and rented space in several turn of the century buildings in what we now call the old River North area of the city. The firm moved here to this location in the late seventies. Then as now, you know that Davis Publishing still believes in developing new writers and we will continue to focus on publishing titles with a lasting value."

Robert gave them a conspiratorial grin. "We have been known to take a chance on controversial subjects now and then, and a new hire like Katherine here, might seem to some of you who know how impossible it will be to fill Vanessa's spot, like taking another chance. I promise you, Katherine is a sure thing." Everyone but Sandra Dune gave Katherine a nod to indicate they were sure Robert was right.

Robert turned and looked directly at Katherine. "I will finish by saying that most of our bestselling books have been in print for at least twenty years. As publisher, I continue to acquire books and oversee our editorial and production staff." He reached over to shake Katherine's hand. "I know my parents would be proud of the midsize publisher we have become. Welcome aboard to a fellow book editor with prospects."

Katherine listened carefully as each of the editors explained how they fit into Davis Publishing. Sandra Dune spoke last and was introduced again as one of the senior editors. "I acquire adult and children's nonfiction, some popular science and activity books. That's about it for me." Katherine almost felt sorry for this woman. Regardless of her, ...um, editorial skills, Sandra Dune would not fool Robert into a marriage if that is what she was hoping for.

The first hour of Katherine's new job was sobering. To say she was no longer in Kansas, however clichéd that may be, said it all. She thought to herself, *Welcome to Chicago and to Davis Publishing.*

When the meeting adjourned, Robert beamed. "That went well, don't you think?"

"Quite well, thank you." In was a rude awakening for Katherine, whose reputation was nonexistent as far as these young people were concerned, and though they had nodded and smiled, Katherine guessed they were singularly unimpressed. Whether she was meant to hear, or not, Katherine heard Sandra Dune say to a coworker outside the conference room door, "She won't last. Robert will be sorry he took her on." In a few moments Katherine heard a door slam. She guessed at the significance of the noise.

7

Robert Davis was sitting at the same walnut table his father purchased in the late 1940's after he moved his publishing company from the basement of their home to Chicago. It had been in use in several locations ever since. Outside this corner conference room, surrounded on two sides by windows, fall was losing its yellow and red glow. Soon Robert would have to stop driving his old, but cherished, BMW downtown. He dreaded the smell of wet wool top coats and generously padded seat partners, the rattle of folded newspapers and the predictability of conversation while riding the same train, with the same people, everyday from Kenilworth into the city.

Driving in today he felt the exhilaration of still being able to be on his own, but this state of well being was fast disappearing while he sat in this nine o'clock meeting. Having set the highest standard for his own work, he expected the same from everyone else, and just now his staff was letting him down. No one seemed interested in the final details of Jessica Ann Lovejoy's latest book, the sole purpose of the author's flight from California to Chicago.

Robert observed Katherine from the corner of his eye and found her still staring out the window. It amazed him how this bright and enthusiastic woman had settled into her job almost over night. There had been maneuverings, as he liked to call them, while the other editors learned to share their toys. Katherine's maturity trumped their youth. She endured extreme rudeness from Sandra Dune, who liked to suggest that Katherine was not up to taking on any extra work, her age being what it was. Having had enough, Katherine's reply set a boundary Sandra couldn't tolerate.

"Don't be such an ass, Sandra. Acting like a quarrelsome teenager isn't necessary." It was not this comment that sealed the deal, but the fact that everyone laughed. Katherine proved to all of them that she deserved a seat at the table. When it became obvious that the authors she was working with liked her, and their manuscripts were improved, the battle was won. Robert's decision to hire her to take Vanessa's place was vindicated.

He felt no guilt when Sandra left the firm. Of course, Katherine knew nothing about the circumstances that led to her bad behavior, which was for the best. Sandra, seeing herself as a scorned woman, however unjustified, was no damn fun.

There was an unintended consequence with Katherine's arrival. Her presence highlighted the fact that his life had lapsed into a routine shuffle between home and the office. He saw a few friends on the weekends, but otherwise parked himself in front of his large TV screen watching sports or reading. Katherine's fervor to get up to speed with the learning curve helped Robert reengage, and his flagging energy revive. For these reasons he could cut her some slack this morning where she remained on the periphery of the discussion. When he noticed Jessica's visible irritation he took charge.

Robert caught up with Katherine as everyone left the conference room. "Stop by my office before you head out for lunch, will you?" Katherine followed along after him.

When the door to the office closed, Katherine said, "I wish you'd go in my place. I feel like I need a surf board when I'm with this girl."

Robert settled his erect six-foot frame into a worn green leather chair behind the desk. "You're looking at me, Robert, with the same pair of sparkling blue eyes that all the girls swooned over in the late 1950's at Duke, but this morning those eyes have narrowed. Am I being scrutinized?"

"Are you trying to give me a migraine?" Robert tried to give her his version of the evil eye.

"You ask me such a thing just because I was totally distracted in there? I'll have you know I can multitask."

"Don't try and look chagrined. As her editor, you don't have to like her to provide distance and experience. You know that."

"Easy for you to say."

"I want you to get along with her as you do with everyone else." Robert was now looking stern and formidable, but enjoying this banter they were both good at.

Katherine paid him no attention, but launched into her opinion about Jessica's work. "She has no aspirations to write literary novels, Robert. She's a commercial novelist concerned with plot gimmicks and making money."

"And, she's damn good at it."

Katherine laughed. "Well, you're right about that." Robert sat forward in his chair behind the desk. Wearing the same old, but expensive sport coat, along with a conservative striped tie and his customary white starched shirt, he began to laugh.

"So where were you this morning while the rest of us were being charming?" he asked.

Katherine answered, "Do you remember the Lincoln Park Gun Club?"

Robert appeared to be running through his mind-Rolodex searching for some relevance to Katherine's question. In fact, he knew a lot about the two-story whitewashed building at the mouth of Diversey Harbor where park land meet Lake Michigan, and was once home to the Lincoln Park Gun Club He surprised her when he said, "With amazing views of Chicago's skyline and the lake."

"I spent hours there as a child, while my parents shot skeet."

"Experts as I recall. Wasn't your mother an all-American?"

Katherine smiled and nodded, yes.

"I was thinking in the meeting about what a shame it is that they closed it."

47

"The environmentalists said that shooting clay pigeons out of the sky leaving the broken pieces to fall into the lake was bad. And then there was the shot from the shells. It closed in 1990."

"How do you remember that?"

"My computer chip is filled with useless information, that's why." He stood from his desk. "You better get going. Without rancor he added, "Behave yourself, will you?"

Katherine turned and waved before leaving his office. "Your last chance to go in my place."

Robert sat back down, feeling better after a brief skirmish with Katherine.

❀

Billed as 'Authentic Trattoria,' the sophisticated Italian-bar decor at Bartolini's is synonymous with Chicago, the kind of restaurant where the smell of garlic and pasta greet you at the door, and too much food is presented perfectly.

"Come right this way, Ladies." A man in his fifties, one of the storied Chicago male waiters that Bartolini employs, led them across the dining room. They passed tables of men dressed in expensive business suits and women clothed in designer slacks and smart jackets. Katherine blended seamlessly into the affluent atmosphere. Observing the plates of food on dish laden tables, she had no doubt that Jessica would order a healthy salad with dressing on the side, foregoing a delicious plate of spaghetti.

Seated, Katherine verbalized the observation she'd been thinking about as they made their way through the restaurant. "I'm afraid these Chicago-style waiters are a vanishing breed. They're known for hovering at a discreet distance and offering impeccable service." Though Jessica showed no interest in this bit of Chicago trivia, Katherine went on. "After years of all their faithful service, I hope the old waiters are in retirement homes out west of the city being well taken care of."

"Can you imagine how boring it must be talking about nothing but food and the celebrities they waited on." Jessica dismissed the subject with a smirk.

Katherine, who had sized Jessica up on her prior visits to the offices, knew she was never interested in much beyond herself. Mentally absent from the meeting earlier that morning, Katherine was determined to make it up to this self-absorbed woman. She started in again.

"I met a new author the other night. He said boys insist on playing games by the rules while girls tell a friend who's just struck out, 'Go ahead, take another turn.' I love that about us, don't you?"

She wondered if Jessica was sharp enough to sense that in telling this story, Katherine was offering her another turn at bat, to make a better impression than the one she'd made thus far. Instead Jessica was more interested in a basket of luscious warm bread that Tony placed on the table. He poured rosemary olive oil onto butter plates and shaved some fresh Parmesan cheese. "This smells delicious," was the only thing Jessica responded to.

In spite of the sunny day, it was barely sixty degrees outside. Katherine refrained from asking her if she was cold wearing only a black sleeveless dress.

While they waited for their lunch to be served, Jessica made some effort to tell Katherine about home. "I write in the mornings and play tennis every afternoon." By the look of Jessica's brown and toned arms, the tennis part must be true. Her bleached and damaged hair, dark roots showing, and pinned haphazardly on the back of her neck did not escape Katherine's notice. Usually fond of young people, and tolerant of generational differences, Jessica's contrived carelessness was of no interest to Katherine.

Tony appeared and without speaking, set an oversized plate of Cobb Salad before Jessica. She did not acknowledge this in any way.

Katherine smiled up at him as he placed the large bowl of spaghetti and meat sauce in front of her. "This smells fantastic, thank you."

A thought came to Katherine while she inhaled the delectable aroma. She looked across the table as Jessica took her fork and mixed a small portion of the toppings onto one corner of her plate. She sensed Katherine was looking at her and looked up with a puzzled expression.

"Something wrong?" she asked.

"This aroma made me think of the spicy smell of incense in church on Holy Days. A few people always voice their objections to this sacramental by placing their hand over their mouth and coughing so others note their discomfort. I just realized that if the incense smelled like this meat sauce, perhaps they wouldn't cough." Katherine registered the blank look on Jessica's face.

Without comment, Jessica glanced around the room. "This restaurant reminds me of the scene in the new book."

"Ah, are we talking about Margaret, my favorite new protagonist?"

"The scene was a true story. I'd taken the train in from Evanston for a lunch date and was waiting on a bench near the front door of the restaurant. An attractive woman in her early thirties arrived with this entourage of four nice looking men, who swept in ahead of her, as if they were clearing a path. She was dressed in a black power suit, before we called them that, and had a great Dorothy Hamill haircut."

After a few bites of salad, Jessica continued. "Watching, it felt like this young woman was taking over the restaurant. It was obvious that whoever she was, she had it made. I, on the other hand, was renting an apartment in Evanston, trying to write my first book. I had no agent and only a writing group made up of Northwestern graduates and pals. I looked at this woman and thought, My God, what am I doing? I've landed in a rental apartment, mostly alone, and without much of a life. I want what this woman has; she's affluent, powerful."

A second glass of wine was poured and the wicker basket refilled with fresh bread. Though Jessica was a salad girl she'd eaten her fair share of the breadbasket. She went on with her story.

"As luck would have it, I saw her photograph in the Tribune a few months later. She should have sued them because it was a terrible picture. It reminded me of that expression, 'ridden hard and put up wet,' but I tore the picture out anyway and pinned it on my bulletin board above my writing desk. For the next several weeks I did some soul searching. I came to the conclusion that I still wanted to be a writer; I wasn't all that unhappy. If I kept at it, someday, I'd be successful too."

"Sounds like that woman helped you to reaffirm what you wanted out of life; you should dedicate the book to her." Katherine finished another bite of pasta. She looked across at Jessica. "Let's hope her life turned out better than Margaret's in your story."

"I doubt it. I've known women hell bent to succeed in a man's world. The life they set out to have is taken up with meetings and getting home from the office at 9:30 at night too tired to eat. I think she and Margaret could be one in the same."

"And you, unmarried, without children, are you telling me you are no longer happy with your choices, your life style, and the writing life?" Katherine instinctively knew she'd gone too far by the look on Jessica's face. A look that said she did not appreciate having this tail pinned on her donkey. Katherine quickly added, "What if you misread the entire scene that day?"

"The woman you saw in the restaurant was dressed in her St. John suit because that evening she was headed to the opening of an exhibit over at The Art Institute. She was dating a man who by now has become a famous artist; they married, soon after this picture was taken at the Saddle and Cycle Club near the Edgewater Beach Hotel, where, by the way, Eddie Waitkus was shot."

"Who's Eddie Waitkus?"

51

"Did you see the Robert Redford movie, The Natural?" Jessica stared back at Katherine with a look on her face that asked what baseball had to do with anything.

"You know, Roy Hobbs, Robert Redford? The movie was inspired by the shooting of Eddie Waitkus who was invited by a deranged woman into her hotel room with the purpose of murdering him. Waitkus survived to play again." Katherine amazed herself when extraneous information surfaced like this. Jessica showed no interest in this trivia.

Katherine returned to her narrative of the high-powered woman Jessica had based her character upon. "I bet you that today this beautiful CEO and her famous husband are living on Astor Street. She did sue the Tribune for printing that unflattering photograph and gave the money she was awarded to Northwestern Hospital for their women's cancer center. What about that scenario?"

"If you're telling me I need to do some rewriting, I would rather accept the terms we discussed this morning; Margaret stays in the book as is. How about that?"

With a genuine smile, Katherine appreciated Jessica's quick response. She was relieved that between them they had found a more lighthearted mood. It did not last.

"Katherine, you're not going to find me sitting next to you on the pew over on LaSalle street at your Episcopal church, but I do believe God sent you back to work just so I could get this book published."

Katherine's demeanor changed dramatically. "Yes, well, believe me, I would have come back with far less notice if that's what he wanted." She reached quickly into her purse for a tissue and dabbed at her eyes. Feeling embarrassed for both of them, she did not look at Jessica for a moment, but when she did, she found Jessica completely impervious to what she'd just said. Instead, she barged on. "I'm through with meetings after we sign the contracts this afternoon. I'm going home to recharge my batteries and start writing again."

...and play tennis, Katherine added silently. She signaled for the bill and complemented the waiter for taking good care of them. Her generous tip probably meant more, but Tony seemed genuinely pleased to have her approval.

Their luncheon had gone better than Katherine predicted. They were part way through their meal when she admitted to herself that Jessica's Northwestern University education had served her well. She liked her forthrightness. A glass of wine possibly helped Katherine slip off her high horse.

Settling into the cab headed back to the offices, Katherine was still recovering from her instantaneous brush with grief. As much as she enjoyed her work as an editor, the thought that the job came at Timothy's expense only served to scratch off a slow healing scab that took constant ointment to heal. Though discombobulated, Katherine did not want to end her time with Jessica as it had started. She managed to summon up enough energy to keep talking.

"When Margaret showed up on the pages of your manuscript, I wondered if she understood that the choices she was making involved a cost." Doubtful that Jessica would have given any thought to such things, she added, "I lived my twenties and thirties as if life were a free pass around go. In my forties, I began to understand that the decisions I'd already made were bearing consequences. It took me years before I accepted that all choices exact a price."

"Are we still talking about Margaret?" Jessica turned slightly towards Katherine in a rare moment of catching the nuances of a language she seldom applied to her writing.

"I'll leave that up to you." Katherine placed her hand over Jessica's and smiled.

The cab stopped in front of the building that housed Davis Publishing and the women got out. As Katherine started for the door, Jessica tugged on her arm to stop her. "Tell me one thing you know for sure about life. Maybe I'll turn it into my next novel."

There were impatient horns honking further down the block and people jostled them as they sidestepped around the two women standing in the middle of the sidewalk.

"I know I wouldn't trade places with anyone."

"You're a better man than I, Charlie Brown. There are numerous people I'd trade places with."

8

Katherine spent time with her daughter when their schedules allowed. She'd been looking forward to seeing Louisa all week. Making her way carefully down the steps at the Davis Street train station, Katherine reveled in this visit, and the invigorating fall air. The onset of October finally brought an end to the awkward fashion season. For as long as Katherine could remember, after Labor Day, regardless of the heat, the women of Chicago were in the habit of trotting out their transitional clothes. Today was the first day these darker, heavier materials, seemed suitable.

Katherine heard Louisa call, "Mom, I'm over here." She waved and headed towards the car. Depositing her overnight bag on the back seat, she climbed into what had been Timothy's brand new Audi, purchased a few months before his death. The car no longer smelled new, and riding in it no longer upset her. She leaned over and kissed Louisa.

"I was sitting here thinking how proud I am of you."

"What a nice welcome that is to hear."

"You shocked the fire out of me when you announced you were moving. Your contemporaries that live here are thinking about retirement and fleeing the cold. Here you are at the beginning of a new life."

"With you in Evanston, it made it a good idea, you know that, right?"

"It's been great. You look great. You're exhibiting flashes of your old self, which is great." Louisa saluted her mother.

"Thank you. The heavy hearted person I've been keeping company with does seem less cumbersome." She paused, laughed, and added, "Which is great."

Louisa asked, "Train ride out okay?" as she backed out of a parking space.

"I was thinking about Injun Summer on the train."

"You used to tell me that children waited every October for the Tribune to reprint McCutcheon's story."

"I'm pretty sure he copyrighted Injun Summer in 1912. The reprint was referred to as a cartoon, but it looked more like an illustration in a children's book. You've seen it, you know."

"After we came across that framed copy you have, when I came to help you pack, I told Beatrice about us sitting on the steps reading the story. She didn't know anything about it. I tried to describe it to her."

"Tell me how you explained the two illustrations." Katherine watched Louisa make up her mind to try.

"I'm not sure I can, you know it so well." Katherine reached over and gave Louisa's arm a pat of encouragement.

"In the first picture, an old man is sitting on a log talking to a little boy. They are looking across a field of harvested corn stalks that are stacked against one another. Smoke is rising from a small pile of burning leaves beside them. In the second illustration, the moon has transformed the scene. There are Indians dancing in the field around a camp fire and the corn stalks are now tepees."

Katherine joined Louisa and they said in unison, "Yep, sonny, this is sure enough Injun summer when all the homesick Injuns come back to play..." They grinned at one another.

Louisa drove west on Davis Street. "I thought you might like to eat at Hackney's."

"You can't imagine what a big deal it was to have a date in high school and drive out to Harms Road for their hamburger on dark rye bread."

"I know, Mom, you've said."

"I suppose I have." Katherine laughed.

Later, when they'd finished most of their dinner, Katherine looked at the large crowd in the bar area near the door waiting for a table. "I suppose we should hurry up?"

"Not until I tell you about Beatrice's phone call."

"Great, how is she?"

"She's met a young man in Greece and she thinks she's in love."

"Oh, Honey." The thought of Beatrice that far away brought tears to Katherine's eyes. "She wouldn't think of marrying and living there full time would she? You did tell her it was a bad idea."

"She's happy, Mom, starry-eyed. You know, first real love and all that."

"I don't wish to discuss 'and all that.' Let's go home and call her."

"I don't expect she'd appreciate hearing from us at this hour."

In her concern Katherine didn't consider the time difference. When they finally stood to leave, a party of four practically knocked them aside. Smiles asking for forgiveness and smiles indicating they understood, were exchanged. Nothing ever changed about Hackney's popularity.

They pulled out of Hackney's parking lot onto Harms Road. Harms woods along the west side of the road looked to Katherine as the woods always had, season after season. This time of year, the dark black trunks of the trees were topped with beautiful yellow, red and rust colors. It was a leaf collectors delight. Katherine knew exactly how the bridle trail wound through the trees near the road. Depending on which horse she owned at the time, she'd ridden these trails for years. Hobby Horse Stables was no longer, but Katherine could have gotten herself there in the dark with no problem. Louisa broke into Katherine's memories. "She sounded happy, Mom." And continued to placate her mother's fears the rest of the way home.

They pulled into the alley behind the house and drove up the driveway. The old green garage doors that once had to be opened by hand had been replaced with an automatic system. The door rolled back and they left the Audi in the middle of the two-car space. Katherine, without much success, was trying to convince herself that Beatrice's news was a temporary state of affairs.

She followed her daughter through the basement door and up the stairs to the first floor of the house. "I'm glad she is happy, but not at this price. To see her twice a year at best, that is if we're lucky; and when she has children, I guarantee, you won't want her in Greece." In spite of her best efforts, Katherine's voice pleaded. "If she could only wait, she'll outgrow this moment. She'll be someone else in a year's time with different needs and desires."

It was after midnight when Louisa knocked softly before opening the bedroom door between the master bedroom and Beatrice's room. "I saw your light was still on. Can't sleep?"

"No, come and sit with me. I keep thinking about Beatrice as a little girl; the playhouse, the European length dresses that tied in the back, those sweet round collars."

Though late when Louisa finally said goodnight, Katherine got the best night's rest she'd had in a long time knowing she was not alone. The next morning, still in her bathrobe, she brought a tray of tea and toast into the breakfast room where Louisa was reading the paper.

"I enjoyed leafing through your wedding album last night. I wish I still had that cranberry dress I loved so much." Katherine set the tray down on the table and slid into the chair across from her daughter.

Louisa smiled and reached for her mother's hand., "You know we could have done all that wedding shopping in Chapel Hill."

"I won't ever forget you looking at yourself in the mirror in the first dress you tried on, the budget flew out the window."

"You were very generous with Dad's Marshall Field's card as I recall." She hesitated and added, "I miss him a lot."

"I think about him everyday." Katherine gazed at her daughter. "There's something more you haven't told me, isn't there?"

"When Clay got ready to go back to Houston on this consulting job he's had down there, he told me that he has met someone, and isn't coming back." Louisa's face was a blank canvas.

"The day we bought my wedding dress I thought he was the pick of the litter. All my friends thought so too. We were wrong."

"Something was right, look at your wonderful daughter."

"Did Daddy like Clay?"

"It was what you wanted, and you seemed so sure. On paper, Clay was impressive; a respectable family, a Princeton graduate. I suppose that made it easier for us to trust your instincts about him."

"Where ever he worked, he was never happy. He always felt that he should be running the place. At first I believed he was under appreciated, but I got tired of hearing about jobs that were never good enough, and why he was still at home. I lost respect for him, Mom. He knew he could fall back on my good salary and trust fund."

Katherine sat quietly for a time holding Louisa's hand. "Then you must feel relieved that this is happening." Louisa nodded her head in agreement.

"I told him I hoped he would have a happy life."

"Yes, let's hope so." Katherine finished her tea. "There were times when your father and I wanted to say something, but we felt we should respect your reluctance to talk about things."

"I dread telling Beatrice. She loves her father."

"She's a big girl now. Big enough to fall in love with a boy living in Greece, I might add."

Louisa stood and came around the table to put her arms around her mother. "Yes, big enough even for that."

"Let's get showered and dressed. I'd love to take a walk around the neighborhood before it's time to go." Louisa unraveled herself from her mother's arms and dabbed at her eyes. "I feel better now that you know."

Climbing the stairs to their respective bathrooms, Louisa said, "Back then we were both a bit slimmer, Mom, but we've still got our natural curls and you still look beautiful in cranberry red."

"Promise me you won't offer Beatrice your wedding dress just yet."

"I promise."

9

With the approach of the holidays, Katherine began to struggle. She telephoned Johanna and invited her for a long weekend in December. She would make plans for her visit and hope that helped. She was making a few new friends in the building; ladies that were starting to include her in their impromptu meals. It was an unexpected surprise in a large building of city dwellers to find friends who knocked on the door with a covered bowl of home made soup. The few times the ladies talked about creating new lives, Katherine's confidence grew that her move had been the right "guess." Still they didn't share a history as she and Johanna did. It would be good to have an old friend come to visit.

Katherine admitted to Fr. Norris one Sunday after church that she was not looking forward to the holidays, especially Christmas. He advised her, "Concentrate on the reasons you have to be thankful, and it will see you through."

"I am thankful. I have my work, my new home, even without the doorman." Fr. Norris looked baffled by the reference to the doorman, but she offered no explanation.

"You see, you have a fine start on your list."

Thanksgiving day Katherine joined her daughter and guests in the dining room where she'd once sat as a little girl. She watched Louisa come back and forth through the swinging door from the butler's pantry and kitchen just as Louisa's grandmother had done before her. The holiday was not without a glitch. Louisa told her, "Don't bother to bring a dish for the dinner, Mom. I've got everything covered."

Before she could stop herself, Katherine cried out, "I always make ambrosia!"

"It's time for new traditions, Mom." Maybe it was.

When the day was over, Katherine wished Timothy could have enjoyed his daughter's gift of hospitality, and the excellent meal she prepared. Thanksgiving had turned out quite well.

In spite of Katherine's initial lack of enthusiasm for either holiday, Chicago at Christmas time was spectacular. Michigan Avenue was strung end to end with white fairy lights. The iconic Salvation Army bell ringers returned to their posts, their red buckets standing at the entrances to the stores. Katherine joined the throngs on State Street to see the Marshall Field's animated story windows. It took a week before a reservation was available for lunch in the Oak Room to sit in front of the Field's Christmas tree. The bouts of swirling lake effect snow that pelted shoppers, and the tired children they dragged behind, took on an Anton Pick quality to what she was seeing. Katherine loved it all, but without Timothy, she had no reason to recreate the lavish celebrations of the past.

The thought of hauling Christmas boxes from the storage area in the basement so soon after unpacking and putting things away did not interest Katherine either. Once Chapel Hill holidays were a Martha Stewart competition, but this year, all she wanted to do was put a red candle on the mantle and let it go at that.

❀

The second week of December, Johanna arrived. She waited in line for a taxi cab outside the baggage claim area at O'Hare Airport, watching a never ending loop of similar make and color of cars drive past. Not only did the cars look the same, but, everyone's luggage seemed identical except for the occasional black bag tied with colorful yarn. The cabs along the curbside appeared as yellow ribbon woven throughout the entire scene, ever changing, yet looking the same. It reminded Johanna of time-lapse photography, a kaleidoscope of streaming color. When she reached the front of the line, she opened the cab door and pushed her own black bag across the seat and slid in.

A young driver, who needed a shave, eyed Johanna in his rear view mirror. He did not smile, but his eyes gave her hope that they would be able to communicate. She leaned forward on the seat and gave him Katherine's address on Lake Shore Drive. The young man nodded that he understood. Settling back, Johanna glanced at her watch and made a quick decision. She leaned forward again. "Before you let me off, I'd like to drive through the Gold Coast neighborhood for some sightseeing." Johanna wanted a sneak preview of the area Katherine now called home.

The driver replied in perfect English, "Sit back and enjoy the ride, Madam," and merged the cab into the lanes with the over-head green sign marked, Chicago and the Kennedy Expressway. Johanna, slightly embarrassed by her assumption that the driver was a foreigner, who could not speak or understand English, kept an eye on him, nonetheless. When she traveled, she tried to give the impression that she was a senior citizen to be reckoned with. In this case, she knew the airport was seventeen miles northwest of the Loop, and they should turn east towards Lake Michigan at North Avenue. Vigilant, she leaned against the cracked leather upholstery and waited for the Chicago skyline to appear ahead of her.

"First time to Chicago?" The cab driver looked at her in his rear view mirror. She pretended not to hear him, too intent looking out the window to have heard him. It might not be safe to tell him that it was her first time. He could drive somewhere and harm her, steal her money, leave her in an alley to die; she'd read about such things. He didn't ask her anything more; they drove on in silence. Less than a half hour later, after exiting the Kennedy and heading east on North Avenue, she was startled when the cab driver began to tell her interesting information about the area of the city she was seeing.

"It's hard to imagine this area was once swampland and that the local doctors thought the nearby cemetery was a health risk."

"Why was that?" Johanna's curiosity overcame her reticence.

"Shallow graves where smallpox victims were buried."

"My friend told me the Palmer House people built a mansion along here."

"You're looking at some of the few remaining ones left along Lake Shore Drive. They started replacing them with these high-rise buildings at the beginning of the 20th century."

"I believe that's called progress." Her snippy voice made it clear Johanna was not interested in succumbing to Chicago's charms.

❖

This was the first time Katherine had driven her car since Thanksgiving weekend. She was learning to depend on public transportation, and often walked home from work, weather permitting. She wouldn't be doing much of that for a while.

On the seat next to her, Johanna sat tightly wrapped in her misconceptions about this glorious city. To hear her tell it, the city was forever covered in ice and snow. They were headed towards Ravenswood, one of the many neighborhoods in the city. Katherine hoped she could elevate Johanna's spirits by giving her a short history lesson. She painstakingly explained, "Ravenswood is centered around the intersection of Lawrence, Western and Lincoln Avenues, and was once home to a large German population." She knew the location meant nothing to Johanna, but Katherine was enjoying her subject.

"Eventually, most of the group dispersed or moved on to the suburbs, but those who have remained carry on the area's German traditions." Katherine knew Johanna wasn't persuaded that Ravenswood was an important stop on the day's itinerary.

"I don't want to put a damper on our adventure, Katherine, but based on what I'm seeing, your enthusiasm for this neighborhood aspect of Chicago is over rated. So far it is urban clutter, unfortunate zoning, hole in the wall restaurants, and a car in the next lane with the bass on the radio pounding. This in exchange for Carolina blue skies and a seventy-two degree warm spell in Chapel Hill. The Carolina students were in shorts when I left."

Katherine was not going to let this wintry gray day or Johanna's summation of things faze her. She ignored the comment and soldiered on. "You know, if you live in Chicago there is no need to travel out of the country. Every language, type of cuisine, music and places of worship from around the world can be found here. You don't have to go to Germany. Just pretend we're taking a day trip there now."

"All this for pastry? I think we've passed a bakery on every corner."

"Ah, but Lutz Cafe and Bakery is famous. They have wonderful things, and at Christmas it should be mouth watering. We'll have lunch and buy some goodies for you to take home for your Christmas tea. Everyone will rave." Katherine glanced over at Johanna long enough to read her expression, which seemed to say, "Are we having fun yet?"

When they walked in the door of the bakery they were flooded with the fragrance of hazelnut, chocolate and vanilla. In the display cases were beautiful cakes, tortes, and cookies of all sorts. Katherine and Johanna moved slowly along the cases, taking it all in.

Johanna finally smiled. "Fabulous."

"They claim they still bake with the traditional European recipes the Lutz family has always used. This is something!"

A stout woman behind the counter, her hair tucked beneath a hair net, welcomed them. She heard Katherine's comment and added, "The Lutz's stay true to the Konditorei method by using only the best quality ingredients that are delicate and light." Neither Katherine nor Johanna had any idea what the word Konditorei meant; their expressions gave that away.

The woman explained, using her hand to gesture around the shop, "Konditorei is the German word for a patisserie and confectionary shop. A Konditorei typically offers a wide variety of pastries and is like a little cafe in Germany. It's a popular custom to go to a

Konditorei to have a cake and some coffee or hot chocolate mid-afternoon."

"Another version of English tea time, I like it." Johanna placed her hand on Katherine's sleeve, "I miss our tea." Katherine put her hand momentarily over Johanna's, and then looked back at the women behind the case.

"You're kind to explain, thank you. I wish there was a Konditorei near where I live." Katherine smiled.

They found seats and had their lunch. An hour later, they pushed through the door onto the street, their bakery bags in hand. Johanna gasped. "My God, it's freezing." Even in the cold, they roamed the streets for another hour ducking into stores along the way. By the time they got back to the car the parking meter had expired. Katherine looked up and down the street for a meter maid, "I got lucky. Parking tickets cost a fortune."

"No Christmas leniency for the businesses to accommodate shoppers?"

"What's this world coming to, right?"

The heater gave off a cold greeting when Katherine put the key into the ignition and started the car. Their breath smoked white. In her side view mirror, she saw a car already waiting to take their space. The driver gave her thumbs up when she pulled out.

"Before we head on back, I want to drive around part of the neighborhood, okay?" Katherine was not really asking for permission.

The trees that lined the streets were bare, and the family lawns had lost their greenness. Katherine appreciated the vintage buildings that now stood side by side with multi-unit apartment complexes, a few newly constructed condominiums, and the single-family homes. They were all crammed together in Chicago fashion. Even if Johanna was unimpressed, it filled Katherine with nostalgia. Neighborhoods like this had been a familiar sight to the little girl that sat on the back seat of her parents' car. There was permanence about these old buildings aged with coal dust and wind blown grim. Here and there steam rose from the pavement grates, and behind dirty windows she could see Christmas trees with large colored bulbs and tinsel. Katherine remembered the past, and presumed the future would alter very little about these small enclaves of Chicago.

Katherine spoke up. "In the years since my parents died, the new buildings downtown would be unfamiliar to them, but a drive along a street like this here in Ravenswood or a similar Chicago neighborhood, would remind them of their youth. I'm sure of it."

It comforted Katherine that something this ordinary retained its forever-after quality. "When I die, if it were possible, and proved necessary, I could find my way back home with the familiar sign posts of the city."

"I don't mind riding along, Katherine. Really I don't. It doesn't mean much to me, I admit, but you should bring Louisa here if you haven't already. She should see these places too."

"I haven't been here in years. That's why I'm struck with the sameness of it all. You're right, I must make plans with Louisa."

"I'm trying to stay positive, Katherine. I guess I still need more time to accept that you're here, that's all. I'll admit I miss you every day. It doesn't help that the new people in your Queen Anne yellow house are from New York and don't speak southern." They both grinned.

Later, in front of the Christmas tree in the living room, Katherine gave Johanna her gift. "I hope you like your present this year. It's a ticket for tonight's Joffrey Ballet performance of The Nutcracker."

"Oh, wonderful. What a treat. Thank you." Johanna stood up long enough to hug Katherine.

"This makes for a long day, but it will be worth it."

They continued to talk until they finished their glass of wine. Katherine took their empty dinner plates and left them in the sink.

"Time to go," she called back to Johanna, who was now stretched out on the couch and nestled in underneath the cashmere throw.

A short time later, a cab drove them down Michigan Avenue where the fairy lights and shoppers mingled together in a blur of light and shadows. Katherine looked over at Johanna who had fallen silent.

"This is amazing, Katherine. It's like watching the beginning of a theatrical production when the curtain goes up and it's snowing on stage. Except we're watching it through the windows of this taxi."

When they joined a festive crowd at the Auditorium Theatre on East Congress Parkway, Johanna said, "I'm beginning to understand the allure of all this, Katherine."

"In time, I hoped you would."

10

Green wreaths and red plaid bows, along with songs of a white Christmas, gave way to biting cold and gunmetal gray. It was down to the proverbial survival of the fittest: Old Man winter versus Chicagoans. Katherine sat at her office desk on one of the coldest days in January. She reached over and picked up the ringing telephone to hear Jessica Lovejoy's voice.

"Good morning, Jessica. Are you calling to rub it in, and ask how the weather is?" Katherine reached for a file. "How's Santa Barbara these days? Are you writing or playing tennis?" She hoped Jessica was up for a little ribbing this early in the morning.

"You don't want to know what I'm up to based on your weather, but, since you're being mean, I'm playing tennis this afternoon. Right now, I'm looking out the open patio door. After this morning's brief rain shower, the air smells of Eucalyptus."

Katherine and Jessica had once talked about the house were Jessica grew up. From that conversation, Katherine surmised that the house held no sentimental value to her. The address was perfect, and that was what was important to Jessica.

"It's a long hard slug here until the end of March at the earliest, if we're lucky."

"I have a marvelous idea and you must say yes."

"You want me to ghost write your next book so you can chase the tennis pro?"

"How'd you know?"

"I'm a good guesser."

"This is about meeting me in Seattle in March for part of my book signing tour. Something to look forward to on a cold windy night."

"There's a thought. Could I come tomorrow?" She heard Jessica laugh. "Why Seattle?"

"I want you to meet several people that live there. Robert will agree, I'm sure."

"Whom are we talking about?"

"Andrew Stillman is a garden-writing friend of mine, and the other is Claire Thompson, who owns one of the bookstores where I'm scheduled."

"Listen, Katherine, I know authors bring their own cookies to book signings these days, and half the people who show up are friends they have invited, but I'm proposing a collaboration between the two of us that has merit. I can promote my book and you can talk about the publishing business."

Ten minutes later, Jessica was winding down. "Tell Robert I'm paying for a room that we can share at the Mayflower, it's my favorite hotel. Most of the rooms have two small, but complete bathrooms. The staff is delightful. We can walk out the front door and down the street a couple of blocks to the bookstore on Pine where Claire Thompson hangs out. She knows how to run a bookshop."

Katherine was interested. "It sounds very enticing, but I doubt the prince down the hall is going to fit this slipper onto my foot It's a busy time this spring."

"You let me work some magic."

An hour later, Katherine walked down to Robert's office. His greeting surprised her. "I think you should go to Seattle."

"Are you trying to get rid of me for another woman?"

"Look for a new talent if you feel you must work." With that admonition, it was settled. Katherine hoped she would not regret what could be a difficult situation.

❀

After talking to Katherine, and then Robert, Jessica walked to her computer and checked the time on the screen. She had two hours to work before her match. She wasn't surprised Robert went along with her idea. For some reason, he'd laughed when she told him she had invited Katherine to Seattle. She wasn't completely truthful with either of them about her reasons for inviting Katherine.

What Jessica didn't say was that she regretted the fact that she'd burned her bridges with Andrew Stillman. She'd courted him and in turn he'd befriended her, thinking she was bright and promising. He introduced her to the world of garden magazines and beyond, all of which expanded her horizons and went a long way to augmenting her income. Jessica got what she wanted from him, and moved on. Now she needed back into his world. She had enough sense to know she could not impose on his good nature again without some excuse.

She would use Katherine as bait; he'd be delighted with an introduction if she served it up properly. Neither of them need know she was attempting her first mystery, toying with the motive for the crime, which would involve the stiff competition for readership in the garden magazine world. She knew a lot about gardens, and with this help, she could get inside the current scene as the setting for the crime.

❦

Katherine thought answering machines were a busy person's best friend. She was waiting for her daughter to pick up the phone. Instead the machine kicked in. "Honey, it's Mom. I want to remind you that I'm leaving in the morning for Seattle. This widowhood thing does have real advantages." Katherine realized too late how this statement must sound.

"Sorry, dear, just trying to be funny." She started talking faster before the machine clicked off. "Love you, bye."

Before hanging up Katherine thought to add, "I'm staying at the Mayflower Hotel in Seattle if you need me." The message machine cut her off.

On the way down the hall to her bedroom Katherine stepped around several boxes she kept meaning to take to her storage unit in the basement of the building. On impulse she picked up the top box and moments later it sat opened on the floor in front of her. She remembered her mother's sewing room, the room with the large deep shelves behind doors where this old Marshall Field's dress-size box was kept. The satin-like cream finish on the box was gray and dingy after all these years.

The box contained some of Katherine's baby clothes, a few wool baby blankets stiff with age, and several pairs of baby shoes. Her mother saved these things between tissue paper turned yellow.

Katherine held up a hand knit pink cable sweater with pearl buttons, buttons her mother fastened. Tears welled as she questioned, what was she to do with these things? She wondered, do I casually walk over and throw all of this into a black garbage bag to be thrown out with the trash? Surely it calls for some sort of ritual before I do that. She couldn't think of what that ritual might be, but she knew that if she threw these things away, she would certainly be parted even further from her mother.

She held the sweater to her chest. The expression, 'Life happens when you're on the way to doing something else' came to mind. Here she was leaving for Seattle to meet an author she did not particularly care for, for reasons that were not clear, and she was feeling like a child again.

Like a genie released from a bottle in the form of this pink sweater, here was an example that widowhood had not extracted the price of losing the child she once was. If anything, the little girl inside her was taking up space she needed for her new life. She said aloud, "You need to get back between the tissue paper in this box. I've got a plane to catch." She then put everything back into the box and closed the lid.

11

The next day Katherine headed for Seattle. Jessica was standing by a SUV parked at the curb when hours later, she came through the arrival doors. The two women shook hands before Jessica hefted Katherine's bag into the back of the car. Katherine opened the passenger door.

"I just have to figure out how to climb in wearing this tight skirt." She laughed.

"Hike it up."

There, as if waiting off stage for the right cue, came a memory of Timothy teasing Johanna as she tried to get into his car in the same predicament. Katherine willed herself not to cry as she hoisted herself onto the tan leather seat.

"All set?" Fastening her seat belt, Jessica started the car.

"Where are we headed?" Katherine fumbled with her own seat belt, trying to sound casual.

"Andrew Stillman has invited us for dinner; he's a very good cook. That okay with you?"

"I think I can manage it." She was back in control now. From experience, she knew it took a little time to recover, enabling Timothy to stroll from the stage. "Tell me more about this Andrew."

"He's a garden writer among many things. I met him ten years ago at a Writers Conference in San Francisco. I was trying to reconcile my net income with my gross habits, and garden writing was the only thing that interested me beyond writing fiction. I'd just moved into my parents' home after they died. It has a fabulous garden, and I know a thing or two about the subject. Andrew was teaching one of the workshops on garden writing."

"I keep garden magazines in business. I have spent a small fortune buying them over the years." Katherine reached into her carry on that sat at her feet and pulled out *Garden Design*. She tapped the cover. "It used to drive Timothy nuts because I would not throw any of them away. I moved cartons to Chicago rather than part with them. But I've interrupted, go on about Andrew."

"He helped me find different ways to write about the color green, which isn't easy, and he encouraged me while I worked to establish some sort of a reputation."

"I had no idea you were interested in gardening."

"It was a means to an end for a while. Andrew and I lost touch."

"Was that literally or figuratively speaking?" Katherine hadn't been able to resist the question.

"He's too old for me. Not that he's old, I don't mean it that way."

"But old."

"Not young. Let's leave it at that."

"You won't hurt my feelings using that word, it has nothing to do with me." Jessica glanced over at Katherine and wondered how old she was. She'd imagined her to be the same age as Andrew. Counted on it, in fact.

It was not difficult to paint an interesting picture of Andrew. "He's lived in the Queen Anne District of Seattle in one place or another since college, and probably always will. He'll tell you about the gardening world here, which he insists is incestuous. Everybody knows everybody, and they're all competitive about their gardens. It turns out to be a good thing because it's enhanced everything they do with their design work and plant selections. It's unbelievable."

"When *Fine Garden Magazine* features one of these Pacific Northwest Gardens I drool on the pages. I have always hoped God made allowances for coveting your neighbor's garden." She laughed, but meant it.

"Andrew's home is in a largely residential community above Puget Sound where the early settlers began building their homes up the hillsides. Many of the early Victorian mansions they built were in an architectural style called Queen Anne, which is how the district got its name. The area has become highly desirable, prices are through the roof."

74

"Ah, yes, of course." Katherine did not elaborate on the fact that she and Timothy lived in one of these picturesque treasures in Chapel Hill.

Part of what Jessica was saying did not register with Katherine while she struggled again to keep some semblance of composure. She saw herself closing the door on her Queen Anne life in Chapel Hill and driving away.

Jessica went right on talking. "The lower part of Queen Anne tends to attract young professionals, artists and students. Upper Queen Anne is home to long time residents like Andrew." By the time Jessica announced their arrival, Katherine was past her brush with heartache.

She looked up at the house that Johanna pointed towards. "This beautiful house?"

"One of the architectural gems of Upper Queen Anne."

"Having lived in one of these gems myself," Katherine said, "I don't need a guidebook to fully appreciate what I'm seeing. The Queen Anne style dominated Victorian residential architecture from 1880 to 1910."

Jessica grinned at her. "Well, look at you miss know-it-all."

"If all else fails I can talk to Andrew about the nineteenth century architect; Richard Norman Shaw. He broke away from designing contemporary Victorian homes when he designed the first of the Queen Anne's. I can tell you this house is perfectly preserved. You're right, this is a gem."

Andrew Stillman was sitting on his one-story wrap-around porch and jumped to his feet when he heard the car doors close. He called to them, "Here you are." His home was the typical asymmetrical arrangement of building parts. The windows were the usual mixtures of sizes and shapes. At the front door Katherine saw a large pane of glass surrounded by small pieces of beautiful stained glass. The steeply pitched hipped roof had a lower cross gable with patterned wood. This house was built with the commonly used brick on the ground floor and horizontal boards and shingles above.

Katherine could see why this man wasn't a romantic prospect for Jessica. She guessed he was in his early sixties, but it was obvious he spent time in a gym working out. Katherine would lay money on the fact that he was dressed, as he had been dressing since college; in a blue oxford cloth shirt with the sleeves turned back, wearing a bow tie. He had on a khaki pair of pants. Katherine knew he was wearing loafers. He was a handsome man. His stance conveyed an energy that greeted them before they took their first steps onto his porch.

"Andrew, I'd like you to meet my editor, Katherine White." Jessica made a sweeping gesture towards her.

"Welcome Katherine, I'm honored." He reached out his hand to her.

Katherine shook his hand. "I hope Jessica hasn't overstated my case. You know how effusive authors can be when they're getting good reviews."

"In your case, I doubt Jessica has gotten it wrong." He reached over and gave Jessica a perfunctory kiss on the cheek. Shifting his gaze back to Katherine, he added, "I'm sure she is dead on about you."

Katherine realized she hadn't seen a man with a military haircut for a long time. What white hair he had was minimized midst the gray. This full head of hair must need a cut at least once a week to keep it in such perfect shape.

Jessica thumped Andrew on the chest and grinned. "Such flattery, Andrew. You know it won't get you anywhere." Hearing a modicum of strain in Jessica's voice, Katherine wondered if she had been completely truthful about her friendship with this man.

"Can a girl get a glass of wine around here?" Jessica asked.

The two women followed Andrew into the house and back to his kitchen where there were three wine glasses sitting on a tray with cocktail napkins that read 'Gardeners Know the Best Dirt.' They stood and exchanged favorite napkin stories.

The immaculate kitchen reflected a precise occupant thriving on order. Filling wine glasses from a bottle of chilled Chardonnay, Andrew proposed a toast. "Welcome, may the book tour be a great success."

"And to Andrew, thank you for your hospitality." Katherine hoped her voice didn't sound too self-conscious.

Several hours later, still sitting at the kitchen table, she felt the effects of the time change. Having savored halibut, fresh tomato and basil salad, a small squash casserole, they topped off their meal with a dish of cut up strawberries, blueberries, peaches and kiwi. It would be a long time before fresh produce like this became available in Chicago. Katherine waited for the right moment to interrupt the conversation.

"As much as I hate to admit it folks, it's midnight in Chicago; it's been a long day for me."

"I forgot all about the time change, Katherine, I'm sorry." Jessica pushed her chair back from the table. "We must get you back to the hotel."

Katherine told herself that there was no correlation between her age and the fact that she might be going to bed earlier than she used to. Truth be told, she was driving a little slower too. Once accused of having a heavy foot, she now preferred a safe and respectable sixty-five miles per hour.

Standing on the front porch, Andrew said, "The time has gone by too fast. I wanted to show you the house, Katherine, and I have a project Jessica thought I could mention to you without being too presumptuous. Is your schedule completely filled?"

"Jessica's in charge of that."

"I'd like to show you several private gardens that belong to friends of mine. Since publishing a book that features them, I am able to call and arrange a visit most any time. Would you like that?" Andrew took her hand and was shaking it.

"That's fantastic." She forgot momentarily she was in Seattle ostensibly to work. Remembering herself, she added, "I'm not sure how much time there will be. We'll just have to see."

As they drove away from Andrew's home he gave them a Richard Nixon, standing on the airplane steps, wave. Tired as Katherine was, she laughed.

"Good time?" Jessica, with a grin, looked sideways at her.

"Very. He's a charming man. It was a pleasant evening. I see why you value his friendship."

"I don't want to preempt him, but he has a book he wants to write about English gardens."

"It's been done."

"That's why I suggested he run his ideas past you. You don't object do you?"

"No, of course not. I'm happy to listen if you think he won't mind what I might say afterwards."

"Your suggestions would be a great help to him, I'm sure."

Walking into the lobby of the Mayflower Hotel, Katherine was happy to hand her bag over to the bellman. Though feeling tired, the evening had been energizing. Within minutes of getting to their room, Katherine climbed into a lush and comfortable bed while Jessica turned out the light on the nightstand between them. Relishing the first moments of sheets with a high thread count, Katherine stretched out. Finding the pillows to be just right, she turned on her side with a satisfied sigh. "Honestly, Jessica, with two bathrooms and this heavenly bed, I may never go home."

12

When the phone rang the next morning at seven-thirty, Katherine fumbled for the receiver. She whispered, "Yes?"

"Katherine is this you?"

Sounding incredulous, Katherine answered, "Andrew?"

"I apologize for calling early, but I have a proposition?"

Eyeing the bedside clock, Katherine now fully awake, said, "I should have mentioned last night that I'm not a seven-thirty in the morning kind of girl. Call back at nine, it's much more civilized."

"I want to pick you up at the hotel at nine. We will take the ferry to Bainbridge Island and visit several of the gardens I was telling you about last night. Will you come?" He paused a moment, "And tell Jessica, you don't need a chaperone. I promise to have you back in plenty of time to have your dinner and get to McCoy's Bookstore by seven. It's just down the street."

"I'm accompanying her to a radio interview at eleven o'clock."

"I wouldn't go if I were you, it's going to be ass numbing dull. Just tell her something came up you can't refuse." Katherine was amused with Andrews' double entendre but realized before she laughed that he couldn't be making an off-colored joke with a stranger. She was embarrassed to have thought of it.

"You will feel more agreeable after a shower. I'll call you back." That said, Andrew rang off.

Any notion of going back to sleep was over. Katherine with an aversion to walking on hotel carpets, regardless of how lovely the room might be, began to shuffle her feet beside the bed until she found her slippers. Jessica had drawn the drapes back to reveal a brilliant day. Did people exaggerate the amount of rainfall here?

From the bathroom Jessica rounded the corner. "I didn't think you'd be up yet."

"Nor did I. Andrew phoned."

"This early?"

"My point exactly. He must be one of these early risers that has the crossword finished by six."

"Why, when do you finish yours?"

"Not by six."

"What did he want?" Jessica reached over and turned the television on.

"He propositioned me."

"Are you serious?" Jessica spun around to look at Katherine as she headed for the second bathroom closing the door behind.

She stood looking at herself in the mirror above the sink. She was interested in mirrors as a vehicle to tell a story about three generations of women who all had gazed into the same antique mirror. This modern bathroom mirror wasn't what she had in mind, but, it told the truth. Seeing herself grown older in the mirror was like watching the Presidents age during their terms of office. She doubted they could use makeup, but she could at least cover up some of the deterioration with a little Laura Mercer and Bobby Brown thrown in for good measure.

Since the day she'd driven away from her life in Chapel Hill, Katherine had been repeating a mantra, "I'm going to be okay." Her goal was to be able to say, "I am okay." The reflection in the mirror said, "You're not there yet." Twenty-five minutes later she was showered and dressed. This time she was prepared when the phone rang.

"I will pick you up in front of the hotel at nine o'clock, okay?"

Jessica seemed unconcerned when told about the plan. "I hope you don't mind me running out on your interview and lunch with the Book Section guy from the paper."

"The weather channel promises a glorious day; seventy-two degrees and sunny, where better to spend it than in a garden."

Katherine was grateful for Jessica's good will. It was a fine day for a private tour of a Seattle garden. Picking up her purse and a scarf, she grinned, "I'm not going to tell Robert how I spent the first day on your book tour."

Headed down in the elevator, Katherine was glad to exchange a day with Jessica for a garden visit, and yes, a seemingly lovely man. In her late twenties and early thirties she'd preferred the company of men. They talked politics and sports, and it was a welcomed relief from conversations about baby bottles and wallpaper samples. In the intervening years, that had changed. She profoundly appreciated the company of women who willingly shared their wisdom. Today, however, she looked forward to this man's company.

While the elevator descended, stopping along the way to let guests on, Katherine thought of a woman who once told her, "The reason I married was to have a date on Saturday night." Katherine was amused at the time, but later she amended this statement for herself; a date on Friday night was even better, it made the weekend seem longer. Was she about to have a first Tuesday morning date in a very long time?

❁

Standing at the rail on the upper deck of the Seattle-Winslow ferry, Katherine was delighted with the view across Puget Sound. It was a little over eight miles from Colman Dock in Seattle to Bainbridge Island at the Winslow terminal, plenty of time for the anxiety she was feeling to dissipate after being rushed into this morning's arrangements.   Andrew stood beside her. "Nice, huh?"

"This could ruin other forms of travel." Katherine was beginning to delight is this adventure.

"There are only a few main blocks in Winslow where we dock. It's lined with art and antique shops, clothing boutiques, and cafés and restaurants. I think the word quaint fits the description." Neither of them spoke for several minutes allowing Katherine to gaze over the expanse of water they were traveling.

She finally turned to look directly at Andrew. "Jessica mentioned you want to write a book about English gardens."

"I have been playing around with an idea."

"Forgive my bluntness, Andrew, but there are a lot of books out there about English gardens written by authors who are well established in that field. You'd have to have an angle that isn't ass numbing dull, as you so succinctly put it this morning. You think you have something new?" Andrew laughed.

"I'd like to select a number of American and English women gardeners who share a common passion and write about their gardens." Andrew raised his hand to stop Katherine from speaking, anticipating an objection. "Instead of photographs, though, I want to find an artist who can create water colors of these gardens. That's as far as I have gotten."

"I see." Katherine thought of Rosemary Verey, the famous English garden woman who visited America and loved the Northwest's gardens. "People do compare the Pacific Northwest's climate to England, but it would be extremely important who you pick to avoid repetition." It was obvious that she meant it when she added, "I love the water color idea. Maybe some sort of sketch book approach using the margins that surround the text?"

Andrew beamed. "Jessica was right, she said you were the perfect person to give me the benefit of your considerable expertise."

"Why do I have the feeling you are more complimentary than Jessica ever is?"

Andrew grinned, letting Katherine know, she was right. "I haven't heard from her in a while. She called about this book tour and the possibility you would be joining her. She did say nice things." Andrew smiled, "I'm glad you were able to make it."

"Did she tell you English gardens are my passion?"

There was a look of mischievousness in Andrew's eyes. "Have

I caught your attention because of this?"

"Perhaps." Katherine smiled. She turned to the Bainbridge Island shoreline as they drew closer.

When they pulled into a parking space in the charming Bainbridge Center, not too far from the ferry, Katherine closed the car door on Andrew's pristine Lexus. She was transfixed by a captivating collection of varying sized glazed pots arranged in three's that filled the entrance to a group of shops. The pots were glazed in celadon, deep reds, and French blues. She reached for her camera.

"Look at the complementary colors of this plant material, Andrew. Don't you love the leaf textures and design?" Before she remembered she no longer had a garden, she called out, "I have got to have some of these pots."

Later, standing in Carol Johanson's famous garden, Katherine was speechless. She'd seen gardens in Italy, France and England, and there was a private garden in The Plains, Virginia that was her favorite small private American garden, but this garden took design to a new level. Standing in front of the 120-foot-long stone retaining wall that terraced the steep property, she could hardly take in the profusion of Mediterranean plants in lavenders and yellow, pinks and various greens. Johanson's cultural practices and design work in combination with the climate had Katherine running from place to place calling out, "Look at this. Look at this."

Several short hours later, Andrew announced they needed to think about leaving. Katherine, with pleading voice, said, "Do we have to?"

"We do if you still want a late lunch and return to the hotel on time. Of course, you could skip the engagement tonight and have dinner with me."

She accepted his hand as they navigated the sloping property and started back to the car parked at the top of the driveway. "You are a troublemaker, Andrew, I suppose you know that," and then laughed. "Of course, I still want lunch, I'm starving."

Katherine appreciated people who were comfortable with silence. Andrew found it unnecessary to fill the quiet spaces. He remained silent on the drive back to one of the small restaurants in Winslow. Katherine thought the large trees that lined the narrow road lent new meaning to the word majestic. Katherine was homesick for the garden she'd left behind in Chapel Hill; a garden now being cared for by a young enthusiastic couple that knew little about gardening, but insisted they would learn.

"Missing your garden?" Andrew glanced over at her.

"How did you know?"

"I'm a gardener."

Back at the hotel they shook hands and said goodbye. Before Andrew let go of Katherine's hand, he said, "I like you immensely, Katherine White. You are beautiful, smart, and amusing. It has been a pleasant surprise. Not much surprises me these days.

"Such flattery. Thank you."

13

The next morning, Katherine wanted to pop her thumb into her mouth and go back to sleep. She still carried a minuscule white scar on her left thumb from the days of thumb sucking. When she got too old to suck her thumb she began the habit of running her fingers along the edge of the mattress pad, pushing the bed sheet underneath making a nice edge. The soothing effect of this tactile motion relaxed her at times when she was over tired. Now working her way up and down a few inches of the mattress pad's edge, she hoped this old habit would work.

Drifting towards sleep, the blank card she bought at the airport came to mind. An artist had painted a crude stone outdoor altar where things had been placed; a dried flower, a fancy button. Packing up the Chapel Hill house, she couldn't part with her own endless sacred items, like the buckeye she'd picked up in France, or the shell from the beach on a writing weekend. She'd kept a heart shaped stone from Beatrice. To Katherine, these tokens were important markers in her life.

When Timothy joined this floating reverie, all hope of sleep was over. She reluctantly got out of bed and headed for the shower. Waiting for the water to warm up, there was little doubt that she had thrown special items away, unaware of their importance to her husband. She'd found a faded picture of a lovely young girl pushed to the back of his dresser drawer. Katherine had no idea who she was. There was a small, carved box that was chipped and worn. When opened she found a deck of cards, dice, and old shirt collar white plastic stays that no one used any more. She apologized to Timothy out loud before pitching the box into a plastic trash bag that was headed to the garbage.

Katherine stood in the shower letting the water sooth her. It was a shame that death carries away the key to a person's treasure map. Her own life's odds and ends would be discarded one day too. Out of the shower, she made up her mind to create a facsimile of an altar on a bookshelf when she got home where she could place her incidental treasures. There she could light a candle now and then and leave the things in God's care. While she toweled off, she wondered what Timothy would think of Andrew Stillman, and what would he think about the plans she'd made with him at some point each day.

❁

Across the city, Andrew sat at the kitchen table with a fresh cup of coffee. He was up early, in spite of the late hour the night before. He could have slept in, but his internal clock, set for 5:30, never allowed it. Scrawled across the cover of the file folder laying on the table in front of him he'd written, *English Garden Book.* It was dated three years earlier. The idea for this book had given him something to talk about when asked what he was working on. The truth was he had not completed any substantial writing since the publication of his book on Seattle gardens. He continued to write articles for regional magazines. He gave the occasional free lecture for local garden clubs, and continued to give workshops at various writing conferences, talking more about writing than actually accomplishing any.

He was in the habit now of letting his far from boring life supersede his work. The Seattle lifestyle had always suited him; he enjoyed a busy social calendar, and his home and garden. It was a comfortable life for the most part. He never fooled himself that the choices he made were at the cost of things left undone. He'd like to write the great American novel like everyone else. Initially, one more English garden book did not interest Katherine, but her eventual encouragement had him sitting here thinking seriously about committing himself to the research necessary to start a first draft. He leafed through the file pages stopping to read some of his preliminary notes. It wasn't half bad. Pouring another cup of coffee, Andrew wished Katherine didn't live across the country. Perhaps he could talk her into collaborating on the book even still. Her professional interest in the book was one thing, but he suspected it was her personal interest he was hoping for.

He willingly admitted that he liked Katherine. Their garden passions made them kindred spirits. Piecing together things she'd said let him know she'd been recognized in her own right as a regional garden writer. She'd lectured to local garden groups too. They'd encountered similar problems while lecturing; a storm that knocked the electricity out in the middle of their presentations rendering their power point presentations useless, terrible acoustics, and plenty of inadequate sound systems.

It was not just their gardening interests that Andrew was thinking about. He had not given up on the idea that there was still a love of his life waiting for him, but Chicago seemed way off script.

He spent the rest of the morning going through back copies of The English Garden magazine. He had every issue they'd printed, featuring well written articles and stunning photographs about everyone in the English garden world: owners to head gardeners. Christening a new yellow legal pad, Andrew began to make notes. He could not remember when he had last put in a long work session like this. Immersed in reading and checking things on search engines, it was mid afternoon before he rang the hotel to speak to Katherine. With no answer, he left a message on the hotel room answering service. "Katherine, dinner tonight?"

At six thirty that evening, Katherine climbed into the front seat of Andrew's car. "Jessica is happy to be shed of me. Makes me wonder what she might be up to." She laughed, and Andrew, feeling light hearted, joined in.

"I always knew I liked that girl." Andrew was resplendent in a light blue silk sports jacket, yellow shirt and bow tie.

"My, don't you look spiffy." Katherine was never reticent when it came to giving well-deserved compliments.

"Thank you madam. I dressed to impress my date tonight." Katherine liked his forthrightness, but a date? The idea seemed odd at their age, but what did you call going out alone otherwise?

"Tonight we're going to Ray's Boathouse Restaurant on North West Seaside Avenue. I think you'll like it.

"I'm sure it will be great, you have such good food out here, and you're trying to make a good impression, right?"

"Are you making fun of me?" He asked this question in jest, but still, he didn't know what to think if she was laughing at him.

"Let's just say you don't have to work hard tonight, Andrew. I'm already impressed." She did not look at him, but sat, smiling.

"You mean I could have saved this new jacket for another time?" He too was smiling. After a moment he asked, "Have you and Jessica had another good day?"

"She's a natural at these readings. When she finishes with that, I talk briefly on the state of the publishing business, and she gives tips on finding an agent. It makes a nice presentation."

A half hour later they pulled up to Ray's Boathouse. "This is the best place to watch the sunset in Seattle. Come on, you'll see." Andrew led the way into the Restaurant. "I've made our reservation upstairs because it's less formal."

They were seated by one of the many windows looking out on the water. Katherine liked the atmosphere: rustic beams and two fireplaces. She asked, "Is this what they call casual-Northwest? It's wonderful, thank you."

Andrew ordered for both of them, sea scallops, with oxbow farm Swiss chard, and artichokes with fennel pecorino. Katherine talked about Italy. "I have only been to Florence, but it was unforgettable.

"I haven't gone far from home. Over a bottle of wine, with friends, we contemplate trips, but that's as far as it goes. Seattle seems to have first claim on our hearts, and we are loyal."

Over dinner Andrew told Katherine of his foray through the English Garden magazines. "They are perfect for introductory research. The articles are not long, but you get an idea of the gardeners and their interests. I made a long list of candidates that fill my criteria."

"I love The English Garden magazine. I have every issue. I would not have dreamed of leaving them behind in Chapel Hill."

Andrew reached into the inside pocket of his jacket and pulled out a stack 3X5 index cards. "I wrote the issue, page and name of the gardens that caught my attention. He reached across the table and put the cards in Katherine's outstretched hand. "If you have time would you take a look?"

"This will give me a good excuse to finish unpacking several boxes sitting in one of the bedroom closets where I know the magazines are."

Part way through dinner, Andrew asked, "Would you consider writing this book with me?"

Startled, Katherine said, "You're kind to ask, but you can do this on your own, you know you can. I do think you have an idea worth pursuing. Write a proposal to yourself with the ideas fleshed out, a synopsis, and continue with your research. See how you feel about things then."

"Does this mean you are not saying no to the idea?" Andrew sputtered like the air in a sprinkling system when first turned on after a long hiatus; he started and stopped trying to say more.

"You don't need me to make a go of this, Andrew. You just need a push off the side of the pool into cold water, to start you gasping for air. It sounds like you toweled off this afternoon and started breathing an author's stratosphere. I can tell you enjoyed every minute of it."

Andrew wanted to tell her he did need her for reasons he could not name other than the safe subject of writing a book together. He reached across the table wordlessly asking for her hand. When she gave it to him he said, "Let's go to England and find the gardeners for this book." He did not let go for several seconds while he searched her face for the answer he wanted."

Driving her back to the hotel, he would have been grateful for a good night kiss. The doorman was quick to pull Katherine's door open to help her from the car. Unfortunately, she gave no indication that a kiss was on her mind when she turned and smiled. "Thanks again, Andrew, goodnight."

Later, in bed, Andrew placed his hand on the matching pillow. He allowed himself a fantasy. Here was Katherine beside him, smiling as she moved closer. He thought of exploring her body, placing a hand on her breast, kissing her mouth, and feeling himself aroused as she lay against him. It was comfortable and warm. No one had ever been invited to actually stay in this room in Andrew's bed. Not that he had not stayed late at the home of someone he was seeing, but he always returned home alone after a pleasurable few hours. The thought of making an exception for Katherine was out of character, but this was the impact she'd made on him.

14

A few minutes past seven o'clock several evenings later, Katherine and Jessica walked into McCoy's Bookstore. Behind the counter stood a woman in her early fifties, ringing up a book sale. Her hair was a nondescript brown, held back by a tortoise shell clip, and her complexion looked rather gray. There were dark shadows beneath her brown eyes, and because she wore no makeup, the brown spots along her jaw line were noticeable. It was her chocolate brown blouse that contributed to this overall tired look. The woman looked up and saw Jessica, breaking into a bright smile. "You've come at last."

This smile was a quick fix for Claire Thompson's academic, 'I don't care what I look like statement.'

Since Jessica only knew Claire in a professional capacity, her effusive introduction seemed excessive to Katherine. Jessica said, "This is my good friend Claire Thompson." She went so far as to awkwardly hug Claire over the counter between them.

"This is a pleasure." Katherine shook Claire's hand.

"Delighted." Claire hesitated and then said, "Authors are alone on the road these days. This is quite a coup for Jessica."

"We have the generous man I work for to thank for this togetherness." Katherine doubted her trip to Bainbridge Island and the other gardens she'd seen could be equated with a hard day's work at the office. Neither Andrew Stillman nor gorgeous gardens would be listed on her metaphorical time sheet.

"To Robert." Jessica raised her hand as if holding a glass.

"Indeed." Claire and Katherine said simultaneously.

Several people were already waiting in line with Jessica's book in hand. "Back to business, ladies. Make yourself at home." Claire returned her attention to the customers and their credit cards while Katherine steered Jessica away from the cash register.

People were already wandering around the store looking at books on small display tables. Recognizing Jessica as the author they'd come to hear, she was soon surrounded by a group of young professional looking people who asked her questions about her work. Later in the evening, Claire confirmed that this sharp-looking crowd was the core of a healthy clientele that worked in the neighborhood, and regularly stopped in to buy books, and attend guest author appearances.

Downtown Seattle was clearly a thriving place for a bookstore. On the walk over from the Mayflower Hotel to McCoy's, the streets felt safe, a great asset in a city's downtown. There was plenty of activity as people made their way to the eclectic restaurants and other successful stores in the area. It was no wonder that the concierge at the hotel insisted they would need a reservation when going out for dinner, or else stand in line a long time.

The people in the bookstore exuded their healthy lifestyles. Katherine felt the same energy about them that she'd sensed out on the streets. This promised to be a successful evening for Jessica's book, and McCoy's. It turned out to be one of the most remarkable evenings of Katherine's life.

By nine-thirty the last of the books were signed and everyone was gone. The evening had been a delight. Jessica's pleasant voice enhanced her well-delivered and affable reading, offering amusing banter that everyone seemed to enjoy. Katherine was pleasantly surprised, having found Jessica's usual brisk detached manner off putting.

While Claire stacked and stored the chairs in a back room, Katherine picked up the coffee cups that had been left around. She was feeling the effects of another long day, starting with an early phone call from an interesting man, and ending here at this bookstore. Now she wanted nothing more than to crawl into her comfortable bed back at the Mayflower.

Jessica showed no sign of slowing down. "I'm starving. Is there a place close by where we can still get something to eat?"

"Ah youth," Claire said with admiration."

"It's because she plays tennis everyday and is in great shape." Katherine made this comment in a kindlier fashion than she once might have.

"I thought she was a writer living a solitary life locked up in her room with a computer."

"Okay, you two, enough of this, 'I'm so old I couldn't possibly eat at this late hour' routine. You know you're starving.

Katherine didn't know whether to laugh or cry. She hoped Claire would say they were out of luck.

"Follow me." Claire finished turning off the overhead lights, and headed for the door.

She led them on a ten-minute walk to her condo. Inside the door Katherine was astonished that the interior could have anything remotely to do with this plain beige bookseller. She must have the house key of a friend, borrowed for such occasions. In the kitchen they sat at a small pine table that looked borrowed from a restaurant where Katherine once dined in Normandy. The fabrics on the French chairs, even the diminutive shades on the chandelier above the table, were the wonderful gold, blue and cranberry tones straight from the French store, Pierre Dux. Claire's kitchen cabinets were painted a deep cranberry red. White woodwork and ceiling set the entire area off. Katherine could not figure out how this decor appealed to someone who was so colorless herself.

Claire set before them a bacon and egg sandwich. "I grew up eating these, we called them cowboy sandwiches."

The three women talked around the edges of their food, egg yoke dripping down their chins. Jessica declared, "Delicious," and Katherine murmured, "Comfort food." It did not take long to scoff their sandwiches down, afterwards using paper napkins to wipe their chins and sticky fingers. The conversation revolved around their favorite bookshop stories.

Addicted to English mysteries in particular, Katherine told them about the shop called Scotland Yard, a small but complete mystery bookstore on Green Bay Road in Winnetka, Illinois. "I went in one afternoon to buy several mysteries set in Australia to give as gifts to friends that were traveling there. Half a dozen folks who were perusing the shelves began to give enthusiastic suggestions. I left with four books in my package and the fulfilling experience of spending time with kindred spirits. This is what I call a great bookstore."

Claire Thompson was a perfect example of why Katherine appreciated the company of women. She was open and honest, told you enough about herself without overwhelming you with personal and perhaps embarrassing details. When Katherine complimented her on the kitchen where they remained seated, Claire said, "My ex-partner is now living in France." It was the only explanation she gave and nothing more was necessary.

Exhilaration gave way to exhaustion making it difficult for Katherine to listen carefully to Claire's account of leaving Iowa with 'a dear friend,' as my mother preferred to say. We moved to Seattle because I saw a travel program on TV about the area that was intriguing." Was Claire a kindred soul, a woman who risked making changes in order to create a new life as Katherine had done? She wanted to ask her if in the beginning she repeated the phrase, *I'm going to be okay.*

Because it was late, Katherine almost missed Claire's reference about living in Iowa. She'd been focused on what brought her to Seattle, but something clicked and she interrupted her.

"Sorry, did you say you'd been raised in Iowa?"

"Yes, Iowa City."

"My mother was born in Muscatine." She glanced over at Jessica as if to say she was sorry to exclude her from the conversation.

Claire began to talk about her grandfather, who owned the local lumberyard, and the fact that her mother never left Iowa City. She herself had been raised there, attended the University of Iowa, and met my dear friend," she laughed, "right out of college."

"Your parents are dead?"

"Oh yes. They were both gone when we moved here. It made it easier to leave." Claire stood. "Let's get off these chairs and move into the living room." Leaving the table Claire stopped in front of a wall hung with vintage photographs. She pointed to one of the photos and said, "This is my mother."

There in a sepia photograph, which was beginning to fade, stood a woman about five feet two inches tall. Katherine assumed her eyes were brown like Claire's. She was wearing a light colored sweater set over a dark skirt and clunky high heels. Something about the way she was standing seemed familiar to Katherine. She leaned in to take a better look.

"Tell me more about your Mom. What was her name?" The three women were now seated on matching couches in a comfortable arrangement in the living room.

"Her name was Evelyn Miller. And as I said, she spent her whole life in Iowa City."

"You said your grandfather owned the lumber business there, and your grandmother?"

"She was a local girl. She and my grandfather were high school sweethearts and married very young. After ten years of trying to have a child, they adopted my mother from an orphanage. She was three or four years old at the time.

Katherine sat looking at Claire in disbelief. She turned towards Jessica, "I know it's late, but can you hold out for a few more minutes?"

"You're the one I'm concerned about. What's going on?"

Katherine moved over to sit beside Claire. "I'm not quite sure how old I was when my mother first told me about her early childhood. I might have been seven or eight years old. Madeline, my mother, her two older sisters, and one younger sister were sent to an orphanage for several years after their father died of black lung disease. Evidently, it was not uncommon to temporarily place children in an orphanage when a widowed mother couldn't financially care for them. The youngest child was adopted under circumstances my mother didn't seem to understand. It was a terrible loss to her. My mother and her older sisters, Virginia and Edith, returned home in time, but they never saw their youngest sister again. Her name was Evelyn."

Katherine reached for Claire's hand. Later when she remembered the two of them sitting silently side by side, their hands clasped, it seemed like the intentional silence that follows a sermon, giving the parishioners a moment to appropriate a particular word meant for them. Just as that silence is broken when people begin to cough and rustle their bulletins, Jessica cleared her throat and said, "I don't believe this!"

There was more to say, of course, questions to ask and answer, but they agreed it was too late to continue. In spite of this incredulous coincidence, Katherine and Claire could not meet the next day. Katherine would come to the bookstore at closing the day after, and they would have the evening to talk.

In the fifteen minutes it took Jessica and Katherine to walk back to the hotel they hardly spoke. Katherine appreciated the stillness while she tried to get her mind wrapped around what had transpired. Unlocking the door to their hotel room she looked at Jessica and said, "Some people don't believe in coincidences. Do you?"

"Of course I do, they happen all the time." She paused and added, "Maybe not as big as this one."

Katherine, tired and overcome, sat on the edge of her bed looking up at Jessica. "I don't believe in coincidences. This was meant to be."

Within minutes Jessica turned off the light between their two beds. "Let's hope Andrew doesn't call at seven-thirty in the morning."

"I'll kill him." Katherine was already on her side reaching for the mattress pad to run her fingers along.

"Me too."

Two evenings later Katherine sat in a taxi outside the bookshop waiting for Claire to lock up. She watched her turn the key in the door and stop to talk to a couple who were passing by. Katherine recognized them from the night of the book signing. How different she appeared, animated and interested when speaking to people. She slipped into the back seat and smiled. "Can you believe this?" She reached over and hugged Katherine.

The food they ordered for dinner hardly mattered to either of them. They sat talking about their mothers. Claire asked, "Did your mother and her sisters try to find Evelyn?"

"My aunt Edith and mother tried years later, but the records were sealed and the orphanage had been closed. Given the times, and perhaps their lack of sophistication about any legal help that might have been available to them, the matter was dropped, but I was left with a lasting interest in this missing little girl. I began to fantasize that I would find Evelyn, recognizing her as a younger version of my mother. A few years after my Mom died, I knew time was running out."

The waiter came and went from the table largely unnoticed. They finished two glasses of wine as the story continued to unfold, but barely nibbled the fish and fresh roasted vegetables set before them. Katherine said, "I never once thought about Evelyn looking like anyone but my mother until I saw the photograph on your wall. Even with your mother's dark hair pulled back in a bun, looking a bit stern, if you don't mind my saying so, something about her seemed familiar. What's so remarkable to me now is when I went back and looked again; your mother looked exactly like my aunt Edith.

"You'd been searching for the wrong face all these years."

"So it seems."

"Were you close with your parents?"

"There probably isn't a day that goes by that I don't think of them. They're like dust motes floating around me that can only be seen in a certain light." She smiled over at Claire and wondered how in the world she could be having this conversation with a cousin who owned a bookstore in downtown Seattle.

By the time the evening was over and they were headed back downtown in a taxi, Katherine wondered if this sudden discovery was going to lead them to a lasting friendship. Outwardly there were stark differences between them. Katherine couldn't think when she might have last worn a flannel shirt over a pair of blue jeans as Claire wore now, and she'd never owned a pair of Birkenstocks. The backpack Claire carried on her shoulder was a far cry from her own Coach bag.

These differences set aside, Katherine liked Claire's unpretentious speech, and her mid-west politics; they shared similar reading tastes, and what little they had covered, their interior lives seem to resonate. Katherine knew she belonged in Chicago walking down Michigan Avenue in her black cashmere coat, which made a statement. The Seattle lifestyle suited Claire. It would require energy on both their parts to build a relationship and stay connected.

Katherine hoped they both had it in them. She asked, "Why don't you come and visit me in Chicago? It's a wonderful city. Maybe we could take a trip to Iowa and visit Muscatine and Iowa City?"

Claire looked pleased. "I haven't got a lot of extra coverage at the shop, but I might be able to manage a few days." She added, "We'll stay in touch and figure something out."

Katherine wasn't sure if they'd see each other again, but it made their parting easier to think that they would.

15

Like most invigorating travel, the time in Seattle flew by. In spite of the pleasure, Katherine was weary. She and Jessica had maintained a full schedule, and to Katherine's astonishment, Jessica worked hard, extending herself wherever they went. She'd done such a superb job that Katherine was now forced to reconsider this 'California girl,' her work ethic, and perhaps, in time, her literary merit. In the late afternoons when Katherine might have rested, she met Andrew for a glass of wine in the hotel bar. Katherine was also trying to absorb the unexpected turn of events with Claire Thompson that packed an emotional wallop.

The tour was over. Katherine and Jessica were flying their separate ways late in the afternoon. The hotel would hold their luggage while they had a final lunch with Andrew at the Icon Grill on Fifth Avenue. Jessica did not wait for Katherine, but went down to the lobby ahead of her hoping to catch Andrew alone before the three of them ambled their way downhill looking in the shop windows and enjoying another day of sunshine.

It seemed impossible that ten years had gone by since Jessica met Andrew at the writer's conference. She'd signed up for a morning novel class taught by someone she no longer remembered. Among other options, the afternoon session offered a workshop on garden writing taught by Andrew Stillman. He had a long list of impressive credentials after his name. She was sitting on the front row when Andrew strolled into the class.

He had a military haircut, and was wearing a coat and tie. Jessica was accustomed to the total disregard men her age had for dress clothes. They wore blue jeans and black tight fitting tee shirts that showed off the results of their daily workouts at the gym. She was impressed with Andrew's appearance and his informative presentation in the workshop.

The second day she took a seat on the first row again, this time leaning forward slightly, hoping he would notice she wasn't wearing a bra under her low-necked blouse. She'd brushed by him several times outside the door when the class took a break. After one of the evenings of author readings, she stood behind him so that when he turned, he bumped into her. She laughed and said, "Nice move."

"Hardly a move, young lady." He stood his ground and looked down at her.

"Oh, it was a move, you just haven't caught up with the idea yet." She took his arm and steered him towards the crowded bar area where some of the conference attendees were having drinks. People from Jessica's novel class waved them over to a string of small tables lined up along a wall. Jessica could tell the conversation was of no interest to Andrew. She moved her leg so that it touched his knee. She expected him to shift away, but instead he glanced at her and smiled. She took this as permission to continue her seduction.

After an hour, Andrew made his excuses to leave, and Jessica said goodnight as well. She hoped the group would think this exit was planned. Riding the elevator to the eighth floor, she was delighted to find their rooms were just down the hall from one another.

Fishing for her key card from the zipped pocket of her purse, she turned with the intent of handing him the card. She was running out of time and had been intentionally provocative.

He refused the card by pushing her hand away. It had been a long time since he'd stepped across anyone's threshold, and this was not the time or place. Jessica gazed after him as he continued on down the hall. He did not look back, but said, "Good night."

Before the conference was over, however, Andrew relented. On one of the breaks between workshops, he did help Jessica open her hotel door. She slipped a do not disturb sign on the outer doorknob.

Jessica walked slowly towards Andrew who stood at the foot of the king sized bed. She put her arms around his neck. He could feel her breasts against his chest and was embarrassed that his instant response was obvious against her body. She stepped back. "How about you unzip this zipper."

He took his hand and slid the dress from her shoulders. She turned and faced him. "Does this interest you?" She began to loosen his tie. She was fabulous, and knew it.

He watched her lay down on the bed. She looked up at him and whispered, "I knew you wanted this to happen."

"I guess I do." He kissed her for the first time and let her take the lead.

Andrew was not proud of the fact that he'd given in. It was a form of flattery, a younger woman interested in an older man, and he knew he was being used from the beginning. Still, he did not put a stop to it. He began to introduce her around to the right people in the garden magazine world. She accompanied him to several events where she could begin to network; all this because she wanted to augment her cash flow with garden articles while writing fiction. He went so far as to look over her early submissions and give suggestions, which he rarely offered.

A year later, when her first articles were accepted for publication in the California garden magazines, she did not look back. Once launched, she never thanked him, unless you counted their infrequent trysts as payment, which Jessica seemed to think was enough. She taught him a lesson about young ambitious women.

When she telephoned to say she was coming to Seattle, he knew it was a prelude to another scheme, which was of no interest to him until she mentioned her editor, and the Davis Publishing Firm in Chicago. Maybe he would use her for a change. He agreed to host them if the editor joined her on the upcoming book tour. Since their arrival, they had not talked privately until this moment when she joined him in the lobby where he stood waiting.

"Were you surprised to hear from me?" she asked.

"Don't you mean, delighted?"

"That too." She leaned forward and kissed him lightly on the lips. "You know you have missed me."

"This will surprise you, but no, I haven't. You used me, young lady, and you're here to use me again. It's okay, because I'm prepared this time. Besides, your bribe is worth it."

"You mean, Katherine?"

"This the price of admission?"

"You like her, I can tell."

"That's what you wanted, my dear, and I have obliged." Andrew leaned forward. He murmured, "Be careful, Jessica, don't embarrass either of us."

"I would not dream of kiss and tell. Though if you'd be interested."

"What do you want Jessica? I assume Katherine will be here in a minute. You'd best get on with it.

"I have a new book in mind. I want to use the garden magazine business as the setting. It's been a while since I have been in touch with that world. Would you put the word out with your contacts that Jessica needs access? Make some calls, set up a few appointments?"

"That's it?"

"For the moment."

They turned when the elevator door made a dinging sound and watched Katherine walk into the lobby towards them. Andrew glanced quickly at Jessica. "I'd be happy to look into it. Thank you for using Katherine as your bait."

When Jessica said she would wait down in the lobby, Katherine assumed she was going ahead to pay the bill and arrange to leave their luggage until after lunch. Looking at Andrew, she sensed that he was irritated, yet Jessica looked unperturbed. Jessica's questions about Andrew had changed from polite teasing, "How was your date?" to pressing for details about what they'd done while together. Katherine knew instinctively to wrap a professional cloak around herself that

102

drew a line she was not comfortable letting Jessica cross. She was after all, a client of Davis Publishing.

Out on the street, walking towards the restaurant, Katherine was sorry to be leaving Seattle. She would miss the atmosphere of the city. Seated at the restaurant, she looked around the room with approval. "This is fantastic." She was looking at the colored blown glass in different shapes and sizes attached to the ceiling. "Could this be Chihuly's work?"

Andrew gazed admiringly at the ceiling as well. "I was told it might have been a student of his. We'll ask." Turning towards Jessica, he said, "I'm sure you have seen his glass sculptures installed in gardens and museums on your travels."

Jessica appeared amused. "You two are like peas in a pod. I think it has something to do with growing up watching movies when a husband and wife carefully take off their robes and lay them at the end of separate twin beds with a nightstand and lamp between them. The most dazzling thing an audience watched was one of Doris Day's radiant smiles. You guys have this comfortable distance-thing going. Might be a bit behind the times, that's all."

Katherine looked across the table at Jessica and Andrew. She smiled. There was something to be said for the liberated lifestyle Jessica led; she was independent and confident. Katherine gave her credit for navigating these past few days with optimism and energy, both of which ranked high on Katherine's litmus test. She knew instinctively that Jessica was incapable of romance, something Katherine, regardless of her age, hung on to tenaciously. Sex for Jessica, however, was probably another matter, after seeing her undergarments.

Katherine felt a great loss over the exquisite moments of intimacy she'd once known. Whether it was the time she stood in a crowded elevator pressed back against a young boy she was falling in love with, or her long marriage to Timothy, she remembered how romantic it all had been. She felt sorry for this young woman who would never be asked to turn on the car radio station so she and her latest beau could listen to the same music as they drove away from each other. Katherine doubted that Jessica would ever have a special song that years later would make her remember being young and in love.

Part way through lunch Jessica excused herself from the table. Andrew wasted no time in speaking directly to Katherine. "You do realize that she thinks we're both old and irrelevant?"

"What on earth gives her that idea?" Katherine laughed when Andrew grinned at her.

"I know her. She thinks we have already lived our lives. That's what the Doris Day thing was all about." Andrew hesitated then added, "And, she uses people. She's looking for something from both of us."

Katherine was not sure what Andrew expected her to say. Robert would never forgive her if she spoke unkindly about a client.

"I want you to know that she owed me big time for some help I gave her a few years ago. Now that she has introduced me to you, her debt is paid in full. I'd like to prove her wrong about life being over for the two of us. She may have youth on her side, but she will never meet someone and have it mean as much as this time with you has meant to me."

Katherine was startled with Andrew's forthright declaration, but, their conversation broke off abruptly when Jessica returned to the table.

It was time to pay the bill, which Katherine insisted was her treat. The waiter stood patiently while the three of them argued until Katherine nodded that it was settled. Andrew wondered how reluctant he sounded when he said, "Ladies, it is time to pick up your luggage and take you to the airport."

❀

Andrew waited with Katherine at the curbside baggage check-in. After tipping the baggage man for her, they walked a few steps toward the doors into the terminal. While shaking hands, Andrew said, "It's been a pleasure, Katherine. Think about my proposition." They both laughed.

"Thank you for making my Seattle trip memorable."

He reluctantly let go of her hand, and watched her disappear into the terminal. He wanted her to turn and wave goodbye, but she didn't.

The moment he opened his car door, Jessica, who was now sitting in the front seat said, "I told you meeting her was a brilliant idea."

"She is an extraordinary woman." He pulled slowly out in front of a car that was waiting to take his space at the curb. Glancing over at Jessica's face he said, "What, you don't agree? You're the one who said she was wonderful."

"Did I?"

Driving further down the departure lane to the United Airlines entrance, Andrew made a decision to leave Jessica with a compliment. "Katherine was impressed with how hard you worked on this tour; she said you deserved success with this book."

"Really?" Andrew thought she sounded like a child who'd been trying hard to please.

Pulling to the curbside again, he doubted that any advice he had to give would be taken seriously, but he was going to give some anyway. He turned and looked directly at Jessica. "If I were you, I wouldn't do anything to jeopardize your relationship with Katherine. Setting business aside, her friendship means something; it does to me, and I've just met her."

In Andrew's estimation, Jessica owed at least a small modicum of respect for her smart, down to earth, editor, but knowing Jessica, she would discount the enormous help Katherine had been in improving her latest book.

Andrew pulled Jessica's bag out of the back of the car. "You won't forget to make some calls for me to your garden magazine buddies?"

"I'll see what I can do." Andrew bore her no hard feelings in spite of the fact he'd already given, metaphorically, at the office. He'd done his best by her and she had moved on. This time Jessica would not reel him in, but Katherine had. He knew on Jessica's part, this was an unintentional consequence.

When Jessica turned to wave goodbye, Andrew's car was already entering the line of slow moving vehicles.

❈

Traffic from the airport made Andrew late for his dinner invitation. Everyone had a drink in hand by the time he arrived. His hostess, Anne St. John, motioned him to join her on the teakwood bench in their city garden. He collected a glass and poured some Merlot before sitting down.

"Happy to see you." Anne greeted him with a kiss on his cheek.

"Lovely to be here as always."

"Been busy?"

"I've had an interesting week with an editor from Chicago."

"That book on English gardens you have talked about?"

"Talked about, that's been the problem, but I'm encouraged to start in earnest on the research now."

Anne St. John was central to this group of old friends gathered tonight. She and George had been married for over forty years. Their home in the Seward Park Neighborhood of Seattle had long been the gathering place for after work drinks and dinner. In their early years these friends spent all their time together in the out of doors: hiking, camping, riding bicycles on day trips. Now in their early sixties, few had slowed down though none of them were playing singles tennis anymore. Andrew's friendship among them was highly regarded. Any one of these long time friends would say Andrew was a patient, good-natured man, who remained unpretentious as his fortunes increased; he was thought of as a genuinely nice person. These friends were Andrew's family.

It wasn't clear to any of them, including Andrew, why he had never married. There'd been a few women he'd been serious about, but in time, they'd given up waiting for an engagement ring. This saddened him, but never enough to change anything about his life. He avoided conflict and tension if at all possible, which seemed to go hand in hand with relationships. He'd mastered the art of ignoring what upset him, and it could be said, meaning no offense, that he was the essence of a 'peace at any price' man. His friends didn't find this a problem, but any long-term relationship he tried eventually did.

Out on the patio, several hours later, the men stood looking up at a star-filled sky. The laughter coming from the kitchen where the women were cleaning up the dishes enhanced their feelings of well being.

Andrew broke the silence, "I met someone this week, George."

"The editor-lady you drove to the airport?"

"Her name is Katherine White. She lives in Chicago and works for a publishing firm there."

"What's she like?"

"Our age, widowed, smart, good humored, engaging."

"She's going to be one hell of an expensive date, my friend."

On the drive home Andrew felt disquieted, which was unusual. A comfortable evening with friends always filled his cup anew, but tonight was different. Even a glass of wine on his front porch when he got home did not comfort him. He watched his next door neighbor walk past with his two dogs, their last outing for the night, but he stayed hidden in the dark without calling out to him to say hello as he often did. Though lonely, he did not want company. It was past eleven o'clock when he finally went in.

Undressing for bed, he gave himself a serious talking to: *You've got to shake yourself out of this funk, my friend. Can't let someone you hardly know ruin your cheery disposition.* But when he turned out the light, he again put his hand on the pillow beside him and thought of Katherine.

16

The answering machine was blinking when Katherine opened the door to her apartment on return to Chicago. Switching on some lights, she stood by her kitchen table and pressed the button to listen. Claire Thompson's voice greeted her.

"Sorry to have missed you. I wanted to tell you that I went into storage and found a box of old photos from my mother's childhood. I've been looking through them and have selected several that were taken when she was little. I have stuck four or five of them in an envelope and mailed them to you. I wonder if they might bear some resemblance to your mother. Hard to tell in these old black and white things, but I thought you might want to have a look. Call me and let me know what you think. Bye."

Katherine was still trying to work out the statistical probability of meeting a stranger in Seattle that would bring resolution to the mystery of her adopted aunt. Even if there had been a lead detective on the case, what were the chances that clues would have led him to Claire Thompson's door. It was an amazing gift of closure she never expected to have at this late date.

Back at work, Katherine sang the praises of Jessica and the book tour, partially enhanced for Robert's benefit. It was the least she could do in appreciation for her time away from the office. She raved about the friendly people she'd met, and the great food she'd eaten. To hear her tell it, the Seattle gardening world was heaven. She did not mention Andrew Stillman, and hoped Jessica never would either. The story of meeting the owner of the bookstore, where a reading was held, was soon all over the office. Everyone agreed it was an amazing coincidence, Jessica's word again.

A package for Katherine was delivered to the office a week later. Elizabeth's curiosity got the better of her and she lingered in

Katherine's office hoping she would open the package right away, but when it was obvious she was not going to oblige her, she turned to leave the room.

"Thank you Elizabeth, and would you close the door?"

"Yes, Ma'am." Katherine heard the fake southern accent in this time-honored expression. With a mischievous grin, Elizabeth closed the door behind her. The precise handwriting and return address on the package belonged to Andrew. Inside the box with a note, lay a pair of sunglasses wrapped in bubble wrap. Katherine reached for her reading glasses and sat down to read the note.

Dear Katherine: I want you to have this pair of yellow tinted sunglasses. Because of our time together, I now find myself looking at my work through yellow filtered light that makes everything vivid and sharp. Your visit provided me the impetus to start writing again. It is my wish that in wearing these glasses you will see the possibilities of our writing collaboration, and dare I add...the possibilities of our deepening friendship. With warm regards, Andrew.

Katherine once cautioned her daughter that long distance romances were not practical. Twice she'd watched Louisa negotiate the expense and incompatible schedules with men living in different time zones. In both cases, it did not work out.

"You can't get to know anyone that way," she'd warned. "Anyone can be charming for a weekend." Now, here she was sitting with a pair of sunglasses, a pleasing note, quite romantic really, from a very interesting man who lived across the country. She said out loud, "Anyone can be charming for six days, Katherine."

Regardless of the miles that stretched between them, time with Andrew had a tenderizing affect on her, a strange way to put it, but there it was. Tears welled up in Katherine's eyes for no other reason than appreciating Andrew's unusual gift and note. She remained seated at her desk considering the whole matter of Andrew Stillman.

On her computer, the McAfee Virus Scan clicked away. The files flew by, but every now and then the scan hesitated, as if looking deeply into something that had caught its eye. Katherine wondered if this was not the same way God checked on her, casting his eye in her direction, only pausing when he found something that was not quite right?

It was not unusual for Katherine to think about her life like this. She once wrote a piece for a garden magazine about the spiritual gifts she found hidden in her garden's compost pile.

While waiting on the scan to finish, Katherine began to doodle on the legal pad that lay before her. Usually she drew flowers and trees, maybe iris, with their sheath-like leaves. In this absent-minded garden scribble, she thought of Mary coming to the garden tomb early on Easter morning. She doesn't recognize, Jesus, sitting on a rock, until he calls to her by name. In that call she recognizes his voice. Katherine believed this call was tender, almost pleading, "Mary, Mary." The story took on new meaning when Katherine heard God's voice calling her by name. Not Katie, her nickname, but her given name, Katherine. She never used her nickname again. Was her friendship with Andrew a new call in a direction she could not have foreseen?

The telephone rang, which required Katherine to put down her pen and get back to business. The scan was finished, and she was late for a meeting in Robert's office by the time she hung up.

❁

Walking through her front door shortly after six o'clock, she pulled the yellow tinted sunglasses, still protected in bubble wrap, from her briefcase. Looking at the clock, she calculated the time change and made a hasty decision before she changed her mind. She searched for a three by five card in her purse where she'd written the names and numbers of the contacts she'd made in Seattle. Andrew answered on the fourth ring. Sounding excessively bright, she said, "Hi there, it's Katherine."

"Hi there yourself. Great to hear your voice."

"I received a lovely present today in the mail. I think it is from a friend in Seattle, am I right?"

"How did you guess?"

"Because the note was signed, Andrew, and you are the only nice person I could think of that might do such a thing."

"Think of it as a bribe."

"How so?" Andrew proceeded to tell her about his work on matching the right combination of Seattle and English gardeners.

"Katherine, come with me to England? I've thought about it since you left, and I really want you to join me on this expedition to solidify the right combinations."

She slid down onto the kitchen chair near the phone and didn't speak for a moment. "That's a lovely invitation, Andrew, but there is my work, and you hardly know me, and there is the expense, and I'm sure there are other considerations to think about."

"When the time comes I'll write it all off as a business expense; it's called research."

"I wouldn't dream of letting you pay my way."

"Why not? Your expertise would be invaluable to me. Think of it as a working trip if you must, but I wish you would consider it for personal reasons too."

"I can't give you an answer without thinking about it. My work schedule is flexible, it's true, but you've caught me off guard." Katherine could not deny that in the few days she'd spent with this man, she'd been drawn into the aura of contentment that emanated from him. He'd been the most pleasant person imaginable; there was something restorative while in his company.

"Katherine, this is a risky thing for me to say, but it is *you* that have caught me off guard."

When she didn't respond, he asked, "Have I just over stepped a boundary?"

"I think we are too old to play games, don't you? You have done nothing but extend a generous invitation to a place I love, and to the gardens that have always inspired me. There isn't any reason why I can't say yes, but I'm not going to give you an answer just now. If you need to make your plans, of course, I encourage you to do so. If you can give me some time to consider this, I'll get back to you."

"In the mean time, would you consider inviting me to Chicago. I can stay at The Drake or somewhere along Michigan Avenue, and we could continue this conversation."

A few minutes later, after thanking him for his gift, Katherine added, "I have you to thank for adding to my pleasure of being in Seattle."

"The pleasure was mine. Think about that invitation to Chicago, will you?"

"I'll be in touch."

"I hope so, and wear your new sunglasses."

She put the telephone down. Her immediate thought was, *Katherine, do you really want to complicate your new life that is still under construction?* She said under her breath, "I'm sure my building permits don't include an addition like this."

After salad and a glass of wine, Katherine reached over and pulled a yellow legal pad from a drawer. Like an automatic writing scam at a séance, her fountain pen started filling up the pages. Only when she realized how stiff she'd become, sitting too long in one place, did she finally stop. The grandfather's clock struck ten o'clock as she headed for bed. Left behind on the table was an introduction, based on Christopher Lloyd's quotation, 'the long conversation that is the English garden.'

17

Katherine arrived at her office the following Monday morning, to find Robert standing looking out her window. When he turned, she greeted him with a smile. "This is a pleasant way to start the week."

"Katherine, something has happened that affects Elizabeth." Hearing the gravity in his voice, she reached for her desk top in anticipation of bad news. "Did you hear about the decks that collapsed last night?"

"Tell me she wasn't there."

"No, thank goodness, but several of her friends were, and one of them died. I talked with her this morning when she called. She won't be in for a few days."

"I heard about the collapse on the TV news while I was getting dressed for work, but I never thought about Elizabeth. She must be devastated."

"If you were out last night, you know it was a beautiful evening. As many as fifty people, most of them in their early 20s, were crammed onto an apartment's upper second and third-floor porches. The third floor porch dropped out from under them, and one porch collapsed on top of the other, sending people and debris crashing to the ground."

"They said thirteen people had been killed and more injured."

"I don't know if you heard the fire chief say that it appeared to be a case of too many people in a small space, but the city's building commissioner said there was no indication of any substandard problems or insufficiencies with the porch. He did add that the porches aren't made for large parties."

Katherine was now slumped into the chair in front of her desk. "Elizabeth was invited, but she backed out at the last minute. Her roommate left for the party without her. She is one of the injured women." Robert sat down in the opposite chair, and reached over to pat her arm.

Katherine placed her hand on top of his. "I just read an article written on the Chicago porches that the Chicago Architectural Foundation printed. One of my own earliest memories is playing on the back porch in the apartment building where we lived."

"They're so typical throughout the Chicago neighborhoods. When I ride the train down there are places where the tracks run so close to the back of the buildings, you feel you could reach out and touch one of them.

"The article reminded me they came about as an outgrowth of Chicago's characteristic back alleys where milk, and ice and other goods could be delivered. The extra space the alleyways provided made room at the back of the buildings for these wooden porches."

"I know the pre-2003 porches are usually original to their buildings, but in the mid-70s a number of the buildings were changed back into single-family dwellings or 3-flats."

"I think this building on Wrightswood was renovated later then that."

"That's one of the reasons the Lincoln Park neighborhood has attracted students and young professionals into the area. These renovations and, of course, its proximity to Lake Michigan and downtown."

"Which hiked the rents. Elizabeth tells me that is why she lives in Ravenswood. She can't afford anything closer." Stunned that Elizabeth was involved in this way, Katherine said, "I can only imagine how despondent these young people and their families must be." Katherine paused. "To think I once complained to you about her."

"I seem to remember warning you that if you hounded her out of her blue jeans we might have a harassement charge on our hands."

"Aren't you glad you couldn't dissuade me?"

"You can be stubborn, Katherine." He was smiling at her.

"She was capable of much more than answering my telephone."

"She had sense enough to appreciate your interest." Katherine nodded in agreement. "I couldn't decide if you were playing professor Henry Higgins, or providing her with a facsimile of a Masters Degree."

"You're lucky she never heard you call her Eliza Dolittle."

"It got a rise out of you." Robert grinned.

"I knew we'd turned a corner when she added several jackets to her wardrobe. She'd already been reading manuscripts for me, but the day she arrived in a well-cut black pants suit, I invited her to sit in on meeting with one of the clients. She was great from the start; respectful, able to make helpful suggestions about the work."

"The girl who came here straight out of college with her long damaged hair straggling down her back turned into a young woman on the rise, thanks to you."

They sat without speaking for a moment. Robert spoke softly. "Life is fragile."

"Why does it always take a tragedy to remind us of that fact? You know these young people think of themselves as indestructible. Timothy's death was a terrible shock because I assumed we had forever."

"You're better now, I can see that."

"Oh yes, much. He still shows up at odd moments, and I miss him, but I'm better."

"I take my hat off to you." Robert gestured with his hand removing an imaginary hat from his head towards her. "To pick up your life, move back here after so many years; you've made me look at some things, I can tell you."

"You're not thinking about moving?" Katherine half smiled.

"Would that bother you?"

"It certainly would. This is the best job in the city. Interesting work, flexible time, a great boss." She reached over and placed a hand on his knee. "I'm your biggest fan, you know. Grateful that we share this long history, remember one another's parents, our Duke days... and letting me be a part of Davis Publishing."

Sounding like Jack Nicholson, Robert mimicked, "What we have here, Ms. White is a mutual admiration society. I'm grateful to you too. More than I can say."

"You've got so much going for you, Robert. Don't discount it; good health, a successful business, friends and interests." She hesitated and laughed. "It's true, you do set a high bar for yourself, and everybody else. Occasionally, your expectations are unreasonable."

"No, surely not."

"The world needs people like you. I would never want you to settle for mediocrity." Katherine stood from her chair and Robert got up too.

"This was kind, Robert, to wait for me this morning with this news." The one thing Katherine was sure of was that Robert was neither devious nor cruel. He had a tendency to snub people that did not interest him, or bother to hide his impatience. His mood dictated which face he showed to the world; dour or dazzling. Robert might hate small talk, but he gave everything he had intellectually when he discussed things with those few who could keep up with his mental agility.

"Elizabeth and people like Jessica Lovejoy have you to thank for my help. I admire that when you find an author you believe in, you forgive them all their sins, regardless of their eccentricities, their drinking habits or their politics that rankle. When you recognized an author's brilliance, they have your loyalty."

Katherine stood looking at the door Robert closed behind him. He'd left her with a distinct impression that something was amiss. Hopefully, it was only this event that involved Elizabeth.

She reached Elizabeth's answering machine. "Want you to know how sorry I am about your loss, Elizabeth. I'm devastated for you. I know you will be taking a few days, and I don't want to bother you, but if you need anything, you know how to reach me. Take care of yourself." Elizabeth picked up as Katherine was saying goodbye. It was obvious she'd been crying.

"I'm here."

Katherine grabbed a Kleenex and dabbed away her own tears when she heard Elizabeth's voice. "Thank goodness you're safe," she said.

"How could such a terrible thing happen?"

"It doesn't help you this morning, but, I feel certain this calamity will bring about new codes and stiffer inspection policies that may be needed."

Elizabeth talked briefly about the death of her friend. "My roommate is going to be okay. Her parents took her home early this morning from the hospital; what a blessing they live up north. They were able to be with her quickly."

"I'm already praying for everybody, Elizabeth."

"Pray for me too."

❁

Four days later, Katherine was home from a 4th of July picnic in Evanston where Louisa had entertained neighbors and their visiting families. It had been a lovely day, not too hot, perfect for the tennis matches at Ackerman Park in North Evanston. Katherine could remember plenty of 4th of July fireworks in Dyche Stadium, Northwestern's football field, when people wrapped themselves in blankets.

Through her living room windows, she stood looking south at the fireworks just starting over Navy Pier. At 9:00 PM, it was almost dark. The living room lamps behind her reflected on the glass, interfering with what she knew would be a spectacular show. She turned the lights off and sat back down. She held a silver framed photograph of Timothy she'd picked up from the small table beside her. He loved this holiday; flying his flag, cooking on the grill, serving beer and brats to friends.

Four years ago Katherine would never have envisioned herself sitting alone looking at the fireworks in Chicago. She and Johanna had laughed about rocking together on the porch at some old folk's home, which wasn't a bad prospect. The men would still have their offices at the hospital where they could get away and talk shop, write papers, and lend a teaching hand with the latest residents. Retired, it would be a welcome relief to have the full burden of their responsibilities shifted. The women would carry on with their latest passions, and the couples would take advantage of some of the enticing trips the University offered. In these scenarios no one ever talked about one of them dropping over at the age of sixty. Katherine pulled a Kleenex from her skirt pocket and dabbed at her eyes.

The finale to the fireworks display filled the sky with red, white and blue light. Katherine placed the silver framed photograph back on the table and headed back to her bedroom. She wondered if holidays would ever be just that again, without sadness or feeling something was not quite right.

The following Monday evening, Katherine and Robert, walked down Michigan Avenue towards The Four Seasons Hotel at One Magnificent Mile. They were representing Davis Publishing at a cocktail party and book launching; a costly affair that the author himself was hosting. Over the years, after attending countless affairs like this, Robert said, "I have considered giving myself hazardous duty pay."

Katherine knew these events left him bored and irritable, which is why she said yes to him when he asked, "You wouldn't consider saving me, would you?"

"Should I be careful and say, it depends?"

"Would you start accompanying me to some of these book launchings?"

Katherine walked ahead of Robert into these gatherings, meeting and greeting, smiling and laughing, which provided cover for his usual grunts and head nodding at people. It was a pleasure meeting new people, and reconnecting with someone she'd grown up with on the North Shore.

This evening they stayed an obligatory hour and were now standing on the street in front of the hotel. "Honestly, Katherine, I don't know how you do it. You actually enjoy these stand up things."

"The standing does get to me, but yes, I'm happy to go with you."

"You have made it easier for me to bear, I can tell you that. Thank you." He took Katherine's elbow and steered her out of the way of others who were leaving the hotel.

In those few steps, Katherine decided to say what was on her mind. "If you don't mind me saying so, Robert, I think you have lost the art of listening." She gave him a nudge with her elbow.

"Nobody says anything worth listening to."

"How do you know? You rarely pay attention."

"So you're saying I'm a lousy listener and what else?"

"I'm just saying..."

Robert glanced at her, smiled, and nudged her back. "Not sure you can teach an old dog new tricks, but I will give it some thought, in spite of how unkind you are to point this out to me."

A young man brushed past Katherine rather aggressively, but immediately apologized. "It's okay," she said, and he turned back in the direction he was hurrying off in.

"Did I tell you about the young man that stopped me over on LaSalle when I was coming out of Ascension?" Katherine put her hand on Robert's sleeve to slow him down as they headed for the corner.

"What do you mean stopped you? He tried to mug you?"

"No, nothing like that, but I was walking away from the church, and he stepped from behind a car and asked if he could talk to me for a moment. I stopped and stepped towards him. I told him of course he could. He said he'd just gotten out of jail and needed some money to catch a bus back home. Then he said the most heartfelt thing. He looked directly at me and said, "I'm not a bad man, but I made a mistake.""

"For once I had some cash on me, but before I handed it to him, I said, 'If I give you this money will you make me a promise?' He nodded that he would."

I told him, "Don't get into any more trouble."

"What did he say?"

"Yes ma'am."

"Honestly, Robert, this brief conversation was one of those conversion moments in life that you never forget. I will always remember him saying, 'I'm not a bad man, but I made a mistake.' I wish I'd immediately answered, 'Me too.'"

"Why, what mistake have you made? Are you regretting leaving Chapel Hill and moving back here? Are you unhappy with your work?"

"None of those things, but you know, mistakes, things we regret, as the prayer book says, things done and left undone."

Robert reached for her hand. "My father used to say that the only mistake you make is the one you don't learn from. I'm sure you have learned from yours. You are a woman of a certain age, successful, endearing, smart and great company."

Katherine grinned. "I wasn't fishing for compliments."

"I'm happy to offer them."

"The same opportunity to help someone happened once before in the same place. There was a bag lady standing on the steps of the church. She asked me for money and I told her I didn't have any, which wasn't true." Katherine paused, "Have you ever noticed the magnificent sculpture of Jesus that hangs on the exterior wall facing LaSalle?"

"I suppose I have seen it, but, no, I don't *know* it."

"Underneath the sculpture of Christ on the cross it says, *Is it nothing to you, all that pass by*. With my imagination, I can see myself standing at the pearly gates being asked, "Do you remember the day you refused to help me?"

Robert raised his hand to hail a passing cab. "I'll vouch for you if needed." He smiled. The cab pulled over to the curb. Robert gestured, "Come on, it's just a few blocks, I'll drop you." When Katherine got out in front of her building she leaned back in. "I had a good time." She knew Robert was simply relieved to have the party over.

"Goodnight." She waved goodbye as the taxi headed for the Northwestern Train Station.

18

September arrived before Katherine had any interest in changing her wardrobe around in anticipation of cooling temperatures. How could it be September 9th already? She stood before Elizabeth's desk. "Come on, we're going to a protest on our lunch hour."

"What are we protesting?" Elizabeth grabbed her purse from a bottom drawer and caught up with Katherine at the elevator door. "I have bail money in case we get thrown in jail."

"I'm prepared to do what ever it takes." Katherine took Elizabeth's arm and marched her into the elevator. Out on the street the two women got into a cab. Katherine told the driver, "Marshall Field's, State Street, please."

"You're joking, we're going to protest at Field's?" Elizabeth began to laugh.

"Mark my words, September 9th, will be a date that will live in infamy."

"I thought that was Roosevelt's line."

"Changing the name of the store from Field's to Macy's, is a terrible idea."

In the cab Katherine sounded like a docent after her foray into the history of the famous State Street store. "During World War Two, the visual team at Field's had a new idea. They began to design theme windows that spanned the length of State Street that told a story."

"I remember the Cinderella windows." Elizabeth exclaimed. "My grandmother brought us every Christmas. We dressed in our Christmas best, velvet dresses, white socks with lace and patent leather shoes. We'd ride the train down and walk the streets looking at all the beautiful store windows. One year she got us rabbit white muffs to carry. I still use mine when I go to Christmas parties."

"That's my point. My mother brought me to see the Field's Christmas windows, and I brought Louisa, and eventually, Beatrice. I will admit, Field's is not what it was when my mother and I rode the El train at Christmas. The help is not as obliging, and the candy department has eliminated the Vermont maple sugar pieces that were always in my stocking. I'm telling you, a century of memories should not be trifled with."

Elizabeth agreed. "It's called making memories. Beatrice won't forget, nor will all the other children who have eaten in the Walnut room and seen the Christmas tree."

When the cab pulled up at Field's, over two hundred and fifty protesters were gathered under the famous Field's clock at State and Randolph. Katherine led Elizabeth into the throng. Everyone was sharing their stories. A woman standing next to Katherine said, "I brought my granddaughter here when she was little to buy a Rothschild coat, and was told they no longer carried them. I was indignant. I told the sales woman, 'My mother bought my Rothschild coats here, I bought my daughter's coats here, and I am here to buy my granddaughter a coat!'"

They stood for over an hour listening to one another's remembrances, united in their deep regret that Field's would no longer be called Field's. When it was time to head back to the office, Katherine said, "Chicago cares about local lore, forget official titles. It will be a long time before Comiskey Park is called the U.S. Cellular Field or Marshall Field's is called Macy's. You can count on that."

Ensconced in a taxi once again, Elizabeth placed her hand on Katherine's thigh and gave it a pat. "Everyone that was there today brought with them the ghosts of Christmas past, don't you think?"

"Absolutely, I certainly did. When I'm on the escalators between floors in the store, I often feel my mother's presence. Missing her, I usually shed a tear, and wish we were headed to see the dolls in the toy department again."

"What toy department?"

"Oh, long gone. The big box stores took care of that. But, for a little girl in those days, it was extraordinary. Toy trains ran in closed cases at eye level where the children stood watching. The kids hated being dragged off to some other part of the store. The dolls were in glass cases that lined the walls. One year I got lost and they announced my name over the loud speaker."

"You must have been terrified. Can you imagine if that happened today? Children are taken in the blink of an eye."

"Not back then. People would come to a weeping child's rescue and take them by the hand to find their mothers."

Outside Katherine's office door, Elizabeth replaced her purse in the bottom desk drawer. When she straightened up she gave Katherine a grin. "Any time you want to go back and protest, I'll go with you."

"Thank you, Elizabeth. I'd like that."

❁

Later in the month, Robert was at home sitting at his desk in the study. He scrawled in large bold lettering across the top of a legal pad: SAME OLD-SAME OLD. On the fireplace mantle a ship's bell clock struck ten times before a brown and white springer spaniel crossed the carpeted floor to rest a head on his master's lap. Absentmindedly, Robert scratched behind the dog's ears, but ignored this invitation to take a walk.

It took him most of an hour to painstakingly write a list of the things he once enjoyed, but was no longer doing. Part of the list read; season tickets-Northwestern football games, golf on Saturdays (in good weather), followed by social events, (downtown after work), and the name of a few friends he was no longer seeing. The only thing he wrote down that he still enjoyed was yard work. If not for the worn pair of Docker pants and the weathered plaid shirt he was wearing, he might not have come up with that. Discouraged, he put his pen down. "Come on, Davis, out we go."

Walking south down Sheridan Road, Robert knew by the wagging tail and adoring eyes, he was back in the good graces of this endearing creature that shared his bed. For the remainder of the walk he thought about the irony of frugality. When they returned home, wanting to sit for a few minutes, he took the dog off the leash and made room for him on the front steps. Davis leaned against his leg, tail thumping.

Under his breath Robert muttered, "Damn." The pile of damp and pungent leaves he'd raked after breakfast were now blowing back across the yard. The next wave of leaves that were fluttering to the ground would soon erase all evidence of his earlier attempt to clean up the front yard. Looking at his watch, there was no time to start over. The dog reluctantly followed him inside the house. Robert returned to his desk and wrote on a fresh piece of paper, COUNTING THE COST.

He hated doing it, but he began with the word marriage, followed by several women's names. Next he wrote, The Hideaway, the name of his parents' cottage in Michigan. He'd traded a lifetime of memories and family traditions for the killing he'd made when he sold it. Lastly, he wrote Club Membership, because he'd recently resigned from Indian Hill Country Club. If you only play one round of golf a season he couldn't justify the membership any longer. Looking for some evidence of excess to cheer him up, he wrote down, clothes.

When the clock struck twelve, he put the legal pad in the top drawer of the desk. Davis bounded out the door ahead of him and waited in the hallway unsure of Robert's next move. Together they climbed the stairs to the bedroom and stood before an immaculate clothes closet. Robert believed in buying good things that lasted a long time; his wardrobe was a testament to longevity. After showering, he reached for a pair of lightweight gray flannel pleated pants, and pulled a yellow oxford shirt from a drawer. He selected a V-neck cashmere sweater and began to dress.

It was quarter to one when he left the house in Kenilworth and drove south on Green Bay Road towards Evanston. Waiting at the light at Kenilworth Avenue, he glanced across at the Train Station. Little had changed about the area since his graduation from New Trier High School. Today the only traffic crossing in front of him came from the Church of the Holy Comforter, the Episcopal Church, which he hadn't attended in years. As a nod to his parents, he still sent pledge money once a year, and there was a reassuring niche in the churchyard columbarium where one day he would join them. When the light changed he said aloud, "Oh Lord, I believe, help me in my unbelief."

A few minutes after one o'clock Robert rang the doorbell on Asbury Avenue. He watched Katherine as she hugged her daughter goodbye, and wondered why they clung to one another an imperceptible moment longer than seemed necessary. They didn't speak, but in letting go, Katherine's daughter said, "I'll be okay."

He picked up Katherine's overnight bag that sat by the front door and slung it over his shoulder. When they reached the car parked at the curb they both turned and waved goodbye.

"She's a lovely young woman, Katherine."

"Her whole life is about to change." She offered no explanation for this comment.

Robert drove down Asbury Avenue getting ready to turn east towards the lake at Church Street. He remarked about the substantial houses on either side of the street. "All these big houses still look strange without the mature elm trees, don't they?"

"When I was growing up their canopy covered the street like a tunnel." Katherine pointed out the window. "Playing one night, I ran into one of the trees so hard that I almost knocked myself out. The trunks of the trees were immense."

"The City of Elms, did you know that?"

"If you have 22,000 of them, it is a good name. I had no idea when I left for college that the Dutch elm disease was insidiously making its way through the tree-lined streets. I feel terrible I didn't say goodbye to every tree on Asbury that stood guard over my growing up."

"It's gone by too fast." There was a note of regret in Robert's voice.

"I saw an old film clip the other night of the first Presidential debate between Nixon and Kennedy. It made me think of children playing hide and seek, and calling out, 'Here I come, ready or not.' That's what the years cry out, don't they? 'Here I come, ready or not.'"

Robert took his right hand off the wheel to reach over and touch Katherine's arm. "I was going to wait until after lunch, but I've spent the whole weekend rehearsing what I want to ask you. You have raised the issue of time, and that's part of my problem."

"You make it sound ominous."

Robert spotted an empty park bench facing Lake Michigan as they drove past Evanston's Centennial Park. He pulled into a space on the street and pointed towards the bench. "Come on, let's sit for awhile."

They walked over to the bench that sat sheltered from the bright sunlight filtered through the leaves of the over-hanging branches of a tree. This cut the glare on the tranquil lake before them.

Robert sat beside Katherine with his eyes closed. He inhaled the fall day as if taking a drag from a cigarette. He was perspiring, and took a handkerchief from his back pocket to wipe his upper lip and forehead.

"Best get on with it, Robert."

"I have a favor to ask." He paused knowing that if this favor was granted, it would be the riskiest departure from his methodical pace that he'd ever considered.

"You moved here to rebuild your life and while you have been doing that I realize that I have no life, not really. I did have one once upon a time, but not any longer. I want to leave the firm in your hands for six months and take a sabbatical. I've got to get away. I'm not sure where I will go, but I can afford to do almost anything I want. If you do this, I can leave, and not worry about the business. Of course, we'd make it financially worth your while." Like the air being let out of a balloon, Robert's intensity dissipated.

"My goodness, I had no idea you were in this kind of a fix, Robert. You've burned yourself out." Katherine's face reflected her concern.

"Yes, I suppose I have."

She took his hand. "Come on, let's get some lunch and talk more about this." They drove to Howard and Asbury where they sat in the parking lot eating a Chuck's hot dog on a steamed bun with mustard, chopped onion, tomato, a strip of dill pickle and celery salt. Katherine said very little while they sat eating and drinking root beer. Finally, she said, "This is a lunch I yearned for many times over the years from long distance."

Between bites Katherine said, "I'm not sure the folks at the office are going to like this idea, Robert. It's taken a while to win them over. What will they think of the new girl on the block in charge? Elizabeth may be the only one who will be happy."

"That's not true. Certainly the women realize you are in their corner. They owe their latest raises to several conversations you and I have had."

"Really? You listened?"

It was mid-afternoon by the time Katherine agreed to Robert's proposal. He insisted on driving her back downtown. When he began to laugh, Katherine waited for an explanation.

"I can hear my father saying, "Have you lost your mind?"

"You have to promise to come back in six months. If you leave December 1st, I expect to see you in the office the 1st of June."

"You wouldn't want to keep Davis by any chance?"

Before getting out in front of her building, Katherine said, "That would be a no concerning Davis."

19

Katherine had given a lot of thought to traveling with Andrew to England. The crux of the matter was not visiting English gardens with a charming man, but consenting to more than collaboration on a book. She fantasized about sharing a bed with him and admitted this was a compelling reason to go. The whole matter would have to be postponed now that she had agreed to Robert's plan. Though she had not given her answer, it was only fair to let Andrew know right away that during her six-month agreement, a trip to England was not possible.

Home from the office she stood at her windows, mesmerized once again by the water that was churning on the lake from the easterly wind. She was sorry to have to postpone this trip with Andrew, which let her know she'd made up her mind to go. She decided to call him.

"Katherine!" He sounded pleased. "I wouldn't have picked up for anyone else. I'm working here in the kitchen with papers strewn over the island counter top."

"Shall I call back?"

"Don't you dare. I have things to report. Between research, phone calls, and keeping track of information on a spread sheet, I'm on a roll."

"I'm impressed."

"Good, that's the whole point. I want you to be impressed."

"I mean, I'm happy for you. You sound energized."

"I'm still looking through the articles in the English Garden magazines. If I like something I read, then I Google for additional information. These search engines are astonishing these days."

He rushed on. "I have spent time checking on how much has already been published about the gardens on my list."

"At least I have hauled my magazines out of the boxes. The problem is that now they are sitting on the floor in piles. I've found a few possibilities too, but I should check what's already out there about them."

"The one thing missing in all this fun is your company, Katherine."

"You're nice to say so, thank you." She knew she needed to get to the point of the call. "I have called to tell you about something that's happened at work." When she finished explaining about Robert's sabbatical plans, Andrew did not try to hide his disappointment.

"Six months? I hoped we could go in May, when the roses are in bloom."

"There was no way I could say no to him." There was no immediate answer.

"The only positive thing I find in what you're telling me is that you have made up your mind to make the trip?"

"Seems foolish not to go, doesn't it?"

"Foolish indeed. I'm not sure how I can concentrate on my work until we can schedule the trip."

"I'm going to have my hands full, but I will do my best to help you when I can."

"Robert relying on you like this is a compliment; you have given him a great gift. You're a good person, Katherine."

Before saying goodbye, they planed a trip of another kind. Andrew would come to Chicago after Christmas. He began to chuckle. "My friend George St. John said you were going to be an expensive date."

❁

Based on nothing more than the fact that he loved Italian food, Robert decided he would spend his six months away from the office in Italy. He told Katherine, "I'm going to fly to Rome, and make my way from there with no further reservations or itinerary. I'm determined to stroll out each morning and get lost, if need be, in order to find what I'm looking for. Does that sound crazy?"

He made no mention about his fantasy of meeting a woman in one of the piazzas that would not only sleep with him, but share some of the journey, in that order of importance. After all, there would be no one to stop him from doing as he pleased. Unknown and invisible, he hoped to slip away from his father's life, and spend the time determining what the future might look like on his own terms. A little female company could only enhance the odyssey.

The day before Thanksgiving, Robert sat across his desk from Katherine. "One moment I'm excited, and then terrified. The only thing I'm certain about is leaving everything in your hands." They had been meeting every week. All the necessary paper work had been signed, the projected schedule for authors and their projects double-checked. The day the staff was informed that Robert was taking time off, their reaction seemed positive. What was being said privately, neither of them had any way of knowing.

Katherine leaned back in the chair in front of Robert's desk. They had come to the end of their business. They both smiled in satisfaction. Katherine felt prepared to take on the job. Robert patted his sport coat pockets as if checking to be sure he had not forgotten anything.

Though Katherine sensed he was eager to be on his way, she asked, "May I make a suggestion?" It seemed to her that Robert's intensity blocked out the (*little ordinary things that everyone ought to do,*), as the line in the song says. Preoccupied most of the time, he rarely looked beyond the top of his desk.

"Whatever you do, try and notice something new everyday. Something you normally walk right past." Robert gave no indication he knew what she was talking about.

"Listen to someone who can teach you something you don't already know." This comment elicited a nod of understanding.

"When you return I want to hear how things looked and smelled, tasted and sounded. Take notice of everything."

Momentarily silent, Robert checked his watch and then rose from his chair and walked around the desk to take Katherine's hands into his. "I want you to know I always notice you. You have inspired me to look for something I think is waiting for me if I would only show up. You will be my morning star each day." He leaned towards her and gave her a kiss on the cheek. "Thank you for probably saving my life."

"Go in peace, Robert." Katherine kissed him back on his cheek as well. "When you return from your travels, bring me the gift of a new man, once blind, but now who sees."

She walked with him to the elevator and watched the doors close behind him. He was headed to the ground floor where a neighbor was picking him up, his luggage already stowed in the trunk of the car. Katherine said a quick prayer for safe travel for him, believing that he was headed towards the possibilities life could still offer him.

20

On the shortest day of the year winter wrapped its arms around the city. Out of the growing darkness, a stiff easterly wind hurled snow against Katherine's tenth story Gold Coast window where she stood looking down on the Outer Drive. She was glad to be home safe and dry.

The weather forecasters were right this time; this was not a typical lake-effect snow she was watching. Mayor Daly's Public Works crews were already at work trying to keep ahead of the trouble this storm promised. The admonition, "Plow the streets, or you'll end up like Mayor Bilandic," was probably calligraphed on a plaque on one of Daly's office walls.

Katherine observed the headlights of the cars creeping north, which indicated how arduous the driving, had already become. The bourgeoning storm would soon make windshield wipers as effective as sweeping the ice with a broom at the United Center before a Black Hawks game.

She knew by now that throngs of huddled shapes were fleeing towards the Union and Northwestern train stations, counting on public transportation to get them home. Would the passengers riding in bumper to bumper cabs along Michigan Avenue notice that the fairy lights along the way were slowly being extinguished, their magical powers obliterated by the snow?

It had been the right decision when at three o'clock Katherine sent a grateful staff home from Davis Publishing. Preparing to brave the weather, everyone began to layer themselves into the efficient wardrobe that Chicagoans wear well; a fashion runway of sorts, show-casing the famous labels attached to outer wear, gloves, scarfs, and insulated boots.

Since returning to Chicago, Katherine's memories of growing up north of the city infiltrated this present incarnation of her life. Here she stood looking out on this winter scene wondering how many times as a child she'd lost one of her mittens? She thought of the small, narrow coat closet beneath the staircase on Asbury Ave where coats were hung and old boots stashed. It was in this closet that her navy blue snow pants and red Eisenhower ski jacket made room for a camel hair Polo coat she took to college.

The scene before her had shifted to previous winters, when perched atop the warm radiator cover in her childhood bedroom, she watched the lawns and parkways disappear beneath the snow. A snowplow's headlamps illuminated the falling snow in the short distance ahead as it pushed the snow's accumulation to the curbside. She could see the sidewalk plow excavating narrow knee-high paths as it passed the house. She could hear a car's spinning wheels trying to climb the hill on Lyons Street beside the Georgian house, the only sound in the hushed darkness. It was as if years of snowfalls had preserved the sights and sounds of these vivid scenes, and protected the past.

Her childhood elm trees along Asbury Avenue held narrow stacks of snow suspended on their glorious branches. In the luminescent white light of the street lamps, Katherine could imagine a stack topple over in a slow wet descent poking holes in the lustrous snow below.

She remembered when the Chicago temperatures would hit the freezing mark, which meant the park district employees would begin working on the ice rinks across the city and suburbs. Children would keep a vigilant eye on the progress of the workers who sprayed water from hoses to make the frozen ponds. Using her imagination, Katherine, could feel her ice skates, the shoelaces tied together and slung over her shoulder as she walked from home down Wesley Avenue to Mason Park on Church Street. The potbelly stove in the skate hut warmed her tired ankles and cold feet. This memory was as memorable as the crunching sound of someone's hurried footfall past her darkened radiator roost.

Luxuriating in a warm bath could not have comforted her any more than these memories on this blustery night. Rousing herself, Katherine drew the paneled silk drapes across the windows as if it were the final curtain of a theater production. She turned the gas logs on in the fireplace with a remote switch, causing flames to come alive with an explosive whoosh. With several more table lamps lit, she felt warm and tucked in.

❀

Returning to work on January second, Katherine sat behind Robert's desk watching more lake effect snow swirl past the upper story windows of the surrounding office buildings. Feeling chilled, she pulled a Pashmina shawl from a bottom desk drawer and draped it around her shoulders. It seemed unnecessary to occupy Robert's office during his absence, but he'd insisted, and she acquiesced. She had five months left to go. Every indication was that she'd been accepted at her new post and people were keeping their focus, working hard under her watchful eye.

The intercom on the desk startled her. "You have a call on line one from Andrew Stillman. Do you want to take it?"

She grinned and picked up the phone. "Hope you brought a warm coat."

"I've got my love to keep me warm." Katherine was happy to hear his deep laugh.

"Chicago in January is great isn't it?" This time Katherine laughed.

Katherine confirmed she would meet him at the Ritz Carlton Hotel at Water Tower Place as close to four o'clock as she could make it. On and off the rest of the day Katherine watched as the weather worsened. From experience, she knew it would become increasing difficult to find a cab. A last minute phone call held her up when it came time to leave the office. In the elevator she prayed for a taxi. It was not beneath her to pray for parking spaces either.

Bundling herself into the back of the first vacant taxi that would stop, they drove erratically over to Michigan Avenue and turned north towards The Magnificent Mile. In the snow the fairy lights sparkled in the trees along the route. She would have liked to trade the taxi for a sled and ride the rest of the way with horses borrowed from a Courier and Ives print.

She was blown by the wind into the entrance a half hour later, Taking the elevator up to the lobby, Katherine brushed the snow from her coat and ran a hand through her damp hair. It was an inconvenient time to appear bedraggled. She lifted her shoulders up tight around her neck and squeezed hoping for relief from the nervous tension lodged in her shoulders. She spotted the back of a man she thought was Andrew and looked for some sign of familiarity to confirm he was the same man she was eager to see.

Across the marbled expanse, this man turned, and in recognition, he smiled at her. All the things she'd forgotten about him returned in that instant. Meeting in the middle of the lobby, Andrew held her at arm's length. In spite of Chicago's winter cold, Katherine felt warmed by this smile.

"Care to offer me a glass of wine?" Katherine slipped her arm through Andrew's and looked for a sign that would tell them where the hotel bar might be.

"Or hot chocolate? It's damn cold here, Katherine." She was happy to tuck her arm close to his side. "This coat isn't going to be warm enough. I'm thinking of investing in a new one where the label inside says, good for Chicago weather." Several hours later, they moved from the bar area to a restaurant in the hotel.

Just after ten o'clock Katherine came through her front door and flicked on a wall switch that turned on lamps in the living room. Brushing past the hall closet, she placed her damp coat over a chair and saw the red light blinking on the telephone. She guessed it was Andrew. Acting impetuously at her age was definitely a good idea, after all, if not now, then when?

Before listening to the message, she put the kettle on to let the water boil for tea, and then pressed the play button. Andrew's soothing voice began to speak, "Katherine, I hope you don't mind me saying so, but I hated to put you in the cab tonight. I will see you at your office tomorrow, but know ahead of time, I am not going to let you out of my sight. Good night, again."

Katherine was tired, but not sleepy. It had been a long day filled with anticipation and then worry that the bad weather would cancel or delay Andrew's flight into O'Hare. After listening to his call she was surprised there wasn't another message from Johanna who usually telephoned after seeing a bad Chicago weather report on her TV. It was always the same, to insinuate that a move from Chapel Hill, with it's temperate climate, and was still a mistake.

She wandered around the living room, teacup in hand, and looked at the individual photographs of her family sitting on tables and tucked on book shelves. In a silver frame on her writing desk was a favorite picture of Timothy taken not long after they'd married. Here he was handsome and confident, the world at his feet after finishing his medical training. Katherine continued to miss him.

Riding up Michigan Avenue to the hotel that afternoon, she admitted that she also missed being in love. The excitement of meeting for a quiet dinner at a neighborhood restaurant, and afterwards, holding hands while walking up the street, anticipating what awaited her at home once the door was closed; she would not mind that again. She'd become increasing envious of the couples she noticed, that were satiated with one another, love enveloping them in an exclusive bubble.

Katherine lay in the dark for a long time after going to bed. She looked forward to the plans with Andrew during his visit. Before falling asleep, she remembered a story she'd once heard from a monk friend who awakened one morning to ask himself: Is this the day I might fall in love? Was there not an opportunity to fall in love everyday with life and perhaps an engaging man from Seattle?

Though Katherine suggested he buy a warmer coat from Joe Banks, Andrew did not like shopping in stores where no one knew his name. The coat might have been a wiser investment than taking a taxi everywhere they went, but since money was not the issue, a cab was less of a problem for Andrew than changing his shopping habits.

Viewed mostly through a taxi window, Andrew recognized that, even in January, Chicago was an architectural delight. Katherine's enthusiasm for the city did not blind him to the reality, however, that visiting for a few days was far different than living in Chicago year around. He had not only brought the wrong coat, but he didn't own a pair of boots that would have protected the pair of shoes he was ruining in the wet slush. He caught on quickly that where possible, he could ask the cabs to let them out directly in front of restaurants where they dined, or on their outing to The Chicago Art Institute and Shedd Aquarium. If he was honest, and he needed to be, the winter weather was a complicating factor in this long distance romance, which he hoped he was having. He could fantasize about a marriage, but in reality it was impossible to think of living anywhere except in his beautiful home in the Queen Anne District of Seattle.

Andrew hoped he was doing the right thing when he checked out of the hotel, the handle of his suitcase extended, ready to roll out the revolving doors into yet another cab to take him to Katherine's address. He was taking a chance that this close proximity would reveal something about himself she did not like. Maybe keeping some distance between them, which they were accustomed to, was better. Her invitation to stay with her the last few days of his visit was irresistible, however, and what he'd hoped would happen.

He'd pressed her the night before when she said she was sure this was what she wanted. She could have changed her mind since they lay together in her bed. He expected a phone call all morning telling him not to give up his hotel room. The phone remained silent. Maybe she truly shared his tender appreciation of this first occasion between them, blessed perhaps by their combined wisdom, that didn't allow the absence of youth to hamper their gentle coming together.

Katherine answered the intercom when he buzzed her apartment from the lobby. "Am I still invited?" He tried to keep his voice light; apprehensive she had changed her mind.

"I have unplugged the telephone, stocked up on salad fixings and salmon, and have a bottle of wine uncorked and waiting. Come right up." She laughed and the buzzer unlocked the door. Andrew took the elevator up to the tenth floor to find Katherine waiting when the doors opened.

They were both nervous, but Katherine's innate sense of hospitality saved them. "Here let me take your coat. Roll your bag down the hall if you like, you know the way." She smiled at him. He leaned forward and kissed her on the cheek.

When he returned to the living room, Katherine called from the kitchen, "Pour some wine will you, while I get some good old fashion cheese straws that you have probably never heard of. Made them myself, thank you very much."

Andrew stood looking out at the lake. "I know this 'borrowed view' is costly, but aren't you glad it's yours to enjoy whenever you want?" He was pretty sure there was no one in Katherine's Chicago life that would make a garden reference like this.

21

Robert let his feet dictate the direction he set off each morning. He carried a guidebook and a decent map in a small backpack, but since he felt no obligation to seek out any of the tourist sites in any particular order, he took them as they came. Thinking he would begin the day with a good breakfast, he soon discovered that instead of bacon and eggs he would have to settle for a strong espresso or cappuccino and a light sweet roll called a cornetto. It took him a week to adjust to the fact that there was no breakfast served in the places he tried.

After discovering the centro storico section of Rome, he found a cafe on the quiet Piazza Fernese that suited him perfectly; he returned there most mornings. He would leave the cafe and walk the narrow streets nearby that ran at random angles, all the while listening to the melodious Italian language that he understood little of.

One morning a question from the desk clerk at his pensione would change that.

"How long are you staying in Italy, Signore Davis?"

"Six months."

"You must learn our language. You can be one of us by then." Leaving his key, Robert turned to go. "I can suggest a tutor if you like."

He considered the idea for a moment. He knew a few fundamental words: *buongiorno* to greet people, *grazie* to thank them. Katherine sent him off with a few phrases written on a 3x5 file card that included "Mi sono perso, I'm lost," and "Potresti aiutarmi, Can you help me?" They laughed together over the phrase she'd added at the last moment.

"You better know this, Robert. "Dove posso trovare il bagno- Where is the bathroom?" This small smattering of vocabulary, and words he was slowly picking up were hardly adequate.

Robert took a few steps back to the clerk. "I like the idea of a tutor. Yes, please, make an arrangement for me. Let me know when I can start."

He continued his morning forays and with the names of four English language bookstores, he began to visit them one day at a time. Feltrinelli's not only had an extensive selection of books, but a cafe on the second floor where he enjoyed a view of the Largo Argentina with his cornetto and cappuccino in hand. He used their ticket office service to buy a ticket to the opera. Feltrinelli International had a flagship shop at Piazza Exedra where their English-language books went beyond literature. It was when he found the Lion Bookshop that he began to buy books. The man behind the counter told him that The Lion was the oldest English bookstore in Rome. In their cafe he made his first acquaintances. A couple invited him to bring his coffee and sit with them where they continued to talk books for the next hour. They were both Americans living in Rome. Thomas Stone. the young man, encouraged him to buy George Eliot's *Middlemarch* and Edith Wharton's *Roman Fever.*

Deborah Stone, Thomas's wife, suggested he try a travelogue or two, "Dickens's *Pictures from Italy* or Mark Twain's *The Innocents Abroad.* Maybe Henry James' *Italian Hours.*" Robert scribbled these suggestions on a pad he pulled from his backpack.

The second time he ran into them they invited him to lunch. "At one o'clock in the afternoon the main meal of the day, pranzo, is offered. Come along, we will show you how to order."

They started with antipasti of a plate of grilled vegetables with mozzarella and thinly sliced meats. "You follow this up with the carbohydrates, pasta." "This is enough for me," Robert insisted, but they urged, "You should add chicken or fish."

Over lunch listening to Robert explain his sabbatical, Thomas said, "Watch out, a man I know moved to Rome from New York where he'd worked for twenty years on Wall Street. His year sabbatical has stretched to a three-year residency. He says he has begun a new chapter in his life that helped him to find some balance. If you like I will introduce you to him. His name is George Willis.

Deborah Stone had been raised in Nashville, Tennessee. "I have a Bachelor's degree in Italian Studies from Southern Methodist University in Dallas. I'm about to finish up a Master of Business Administration in Finance here in Rome." Robert was impressed with her academic credentials.

"I came to Rome for the first time the summer after high school with my family. I knew then that I would return. I began to learn Italian by renting Italian movies and subscribing to Italian magazines. When I came here after SMU, I was going to stay for a year. Four years later I'm still here."

The three of them, over a leisurely lunch, continued telling their stories. When the waiter took their plates away, Thomas said, "Pranzo is topped off with another cafe, never a cappuccino."

Over their coffee Deborah said, "This will be enough until the evening meal, cena, at eight or nine o'clock. You will want to order a light dish and finish with fruit and more coffee." Robert laughed. "Then prepare to stay up all night after all the caffeine I'm drinking."

He asked them for suggestions for where he should eat. "Choose a place where you see Italians eating. Follow a group of them into a restaurant if need be. Cooking for tourists in the obvious places, not so good. They don't expect to see you again. The chefs want to please the Italians so they will come back."

"I sit outside when I can. Am I lucky or is the weather always this mild?"

"February can be rainy, but we like that because the city isn't as full of people. Like the weather, the local cuisine is dependent on what produce is in season, so what you eat will keep changing." Robert was grateful to these smart young people who had taken him under their wing. They continued to make plans once a week and each time they introduced him to another of their favorite hangouts in the city.

A pattern began to emerge in Robert's days. There was a different feeling in each of the wards of the city that he wandered through. His favorite restaurant thus far was near the Spanish Steps, the historic Antico Caffe Greco on Via Condotti. He could not resist the fact that writers like Goethe and Stendhal and Bryon had once eaten there as well. Tinted mirrors and marble-topped tables, along with pastoral paintings, fed Robert's imagination. He'd made the right decision to let his love of Italian food solidify his decision to come to Italy. Taking Thomas and Deborah's advice, he had not been disappointed one time.

It was seeing the juxtaposition between a motor scooter parked near an ancient stone column that reminded him that he was here to put old habits aside in favor of a new approach to his life. A few weeks of traipsing around day after day was enough time spent on adapting to this new culture. This was the day he needed to get serious about the transformation he was seeking.

"Signore Davis?" Smiling, a man about Robert's age stood with an outstretched hand. I am here for our appointment."

"Signore Antonio, good of you to come." Robert stood and shook the man's hand. They both sat down at the table where Robert had been waiting.

"Tell me one word in Italian you wish to learn, Signore."

"I want to learn to ride a motor scooter. What do you call them?"

The tutor laughed. "In Italy, you are never too old to learn to ride a Motocicletta, I have a friend who rents them, I will take you to see him."

Throughout an easy and relaxed conversation the two men drank their expresso. Robert was relieved that the man sitting across from him was easy going and unpretentious. He explained to him, "I have no definite plans, and I don't know how long I will be in Rome, but while here, do you have time each day to give me a lesson?"

"For you, I will make the time. As you say, I have no definite plans either."

"I'm not here as a tourist, not really." Robert did not know how to explain what he meant by this statement and made no further attempt to do so. He changed the subject by asking, "Where do you and your friends dine in Rome?"

Antonio glanced at his watch and pushed back from the cafe table. "Come with me, we will have our first Italian lesson over a menu. You will buy my lunch and I will teach you. How is that?"

"It sounds perfect."

Antonio led Robert to Trattoria der Pallaro near the Pantheon. "There is no menu here, but whatever Paola Fazi is cooking today, you will like." He pushed open the door to the restaurant. A short square woman in a well-worn apron greeted them. "*Benvenuto!* she called to them, welcome!

Two hours later Robert had enjoyed a delicious meal of porchetta, a boneless pork roast served with vegetables. They remained at the table where Antonio continued to discuss in English Italian food, sprinkled with Italian. "Northern Italian cooking is based on butter, meat, and fresh pasta. Southern cooks use olive oil, vegetables and dried pasta."

Antonio explained, "The regional differences in Italian cooking have everything to do with geography, and reliance on locally produced food. A limited amount of pastureland makes it impossible to raise beef cattle in southern Italy. They raise smaller animals, and the milk of goats, for example, is used to make cheese."

The discussion of regional differences led to a plan for the next morning. "You must see a local food market called a mercati. I will give you directions to our famous market here in Rome, Camp De' Flori." Finishing the last of his wine, Antonio asked, "Would you like company at the mercati? I will not charge you because I would enjoy showing you around. It's a good place for recipes and cooking advice, you can ask for restaurant suggestions too."

"If you have the time, of course. How better to see the market, ah, mercati, than with you. I have no place to cook, of course."

"You will come and cook our lunch at my home with what you buy. You cook, I will teach, is a good deal, right?"

Robert agreed. "It is a good deal."

The mercati was the best market Robert had ever seen. The fruits and vegetables that were displayed in their crates appeared polished. There was fish and meat spread out in refrigerated cases. Antonio took him to a mushroom man where he was told to buy dried porcini mushrooms.

"If I buy them, what then? I don't know how to cook with porcini."

Antonio explained, "You soften whole dried mushrooms in hot water for at least 15 minutes before adding to a dish. You can use the flavorful soaking liquid as all or part of a recipe's cooking liquid. I will show you while making mushroom risotto."

Antonio lived in Monti, Rome's first ward. Walking along Via Panisperna, Antonio pointed out the Basilica of Santa Maria Maggiore, a slice of which they could see through 19th century apartment buildings in the narrow street ahead of them. They passed a butcher shop that Antonio said sold some of the best meat in Rome.

"As you can see, the tourists prefer Campo De' Fiori and Piazza Navona, but this is Rome, a working-class neighborhood in the heart of the historic center. I live in an apartment down the hill on Via Baccina that is between the Roman Forum and our little Piazza della Madonna dei Monti. Come I will show you."

There on the cobblestone pavement was a simple, two-tiered Renaissance fountain with a spigot constantly flowing. A dog was drinking from it. Several young children were kicking a soccer ball, and a gathering of old women dressed in black sat together gesturing with their hands and laughing.

"There is a festival that takes place right here each April with music and jugs of wine. You will come, you'll see."

They stopped and looked in the window of a cramped casalinghi, a new word for Robert, that he took to mean a 7-11 type of store in the states that sell everything from toothpaste to dish soap. "The woman that owns this store lives across from me." She waved at them and motioned them inside calling *Benvenuto!* Antonio instructed Robert to

146

say, *"Ciao, mi chiamo Robert."* They stood and talked a few minutes. When Antonio said, *"Come vanno le coos,* how are things?" the woman launched into a manic gesturing and torrent of words that Robert could not fathom. This neighborhood was what Robert had hoped to find, a perfect place for long walks and a quaint atmosphere. He would give it some time, but Robert thought he might leave his present living arrangements and relocate here.

On one of the ensuing trips to the market, Robert stopped to talk with Rosa, who sold olives. After discussing the virtues of her product, she asked, "Would you like me to introduce you to the man who makes this oil? His farm is outside Rome. Take Antonio, he knows the place."

A comfortable friendship began to grow with Antonio and a daily pattern built around Robert's Italian lessons. There were few times in the following days when Antonio was not available after a lesson to share a meal. He went out of his way to introduce Robert to congenial friends. Most evenings they sat late into the night drinking wine and enjoying the camaraderie at Da Valentino, a small, old-fashioned trattoria on the Quirinale Hill side of Monti. At midday, the place was packed with bank and government ministry workers, when a single pasta dish was offered, and meat and chicken dishes that were served by friendly waitresses that bounced from table to table kidding and flirting with everyone. At night, the same restaurant was filled with flickering candles, and laughter. Robert was beginning to understand more Italian than he could speak, immersed in the city. He was learning exponentially.

The day Robert visited the Olive man alone, he was told about an apartment for rent that was part of a agricultural tourism program, an agriturismo, that would allow him to stay, as long as he wanted, and participate in the day to day work. Robert was intrigued, "I need to get my hands dirty, thank you, it is the kind of experience I would relish. I'll let you know in a few days."

That night, back in the city, Antonio dropped Robert at his Pensione. Pulling up in front, Robert surprised himself by saying, "Why don't you come with me?"

"You are serious about going?"

"Yes, I think I am. I haven't explained much about this trip, but the short version is I needed a change, I need to change."

"You go, Roberto. I am here when you return. You need the space to work and think, no?" The two men shook hands, and said goodbye.

"Grazie, Antonio. See you when I get back." Robert stood on the pavement and watched the car drive away. Turning, he entered the pensione smiling to himself. So far there had been no beautiful woman in the piazza, but perhaps even better he had made a new friend with the Italian gift of making the most of what he had.

The next day, however, Robert did meet a woman in the Piazza di Spagna below the Spanish Steps just as he imaged he would. Her name was Maria. They entered the Caffe Greco at the same time. She was wearing stiletto high heels and a short black skirt with a quilted jacket that looked like a Burberry, the kind that women in Chicago paid big bucks for in order to pass the label test. Robert recognized a Gucci scarf artfully tied around her neck. Waiting to be seated, he asked if she might join him. "Tired of eating lunch by myself." Which, was not exactly true, but he was way past knowing what pick up lines worked these days. She laughed and agreed. "You must practice your Italian, and I will practice my English." They shared a bottle of wine and he was hopeful she was flirting with him while they waited for the pasta he had ordered in Italian with no assistance. By the time the waiter brought their meal, they both had settled in comfortably. Robert watched the waiter grate cheese from a wedge of pecorino Romano over a pasta that had pancetta, a local bacon, onions, garlic and olive oil, and smelled delicious.

After lunch they wandered around the area, stopping in front of high-end storefronts that Maria pointed out to him. Robert was not interested in the shopping tips, as much as he was in this young woman in her early forties.

"Would you like to see my art work?" Robert laughed and said, "Don't you mean etchings?" Maria didn't seem to understand Robert's joke.

"My work," she repeated. "I am an artist. You must buy one of my paintings, which I will charge you too much for. Tourists, they expect this."

"I'm not a tourist," but, of course, he was. He followed her into a small courtyard that was concealed from the street by a bright blue gate that she opened with a key. She led him up a flight of steps to the second floor where they looked down on the courtyard from the wrought iron balcony that ran completely around the inner side of the building, with other blue doors and vines growing on the earth tone walls. Inside the apartment the walls were filled with lovely watercolors of architecture, gardens and people.

She motioned towards the couch and told him to sit down. "I will get some wine." When she returned she had a small plate of crostini toasted with olive oil and two wine glasses on a tray. They sat beside each other on a small couch with a spread thrown over one edge in a colorful pattern. Her knee rested next to his. Robert liked the feel of her warmth between them. When she allowed the first kiss, she was exactly what he had hoped for; someone who laughed easily and seemed passionate about her life. Robert could learn from her, and besides, here in Italy, it seemed wrong to waste time with a woman who took things too seriously.

Maria set her empty glass down and took Robert's glass from his hand. She stood up and pulled him up beside her. Smiling she led him into a small bedroom where he sat on the end of the bed. She brought a nude painting from behind the door. "I want to show you something. Do you like it?"

"This is you?"

149

"Of course, an artist friend gave it to me at the end of our affair."

Robert watched her slowly undress never taking her almond colored eyes from him. She reached up and pulled a clip from her hair that fell to her shoulders. This young woman was what Italians meant when they spoke of la bella figura; it was not just how she looked, it was her attitude; the way she had behaved in the restaurant, and out in the piazza. She was perfection. She stood before him naked. "I like this better than the painting," he said. He reached up and cupped one of her breasts in his hand.

She smiled down at him. "I will let you buy the painting for a generous amount of money, and you can take it back to America to remember your time here. A good purchase, yes?"

Robert kept Maria to himself. He told no one about her. She allowed him to come to her after his day of exploring the city. He put thoughts of the agriturismo on hold. Leaving Rome could wait a bit longer. With her kindness and laughter, her handling of him that was passionate and appreciative, he was in danger of spending the time he had left in Italy in her bed. After several weeks of sleeping with her she began to insist that he should arrange to go and stay at the agriturismo that he talked about the first day they met. Afterward, he should visit two of her favorite small cities. He all but begged her to join him. "I will pay for everything, you must come too."

"If I tag along you might as well stay here in my bed that is free. You have been holding back all this love you have to give. What's wrong with American women? They have missed a good time." Robert did not explain that everything had been his fault; it was he who made the choice to live as he had been living.

When he left Rome in his rented car he almost turned back thinking he could not do without Maria's constant attention and body. She'd made a remark that she was cutting back on his meds. He realized how true this was. She had been his medication, Antonio and friends his doctors, and he was headed to rehab.

150

Several hours later he reached the Agriturismo Santa Maria di Pienza, a farmhouse at the end of a long gravel road with six rooms, one of them waiting for his arrival. It was a working farm that produced among other things, chickpeas, wheat and spelt, produce the owners and their family used to prepare dinners for guests. In making the arrangements by phone, they assured him he was welcome to help them with the work of the farm. He parked the car and stood looking over a large garden and swimming pool. The farmhouse, in the middle of a nature reserve overlooked Val D'Orcia. These Tuscan surroundings were a perfect place for his rehabilitation to continue.

22

They agreed when Robert left for Italy that they would operate on the premise that no news was good news. If this sabbatical was going to work, he needed to cut the umbilical cord to the office and breathe on his own for the first time, letting Italy care for his needs. Except for a postcard from Rome after the holidays, he'd abided by this decision.

At the beginning of February, Chicago hunkered down hoping to outlast winter's determination to make everyone miserable. Oddly enough, Katherine was unperturbed by the rigors of it all. She loved the city, her work, and the routine she had established for herself. Chicago offered everything she could want in the way of culture, food, shopping, and new friends. So far it seemed a satisfactory trade off for another winter that included bad weather.

There had been several incidents to give her pause since she'd unpacked her bags to stay. On Michigan Avenue, one late afternoon, she was pick-pocketed. Headed into the wind and snow, head down, she realized afterward that the bump she'd felt from behind was not just someone who had walked into her, but the moment her wallet was lifted out of the handbag slung over her shoulder. At home, she threw the bag without a zipper into the trash after deliberating if she should give it to Goodwill. She would not wish on anyone else the time it took her to telephone the credit card companies to cancel her cards. As quickly as she had placed these calls, one of her cards had already been used to buy gas and snacks at a Quick Mart station on the South Side. She liked one of her neighbor's incidents better than her own. That stolen card was used to purchase soccer tickets in Romania.

The most recent incident occurred earlier in the evening when she imagined she was being followed as she made her way towards the Gold Coast restaurant where she was meeting a group of old high school friends to celebrate a birthday. She tensed up, and quickened her steps before realizing, that like a dog that senses you're afraid, she could get in real trouble if she panicked. She was emboldened, and abruptly turned around, taking a determined step back towards the few people on the sidewalk behind her. A startled man had to walk around her, but kept going. There was no need to be afraid. She headed back towards the restaurant, this time amusing herself by thinking of titles for a mystery she could write; *The Man on the Avenue* or perhaps, *The Man Who Followed Too Close.*

Home from the birthday gathering, Katherine was watching the 10:00 news when the phone rang. She had not thought of Robert in several days, so was surprised to hear his voice.

"You're up awfully early. Everything okay?"

"I needed to talk to the woman who has saved my life."

"Are you well, has your time been marvelous?"

"I have met someone, Katherine."

‘   "I hope she's both sophisticated and beautiful with an apartment in Florence where she writes literary works of fiction, and will make Davis Publishing a lot of money."

"It's a man who makes his living teaching Italian to American tourists."

It took Katherine a moment to process this piece of information. "And here I thought you were a ladies' man. Since when have men become your thing?"

The laughter that greeted her was robust and genuine. "You told me to find someone I could learn something new from. My Italian is improving every day. If you have dismantled the firm in my absence, I think I can find a job cooking in an Italian restaurant." He paused and then added, "It's been superb, Katherine."

"I'm glad you haven't completely forgotten about us playing here in the snow. You couldn't stand not knowing what is going on, is my bet."

"No, I know you have it all in hand."

"Just so you're not calling to ask me to put your house on the market and send the rest of your clothes?"

153

"Why not? I can make a living here. It might be the right thing to do."

"Oh, no you don't, we need you, I need you. I can only pretend to be the boss for so long."

There was a hesitation. Robert said, "We need to talk about a few things."

"We are talking, just don't scare me with all this Italian exuberance."

"I'm going to fax you a memo announcing to the staff that they are being given a week off the end of March over Easter, but only if you book a flight to Rome for that week and join me. I want to reintroduce myself, and discuss the company, and its future with you."

Katherine was dumbfounded. "But, Robert..."

"I know you think I'm a stodgy, one man band. You aren't far off, but that's why I want you to come here. I'm saying, please."

They talked another fifteen minutes about some of the things Robert was doing, new friends he'd made through the man he called, Antonio. "I'm staying here in Pienza just now and yesterday I saw a woman who looked like you, she could have been your sister. I called out, believing it was you. When it wasn't, I was devastated. That's why I'm calling."

"You'll need to take a loan out to pay for this phone call, Robert." It was the only thing she could think to say to cover her complete astonishment.

"Don't bother to tell me I'm crazy. That would have been true if I had not offered you a job, and I would be certifiably nuts not to make this phone call. I'm in love with you, Katherine. Probably have been from the beginning, but I could not offer anyone anything. I feel like I have risen from the ashes here, and I want you to see me under these different circumstances in this amazing place. Will you take another chance with your life, and try me on for size here in Italy?"

After the call, Katherine sat in the darkened living room staring into the fireplace where the electric logs burned. One lamp was lit beside her chair. In saying goodbye to Robert, she'd left room for the possibility that she would accept his invitation. If he imagined that she was the answer to his stalled out life, it was only the next phase of his mid-life crisis, albeit a late one, that he was working his way through.

Katherine thought that this was the kind of story line Jessica Lovejoy would turn into a best seller. She would love the part where Andrew comes to Chicago and seduces his editor to further his prospects. She could play up the vulnerability of a woman who'd had no sex since her husband's death. She would probably write that Katherine was having her own late mid-life crisis. Now she could incorporate Robert into the story.

Once she'd asked Jessica about her reasons for becoming a writer. Her answer still rankled because Katherine was looking for something more meaningful than what she was told. "When I discovered I could put my dirty mind to work, I began to write stories that have good sex in them." Jessica's answer was so unlike the one Katherine would give if asked about her own writing life. It still disturbed Katherine where Jessica was concerned. Why would she look at her work in such reduced terms?

Katherine liked to read about, and hoped to write about, characters that over the arc of the story were engaged in life, who came to embrace the good and the bad they'd experienced, which made them who they became. She hoped to give a reader a new language they could appropriate when trying to interpret their own lives. Though good for Davis Publishing, Katherine was not sure why a reader would return to Jessica's work if sex was the major lens through which to view the story. She'd tried to nudge Jessica into using a broader template where the characters and scenes were no longer shuffled around and given a new title. Of course, Jessica's sales didn't support Katherine's opinion on the matter. If Jessica knew what was going on in Katherine life, it would be reduced to a typical Jessica mundane ending. That was not acceptable to Katherine in fact or fiction. She rose from her chair after clicking off the electric fireplace and lamp, and walked over and pulled back the drapes she's drawn earlier to take one last look at the dark lake. There was moonlight sparkling on the water.

Robert's declaration of love was not the least of what had transpired in their phone call. He didn't mean it anyway. It was when he told her he was considering selling the company that she was speechless. He asked her to contact the company's lawyers and accountants on a fact-finding expedition before coming to Italy to apprise him of what would be involved. If he sold the publishing firm, this would be a major disturbance in her peaceable kingdom.

She couldn't sleep. At last she turned the lamp on beside her bed and sat up continuing to mull over what she should do. She certainly did not need two men in order to take a trip to England or Italy. She reminded herself, *I'm a woman of independent means.*

Andrew told her, "I can't manage this project without your collaboration." As for Robert, what could he be thinking, selling his business, living in Italy, and with her? These were romantic scenarios except Andrew would never move to Chicago, and Katherine was not sure she wanted the end of Jessica's novel to be her move to Italy.

Lying awake, Katherine allowed herself the pleasure of an Italian fantasy. Some of her favorite books were memoirs when somebody leaves everything behind in order to start a new life in one romantic location or another. There had been *Under the Tuscan Sun,* about Frances Mayes wonderful life in Cortona or *A Garden in Lucca: Finding Paradise in Tuscany* by Paul Gervais. He left California to find a place in Tuscany also. Wasn't one of her all time favorite movies adapted from Peter Mayles' best-selling novel, *A Good Year?* The movie was the best thing Russell Crowe ever made. She chuckled when she thought of telling Robert that in order to make this work between them they would have to live in Tuscany. There they could write a book together called *Two Fools in Pienza,* and sell the movie rights. She would fly back to the states and give lectures about her new life as Frances Mayes was doing. Why not? If we are what we eat, we can become what we dream. Is this not the American way, perhaps the Italian way too?

What would Louisa and Beatrice think if she told them she was going to England to work, ostensibly on a book, or that she was going to meet Robert in Italy? At work she could lose the respect she'd worked hard to earn from the staff at Davis Publishing, who at the moment were treating her as the woman in charge. "How did you spend your Easter vacation, Katherine?" The smirk on their faces would barely hide what they wanted to say, "What did you have to do to deserve this perk?" This was no example to set for Elizabeth, who was now being paid as an assistant editor to Katherine, and secretary only when needed. *Sleep your way to the top, girl, and you too can get a free trip to Italy.* The whole damn thing was preposterous.

Trying to fall asleep at last, Katherine wondered if she could tell Johanna the next time they talked that she was considering life with a man in Seattle, and with one in Italy. She would shuttle between the two of them from O'Hare International, all the while earning frequent flyer miles, and living happily ever after.

❁

When Katherine encouraged Robert to pay close attention to his surroundings in Italy, it was because she placed great value in trying to live an observant life. Whether it was watching the changing colors of the water on Lake Michigan, or years before, remembering the man who stood in the twilight on a Charleston Street. He was wearing a bow tie and a blue oxford cloth button-down shirt, sleeves turned back, and a khaki pair of pleated pants. At the time she'd seen him, overheard his slow southern drawl, she wondered if he could have flourished in any other setting than in Charleston. She was pleased,

157

therefore, that throughout their conversation she'd had with Robert, he kept mentioning the ordinary details of what he was experiencing; the names of the wine he was enjoying, the circumstance of the people he met in the market. He might indeed be getting the hang of ordinary time.

There was no reason Robert should link Katherine's liturgical church calendar, and the cycle of Ordinary Time, to her suggestion that he look up and look around. The word "ordinal," meant counted time: a time to be counted, weighed, used and invested. It was her personal piety that extended this practice by paying close attention. Surely this was what Robert's sabbatical called for.

She'd just been explaining Robert's absence to Father Gregory over lunch earlier in the week. He agreed with her. "Everyone is meant to spend time weighing up their life, hopefully deciding to use their days for good and investing themselves in others. To your credit, Katherine, you have given this man a great gift."

"You're kind to say so, I just wish I had more to show for my life than I do. It bothers me that when Louisa dies, and then my granddaughter, I will no longer be remembered. The same thing will be true of my mother and father, who I think of most everyday. My father left a mark on his profession, but my mother, won't be remembered for reading books to me when I was growing up."

"Look who else is weighing up her life?"

Standing out front of the restaurant an hour later, Katherine hugged Father Gregory goodbye. Leaning in to give him a kiss on his cheek, she whispered, "Thank you."

"Go home, get your book manuscript out of the bottom drawer, and write about the ordinary things people do in an extraordinary way. Write about what has been particular to you; your path, your journey, what you have noticed along the way. Start there, Katherine, and it will help others in remembering their own lives."

Later, once again propped up in bed, exhausted from several days of sorting through her feelings about Robert's call, Katherine had an epiphany…This should not be about what Robert wants of me, or Andrew, for that matter. The defining question is, what do I want?

She wrote a brief entry in her journal that stayed hidden in her bedside table drawer. *The years are flying by. My life is narrowing down to a small tear in the fabric of my days through which I will slip into the great amen. I can't ignore this reality; I need to be responsible for my own decisions.*

She put the journal back in the drawer before picking up the copy of Isak Dinesen's novel, Out of Africa, where a bookmark marked a revered place that Katherine often reread. *"If I know a song of Africa, of the giraffe and the African new moon lying on her back, of the plows in the fields and the sweaty faces of the coffee pickers, does Africa know a song of me? Will the air over the plain quiver with a color that I have had on, or the children invent a game in which my name is, or the full moon throw a shadow over the gravel of the drive that was like me, or will the eagles of the Ngong Hills look out for me?"*

Katherine wiped the tears from her eyes with the back of her hand. Crying was not unusual when rereading what Katherine thought of as a brilliant prayer; Dinesen, who expressed her fear of being forgotten, also expressed her deep love of Africa. She set the book back on the table. Her tears were now for Timothy, for her parents, and even for the little girl she once had been. Of one thing she was certain, that while she lived on, none of them would be forgotten.

Able to turn out the light at last, Katherine lay in the dark at peace with herself because she'd gotten to the crux of the matter. There would be no conclusive answers about any future Andrew or Robert might play in her life until she prayed specifically about what she hoped for in the years left to her. It was akin to the author who believes that only when the research and plotting are out of the way, can the creative process of writing begin.

23

The next morning Katherine closed the door to her office and placed phone calls to the company's legal counsel, Tom Braxton, and another call to the accounting firm of Arthur Anderson, where she talked with Malcolm McDowell. On her desk lay the fax Robert had sent authorizing her to make inquiries on his behalf. Though they had signed papers with the company's attorneys that spelled out Katherine's role in his absence, neither of them were sure that this would be adequate for inquires into the sale of the publishing firm.

Katherine gave no explanation over the phone other than to say she was asking for an exploratory conversation with both men on Robert's behalf. Since Katherine never thought of herself as a businessperson, she worried that she was not the best person to be representing him. Nonetheless, a meeting was scheduled at the attorney's offices for ten o'clock the following morning. The message she left for Elizabeth gave no reason why she would be coming in late the next day.

She spent a restless night and was awake having a cup of tea by six o'clock the next morning. Standing, watching the clouds gather over the lake, she prayed for Robert, and what he was contemplating. Part of what kept Katherine awake most of the night was realizing that in a short period of time she had invested herself fully in Davis Publishing, and she did not want to lose the stability her work gave her. She had recovered enough from Timothy's death to admit she was happy most of the time now, though not before asking Timothy's forgiveness that this could be so.

At 9:45AM Katherine walked into the offices of Braxton and Braxton. The receptionist led her back to a small conference room where coffee and rolls had been laid out. She assured the woman that waiting a few minutes would not be a problem. "I'll use this time to collect my thoughts, thank you." She took the coffee cup poured for her and sat down on one of the chairs arranged around a chrome and glass top table. This sleek, minimalist, and efficient setting, sent a far different message about doing business here at Braxton and Braxton, than the old boy's club furniture Robert's father, and now his son, perpetuated. Katherine thought the chrome might as well be flashing a sign that business here was cut and dried, and not to expect handholding in this environment. Katherine felt she was in an absurd situation, knowing nothing about selling a business of any kind. She was going to need all the handholding she could get.

Thomas Braxton walked in the door a few minutes past ten. Malcolm McDowell followed on his heels. Both men appeared to be in their late forties. Thomas Braxton, with his fair complexion and blue eyes, was a bland looking man who maximized his tall stature by wearing a well fitted dark blue suit, light blue shirt, and a striped club tie. Katherine wondered if the tie was a Brooks Brothers Christmas gift from his wife, who did not know what else to buy the husband who already had everything. Malcolm McDowell was the flip side of the coin. No taller than five eight, with a stocky build, he wore a V-neck cashmere gray sweater under a black cashmere jacket with gray pleated slacks. All smiles, both men shook hands with Katherine before they joined her at the table. She offered to pour them coffee.

Thomas Braxton, adverse to small talk jumped right in and asked, "What can we do for you, Mrs. White?"

Katherine obliged him, and got right to it. "Over the weekend I received a phone call from Robert. As you know, he is still in Italy. He informs me that he is thinking of selling the company." Both men sat back in their chairs and stared at her with a look of dismay on their faces.

Katherine continued. "I asked for the meeting here because he knew you would provide discretion while he garners information on the steps that have to be taken if he puts Davis Publishing up for sale."

Tom Braxton looked down at the file he'd placed on the table. He leafed through it pausing to read one of the papers included. "I took a quick glance Katherine at the papers you signed. I believe they are broad enough to allow you to represent Robert in this. You can't make final decisions, but we can certainly proceed without a problem. May I ask, has he discovered a health problem?"

"No, no, nothing like that."

"I know he doesn't have an heir to manage the business after retirement, but this is shocking news. My father and his father..." Tom Braxton's voice trailed off and his look of distress was genuine.

"It has more to do with a lifestyle change, I'd say." Katherine eyed both men over the rim of her coffee cup while she took another swallow. She felt ridiculous talking about Robert's motives when she understood so little of them herself.

Malcolm said, "The company is not suffering because of competition, but Robert's net worth is tied up in Davis Publishing. Perhaps he wants to 'cash out' either partially or wholly." Here was a straightforward motive that made no reference to what Katherine thought of as Robert's heart problems.

If Malcolm had listened while Robert talked about the people in the Piazza Navona, where he now walked among the street performers and the artists drawing caricatures, he might understand what was happening. Here was a man who was unchurched, with no visible piety as far as Katherine could tell, drawn to the churches where he sat tucked in a corner observing the tourists walking quietly up and down the aisles, some stopping to pray before side altars. He watched the Italian people with their small children arrive for a mass he knew very little about, though he was beginning to comprehend the words that were spoken.

Tom, who'd had a moment, regained the authoritative edge to his voice. "Robert must consider at the outset what he expects to obtain from a sale of the company. If his answer is liquidity, because he hopes the sale proceeds will generate many times his current salary, that's one thing. Do you think he is considering a partial sale that would provide the company with capital for expansion?"

"He didn't mention expansion, but I would think retaining partial ownership of the company would appeal to him." Katherine's answer had everything to do with what her wishes were in the matter.

"If the decision to sell is made, the next major step will be to identify potential buyers and to market the proposed transaction. He may want to consider hiring a public relations consultant to work for him. He could engage a business broker or investment banker. Both these positions would be significant hires." Tom Braxton looked over at Malcolm. "I'm sure Malcolm would agree that if Robert has confidence in us, his legal and accounting people can help him with the sale."

Malcolm nodded in agreement. "We handle transactions like this all the time. I would just add, if I may, that a key issue during the buyer identification process is confidentiality. Robert must know this since you asked for this meeting away from the office. Any potential buyer would sign a strict confidentiality agreement covering the fact that negotiations are taking place."

Fifteen minutes later Katherine was in a cab headed to the office. There was still no sign of the promised snow, but gray skies seemed appropriate for such a morning. She was thinking about Robert's parents. If his father were still alive, he'd need a medicine cabinet full of antacids to handle this situation. His mother, poor thing, southern lady as she had been, would certainly take to her bed.

Katherine looked at her watch and calculated the time in Rome. With another meeting scheduled for the end of the week perhaps she should wait until then to talk to Robert about what she'd been told. In the meantime, he might realize he was overreacting to what ailed him. By the time the cab pulled up in front of the office, Katherine was certain Robert could split his time, vacations and holidays in Italy, and the rest of the time running his business in Chicago.

❂

Robert's memorandum arrived by e-mail and was addressed to the employees of Davis Publishing. It read as follows: "The firm will be closed April 2-9. A paid Easter vacation is my gift to all of you in gratitude for the ongoing work you're doing in my absence. I hope these few extra days of vacation allow you the leisure and rest you deserve." It was signed, Robert Davis."

The buzz around the office was one of elation. Only Elizabeth asked Katherine what she would do with this sudden opportunity. "I'll have to give it some thought," was her noncommittal answer. What she needed was a talk with Louisa. She tried to reach her late in the morning, but had to leave a message. "Hi, it's me wondering if you are free tonight. I would love to come out on the train after work and spend the night. I have some things I want to talk over with you. Depending on your plans, we can have lunch tomorrow, and then I'll head back home. That way it won't take up too much of your weekend."

Louisa returned the call while Katherine was in a meeting, which said, "Come ahead."

Dark and cold, Katherine hailed a cab to take her home. The cab passed busses strung along Michigan Avenue with people standing shoulder to shoulder in the aisles with every seat taken. Katherine thought how lucky she was to be able to afford the luxury of a taxi when needed. Walking into her warm living room she almost called to cancel her overnight with Louisa. The thought of going back out seemed daunting on a Friday night.

She was tempted to get her car from the garage below the building where it had been sitting most of the winter. Though she learned to drive on snow, her North Carolina hiatus had eroded her confidence. All winter she'd been relying on public transportation or cabs to get around. One more cab to the subway was just the price of doing business. She packed an overnight bag only pausing to look briefly at her mail before heading back out. There was a large manila envelope from Andrew, which she would leave until tomorrow.

It was seven o'clock by the time Katherine got off the train at Davis Street. She followed a mother and her little girl down the steps from the platform to the street below. It seemed long ago now, but Katherine thought of snuggling close to her own mother, head resting against the curly lamb coat she wore as they rode the train home from the city. Would this child in front of her, who held tight to her mother with one hand, and the stair railing with the other, remember this day? Years from now, all grown up, would she step off another train and miss her mother as Katherine missed hers? More than likely this little girl's memory of today would slip away, not intentionally brushed aside, but in order to make room for the life that stretched ahead of her.

Katherine knocked on the car window with a gloved hand and startled Louisa who had left the car running to stay warm. She was reading a book with a small battery operated light clipped to it. Louisa had grown up in a household that never left home without a book, and here she was continuing this habit. Once, when they'd been headed to the mountains on I-40, to see the fall color, there was an accident that stopped cars in their tracks for several hours. The statement, "What would we have done without our books to pass the time?" reinforced the habit that a book was necessary when traveling, waiting in an office for an appointment, or even eating a meal when by yourself. It was necessary while waiting to pick up your mother at the station as well.

Settled on the front seat, Katherine said, "I'd like to buy you dinner after hauling you out like this." Buckled in, she reached over and kissed her daughter, who met her half way.

"I picked something up on the way home from work. Let's get out of these clothes and light a fire. We can eat in the living room if that's okay."

"It's divine. I've had quite a week for myself." Katherine leaned back in the passenger seat appreciating the seat warmer that was operating. "I don't like barging in on your Friday night, but I am in need of your wisdom, which is plentiful, if I haven't told you that often enough."

Katherine had no scientific proof, but believed that she had evolved beyond her mothers' experience in life, if only because she had choices that were available to her that were unheard of in her mother's generation. Louisa, at this age, was wiser in every way than Katherine had been. Beatrice, well, she had moved beyond them all. She took in stride the societal problems that her generation lived with, unperturbed by the furor created over homosexuality, or the gay marriage issues that were emerging.

Louisa drove down the Lyons Street hill and turned right into the alley behind the house on Asbury Avenue. She pulled into the driveway into the garage that was a part of the house, the breakfast room built over it.

Louisa asked, "Are you here because your lifestyle is grander than your pay check, and you've come to ask for money?" They both laughed. "I hate to disappoint you, but that's my problem too. I would appreciate your leaving a quarter on the sink every time you use the toilet." Katherine didn't need this reminder of how much Louisa's sense of humor was like her fathers.

Fifteen minutes later, Katherine sat on the couch with a dinner tray on her lap. She was gazing into the fireplace in the large living room with its fourteen foot ceiling and original glass built-in cabinets that lined the end wall. Part of the collection of the Miesian figurines, and other porcelain that Katherine's parents had once displayed on these same shelves, were back in place again. With the sale of the Chapel Hill house, Louisa could now enjoy some of the china in her own home. One day it would be Beatrice's turn to be the caretaker of the collection.

Many other things about the house were unchanged. Virtually unused, the pocket doors throughout the main rooms stood incased in their thick walls. Katherine looked across at Louisa who was stretched out on the matching couch opposite her.

"I was wondering if memories have DNA; if it's possible that a house retains the collective memories of those who have lived in it?"

"I don't know, Mom, maybe the most recent occupants making new memories over write some sort of memory chip the house may have?"

"I remember when my father took some paint remover to the tiles around this fireplace and found these beautiful redbrick-color etched four by fours. It was a discovery that pleased him to no end. You and I both know how this happened, but those who come along won't. I don't want this to be forgotten."

"The Pages built the house, right?"

"Yes. The little house at the foot of the garden was built for their daughter when she married. I think it was the family that bought the house from Grandpa that painted over the gorgeous oak paneling in the dining room."

Louisa gave a little snort. "Can you imagine the nightmare that must have been to get off? I know the young couple that next bought the house were involved with historic preservation here in Evanston. It took them quite a while to put things right again."

"Your grandparents were still alive then. They loaned those people photographs of the house taken when we first moved in. You have those things, right?"

"You needn't worry, Mom. I have them. Should I leave the photos and bits and pieces of paper with the next owners?"

Katherine heard the word *next* owners and swallowed before going on. "I've forgotten the architect's name, it's in those papers, but he was clever to design the large window that slides up and the paneling below that pulls open like a Dutch door out onto the porch; same thing upstairs in the master bedroom.

"That was a lot of work for grandma to scrub and hose the porch down every spring. I wish whoever removed the screens had replaced them."

"It was a great place to read and play in the summer. Sitting out there in the dark, your Dad asked me to marry him."

"I think of that a lot when I come around the corner and drive down Lyons past the porch."

"Are you thinking of replacing the screens?"

"I just may if I stay." Louisa sat up from the couch and looked across the coffee table between the two couches where they sat.

Katherine could not ignore the *if* since Louisa was obviously waiting for some reaction. With Clay gone and Beatrice living on her own, it startled Katherine, nonetheless, that Louisa might consider moving.

24

Louisa's divorce was granted after more unpleasantness than Katherine thought Clay capable of. Depending on the day, Katherine could take or leave her son in law, but as long as he was there for Louisa and Beatrice, she usually forgave him when he acted like an ass. Trying to get a portion of Louisa's inheritance from her grandparents and father, were another matter. She agreed with Louisa's lawyer that this was worth fighting over.

If Timothy had lived to see Clay try to take advantage of his daughter, she was sure one word from him would have put a stop to Clay's shenanigans. Katherine could imagine him saying, *listen here you little bastard, I've got enough money to hire lawyers to be sure you get nothing, so back off, and sign these damn papers.* It was a side of Timothy few people knew, and was seldom needed. In the end, it was Beatrice who asked her dad to step back and treat the situation fairly.

"I don't want to lose respect for you, Dad. I know this is between you and Mom, but I can't say I'm feeling the love with the way you're going about this. Why act poorly when you're the one who is asking for this divorce?" Her take on the situation prevailed. The combination of her left and right punches to the solar plexus finished Clay off. The divorce went forward with no further acrimony.

Katherine was surprised when she received a call from Clay the day the divorce was finalized.

"Calling to thank you Katherine, you have always been kind to me. I'm sorry about all of this. The truth is Louisa and I grew up and we grew in different directions."

"I like to give you a last piece of advice, Clay, because I do wish you well."

"Do I have to promise to follow this gem of wisdom?"

"I hope you will take it seriously."

"I'm ready, let me have it." Katherine was amused that Clay, who had always sparred with her in a goodhearted way, was still at it.

"If you can't make a success of your marriage, Clay, for God's sake, make a success of your divorce. I've told Louisa the same thing. I hope for all our sakes this will be the case."

"I hear you, captain, over and out. Seriously, you know the Asbury house is paid for in full, part of what Louisa can go on with even though the house is too big, and hard to keep up without help. Though you can't tell her that."

Still sitting in front of the fireplace, now drinking a pot of tea and having cheese and crackers together, Louisa said, "You look pensive."

"I was thinking about Clay's call. Have you heard from him?" Katherine knew Louisa was waiting for some reaction over the possibility that she might sell the house. She looked over at her daughter.

"You're thinking of selling?"

"With Clay gone and Beatrice living on her own, it's crossed my mind. It's a big place just for me, and a daughter who has flown the nest and is settling again in New York."

"Would it help if I moved in with you?" Katherine grinned at her daughter. "Wait a minute, what did you just say? Beatrice is coming home from Greece? You don't mean it."

"I didn't want to get your hopes up until things were sorted out, but yes, she put in for a transfer to the offices in New York and they offered her a position. She will be home the first of May."

"It's over with her young man, or is he coming too?"

"Parting as friends I'm told. After a few years living there, and with the country's economic turmoil, the blush was off the rose, as they say. The reality of living there full time, the children they might have, she realized she could not do that."

Katherine threw both her arms into the air. "God is good! Oh my, this is stupendous. Coming home!"

"The best part is that she's delighted about it, and is no worse for the wear. She will bring home the memory of a romance with a Greek god, not to mention a fine international business experience to add to her resume."

"I have missed her something fierce, and I can get to New York."

"You might as well prepare yourself, Mom, that next we will be hearing about some dashing Italian or the son of the owner of the Jewish deli on the corner.

"Either way she will marry into a big family, and have the benefit of great food. I'd love it." Katherine was ready to discuss why she had come to spend the night.

"An Italian would be an interesting coincidence," she said.

"How so?"

"It's why I needed to see you tonight. I'm going to Italy for a week over Easter." Katherine spent the next half hour expanding on the circumstances of Robert's predicament, and filling in further details about why she agreed to hold down the fort for six months. She wondered if she was beginning to sound nervous as she drew closer to telling about Robert's phone call asking her to come to Italy.

"Wow, Mom, he told you he was in love with you? I should have paid more attention to him the day he came here to pick you up, but Clay had just left, and I wasn't tracking. He certainly is attractive, and you say he's smart. This is why you're here to ask my permission to go meet him in Italy?"

"Something like that. There's more, Louisa. There is Andrew Stillman who lives in Seattle."

"This is the man you are sort of writing a book with except when you are not?"

"He flew here in January for a few days. I didn't mention it because I thought you'd disapprove, and I can't make up my mind whether to have a long distance romance at my age."

"You might write a book, and you might have a romance, and you think I might be of help?"

"It wasn't a romance, but now it might be. At first it was collaborating on the book, which would take us to England for research. But now it is go to England, and while we're at it, explore the idea of something more."

Louisa, who'd been studying her mother carefully, began to laugh and then could not stop, convulsed, both hands covering her face. She finally managed to say, "To think I was worried about you coming to Chicago on your own, your life ruined because of Dad, and here you sit telling me you have been invited to travel with two men and share their beds. I should get so lucky."

Out of relief, Katherine laughed too. "It sounds absurd, I know."

"Not a bit. Why shouln't you do both? Who knows, by the time you are free from babysitting the firm, you may not want to go England with Andrew because you're too busy cooking spaghetti and speaking Italian with Robert." Louisa laughed some more.

"I've at least come to my senses in that I realize the question I need to ask myself is, what do I want in all this? I heard you say *if I stay* in this house, a minute ago. So, let's talk about you."

"I know you'll be devastated Mom, but perhaps I should consider it."

"It has been wonderful to come home again, which proves that you can. But maybe the real reason I have turned up on your doorstep tonight is because I have been sent to tell you that now that your divorce is final, and you will have a daughter in New York, you will need to ask yourself what it is you want. You can work anywhere with your credentials, teach at a college somewhere where it's warm and there is no snow."

"Geez, if you're going to move to Italy or Seattle, what have I got to live for?" Louisa smiled at her mother, and blew her a kiss.

"There's something else I want to tell you. Top Secret you understand. You must sign your name in blood that you won't talk about it."

"There's a third man?"

"Robert is thinking about selling the company. I hope it's just an Italian moment like Beatrice has had in Greece, but he thinks staying on in Italy is the answer to his mid-life crisis, and that if I would fall in love with him now that he feels he has regained his essence, or something like that, everything will be fine. It's quite a romantic idea, which I readily admit to being susceptible to, but then it hit me, this is not about what Robert or Andrew want, but what I want.

At the close of the day it is what you want concerning this house, whether you stay or move. I envy you; you're young enough to have new dreams and act upon some old ones. Once upon a time you said you were going to move to Charleston and marry a man with a southern accent who wrote novels like Pat Conroy without the dreadful family."

"Oh, I'd forgotten about that. Yes, someone with antiques and ancestral paintings on the wall, even if they aren't his."

"There you go."

"Mom, what if Robert does sell the business. Does that mean you lose your job?"

"Not if the employees bought part of the company. I have had one appointment with the lawyer and the financial wizard, and I did understand some of what was being said. They talked about a partial sale where Robert could take his money, live as he pleases, but remain part owner. He could live in Italy part time if that's what he wants and still keep his hand in the business.

"Forgive me, Mom, do you want to take on this kind of responsibility at this stage in your life? Let's say you give it your next ten years. You'll be shy of 75. It's a lot, Mom. What about your writing? You barely have time now to do any. Maybe that's not the number one priority, which is fine, don't misunderstand me."

"I'll have to take this one step at a time. If I go to Italy it will be easier to discuss all of this with Robert. How that turns out will have a bearing on what I will do. The other side of the coin is what I think of his Italian makeover. He's always been a fine person and seems to think I will think more of him. Maybe I will. It's Andrew that I'm most concerned about. I haven't encouraged him, well that's not true, his trip here after the holidays changed some things."

"Careful Mom, in front of the children, and all that." They both smiled.

"I have dithered over traveling to England with Andrew, knowing that it implied more than I might be able to give. Going to Italy to meet Robert over Easter suggests the same thing does it not?"

"I rather think it does. I don't know what to say that is helpful. Let's sleep on it. I have no problem with this Mom. I miss Dad, always will. I know what a loss his death has been to you, to all of us." Louisa thought for a moment.

"You told me when I was growing up that life is full of possibilities and to pursue them when possible." She laughed at this little joke. "You are not exempt from your own possibilities, at least this is what you told me when you decided to move from Chapel Hill to your Gold Coast nest looking East over the lake."

"And I can understand why you might leave this house. If this is what unfolds for you, you know I will support you all the way. I'm pretty sure you will come to a point when you'll miss being in love. You'll notice couples holding hands, absorbed in one another across the table. You will want to be breathless and excited again."

"You speak from experience?"

"Somewhere upstairs on a bookshelf in Beatrice's room there is a copy of Daphne du Maurier's Frenchman Creek. When you're ready, I suggest you find it, and let the pirate take you out to sea once more. In the meantime, help me pray about what lies ahead.

Louisa hugged her mother before leaning over to check on the logs in the fireplace that had burned down to embers. "Too bad we don't have marshmallows." She poked at one partially burnt log and rolled it further back in the grate.

"Come on, let's take the tea things back to the kitchen." Katherine walked across the large entry hall past the music room towards the kitchen area of the house.

"Leave the lights to me, Mom. I will turn them out when I come up. I want to check my messages when we get done." They reached the door of the butler's pantry, and passed through to the kitchen beyond.

"It always startles me that these are the same tall, upper-glass front cabinets after all these years. No one can reach anything on the top shelves. Certainly not your grandmother."

"Just my luck none of the other owners spent the money to gut the whole thing." Louisa had updated the kitchen, though it was far from the efficient designs found in the decorator magazines.

"Your grandmother walked a hundred miles in a year going between the work space on the counter tops to the stove, across the room to the refrigerator and back to a sink. At least there is a dish washer now and the appliances are better situated."

Katherine continued to think about the memories of the house while she dried up the dinner and tea things and helped put them away.

"Do you ever watch that program on TV called, *If These Old Walls Could Talk?* Some of the stories that took place here could be awkward." "You mean the long lectures grandpa gave you at report card time?"

Katherine pointed towards the butler's pantry. "He built a desk down in the basement that he fit into the leftover space where the cabinet and sink stops. He did his haranguing from that spot."

"The little girl with her pigtails that caught hell."

"It's nonsense what parents think they must say in order to do a good job; the starving children of the world speech to make you finish your vegetables."

"I seem to remember some version of that speech."

"Surely not." Katherine started towards the door.

"You go on, Mom. I'll be up in a minute."

Katherine began the climb up the staircase to the second floor. She stopped on the landing and looked out the large window on to Asbury. The lights were on in the houses across the street. She turned and looked back down the steps. She was in Louisa's home now, but her mother and father were always here waiting for her when she arrived.

"I thought of something I want the walls to talk about." Louisa had joined Katherine in Beatrice's bedroom.

"What's that?"

"I want the walls to talk about your grandmother letting me lick the beaters in the cookie dough bowl, or having a pinch of raw hamburger meat with salt on it while the hamburgers were being patted together. I want them to talk about the books she read to me in the breakfast room."

"When you talk about Grandma reading, I always think of the scene from Peter Pan where he explains why the swallows nested in the eves to hear Wendy's stories."

"I wish I knew the exact day I became too old, and slipped off her lap and started to read on my own. I would love to remember the name of that last book."

Now in her nightgown and robe, Katherine joined her daughter in the master bedroom next door. They stood looking out unto the large garden below. The street lamp on Lyons Street cast a shadow across the parkway where the snow lay dingy and unappreciated at this point in the year.

"Did I ever tell you that there was a fire across the way in the carriage house? I stood here with your grandparents and watched from this window while the firefighters put it out. The thick stone exterior was scorched near the windows and doors, and the apartment above the garage space was gutted. It was scary. This is the kind of thing I think about, I want this to be remembered."

"Write it down, a memoir perhaps?"

Katherine smiled at her daughter. "No one will care that there was once a square black lined fish pond in the middle of the yard down there with koi and water lilies. I'm not sure when your grandfather filled it in with dirt; the liner must still be there."

Louisa put an arm around Katherine. "I care, Mom."

25

Andrew had barely been home since his return from Chicago. In the last month he'd spoken to Katherine briefly between two symposiums, one in California, and a week long writing conference in Houston, Texas. This schedule had left little time to sort out his feelings about their time together. Normally he enjoyed these conferences and counted himself lucky that this kind of work not only paid him well, but brought him together with friends. He had to admit it was a kind of rush when sought after in these situations, but well aware that adulation can become addictive, he was careful to enjoy the energizing effects and fun, and let the rest go. Most of the participants at these conferences were eager and enthusiastic. Andrew got as good as he tried to give. Nonetheless, thoughts of Katherine had been a distraction.

When the plane lifted off the runway in Houston to take him home, instead of feeling his usual satisfaction upon completion of these commitments, he was lonely, tired and unsettled. The last thing he wanted was the woman stuffed into the seat beside him taking up any more of his space by talking. This was an opportunity to think about the time he'd spent with Katherine in Chicago. He didn't want anything to interfere. He feigned sleep by closing his eyes. The woman left him alone.

Andrew thought back to the two days he'd stayed in Katherine's apartment. They had worked several hours, both mornings and late afternoons, on the structure of the book, considering the gardens and gardeners to be included. They read each other's input by switching their laptops between them. Katherine showed him the work of several watercolor artists she was recommending. Andrew narrowed them down to two choices. Katherine was able to reach both of them by phone, handing the phone over to Andrew who explained the reason for his call. His favorite choice of the two, a gentleman that had gotten up there in age, was no longer accepting assignments that took him out of the country. He would be interested in the American garden assignment if they were agreeable to letting someone else paint the English gardens. They all agreed they would continue to explore the possibilities of working together. Both artists were intrigued with the concept of the book, which was encouraging.

What was evident during the hours they worked together was that they easily agreed about things, but it remained true that Katherine could not make any plans until Robert returned from Italy.

There where few times when they were quiet, except when they read for an hour or watched WGN news. Otherwise, they talked non-stop while cooking in Katherine's small kitchen and eating on trays before the fireplace. They shared stories from the past and details about their work. It was obvious to Andrew that Katherine was happy with her life, but she seemed happy laying beside him too. Leaving her was going to be difficult, even if he was returning to a life he loved as much as Katherine loved hers. When they turned out the bedside lamps, and turned towards one another, growing in confidence with one another, it was everything he could hope for.

He had questions that worried him. Would he ever be as content again in the world he'd created for himself without Katherine? Could he give up the freedom to do what he pleased when he pleased, for her? He'd never thought he could do so before. Had he become so set in his ways that there was not enough generosity in his heart to make meaningful room for Katherine, thought in this short time he regarded her as a pearl of great price?

Andrew was barely in the door from the airport when the telephone rang and his caller ID told him it was Katherine calling. After thinking about her on the plane he couldn't deny how much he was missing her in spite of how busy he had been. Still he was uncertain what to do about her. He dare not risk a conversation when he was feeling tired and anxious. What if he inadvertently said something that could ruin the possibility of a future together? He let the phone ring. She did not leave a message. After a good night's sleep he would call her back.

There was an earlier message from her that he hadn't erased. He listened to that once again. "Hi there. Sorry to miss you, but I have gone over the preliminary work that you have sent, and I believe you have a viable project here. You don't need me, I keep telling you that, but you can count on me for whatever help I might be." The first time he heard the message, like a teenager, he kept replaying the message to be sure he had not missed some coded language that said something more about him, than the book.

He wasted no time getting himself to bed. At nine o'clock his light was turned off and he felt comforted returning home to his own bed. This would go a long way towards making everything right again with the world. He was awake by five thirty the next morning, showered and fifteen minutes later making coffee. With the time change there should be no problem in catching Katherine before she left for the office.

She picked up on the first ring. "Oh good! How are you, Miss Pearl?" a nickname he'd given her when he left Chicago. The name brought back the scene when they parted. He'd whispered, "You are my pearl of great price, and don't forget it."

He'd been pleased when she replied, "You're making this difficult, Andrew, I'm sorry to see you go."

He made no apology for a none too gentle kiss in their last moments together. It was an attempt to take something of her with him. The shyness they were overcoming made room for an intensity that surprised them both, though they did not speak of it.

Here she was sounding so near, but was so far. "I know you're about to leave for work, but I'm back home for awhile and I want you to get on a plane Friday after work and come out here and stay with me. Stay here, at home, in my bed." He hardly recognized his own voice saying these things. "Please come, I'll arrange for your ticket."

180

When Katherine hesitated, he was sure she was going to say no. Instead she laughed. "You know, I'm going to take you up on this. I will take Friday off and come back Monday morning. But, so we understand, I'll pay for my own ticket."

Andrew sat down on the bar stool at his kitchen counter. "Katherine, no one has ever spent the night here with me. Never! I don't expect you to understand, but this is a very big deal for me." He wasn't sure what he wanted from her in return for this admission.

Katherine moved to the Hitchcock chair beside her small antique table in the kitchen where she could sit down as well. It gave her a moment before she responded, recognizing this was important. She glanced at the clock and saw she was going to be late.

Andrew could not see that she had placed her hand on the table in front of her as if to take his hand.

"You've probably had an experience of trying to speak to a friend that may have lost a child or a spouse knowing full well that whatever you say will never be adequate. I feel that way about your invitation to come and stay with you, because I recognize, as you say, how big a deal this is." Katherine, who was used to talking in stories, seized on one she thought fit the situation.

"I was home for Christmas my freshman year in college and dating a Dartmouth boy. We'd been out somewhere and had pulled up to my house with an eye on the clock because I still had a curfew. This young man asked me to slide away from him because he had something he wanted to tell me. There in the dark I could feel him sucking all the oxygen out of the car in preparation to say, "I'm Jewish." That was it, that's all he said."

Andrew took a swallow from his coffee and thought he understood where this was going.

"The irony is I already knew this about him, but since it never would matter, I never gave it a thought. Looking back I don't pretend to understood what it cost him to make this pronouncement, I only

181

know it was of no consequence to me. My parents' best friends were Jewish, I had grown up with their children, their aunts and uncles. At least I had sense enough to realize he'd agonized over what he thought was a momentous confession that could make a difference to me. All I managed to say was something flip like, "So what."

As if it had happened yesterday, Katherine could see this handsome boy looking at her from behind the steering wheel of his car. "I've remembered this scene my whole life with regret. If only I had been able to say something somewhat commensurate with what took him courage to say."

Katherine paused. "I tell you this story, Andrew, because I have no response for you that is adequate, but I do recognize that it is a very big deal, as you say, to invite me to stay with you. I wouldn't want you to regret this." Andrew remained silent while Katherine waited for him to react.

"Hurry and get here, Katherine. I'll be waiting at the baggage claim for you." After he put down the phone he didn't remove his hand. The connection between them held until he finally let her go.

26

Katherine's United flight was leaving Chicago at 5:58PM. Taking no chances with the traffic, she hailed a cab and was checking her mid-size bag at curbside by 4:15PM. Even if she had packed lightly or crammed things into a smaller bag, there was no point. She could no longer heft a bag into the overhead without a struggle. Knowing that chivalry was problematical these days, Katherine thought it best not to count on someone who would help a damsel in distress. She gave thanks for a hassle free get away when United pushed away from the gate on time.   Before she settled back to enjoy the flight, she was prepared when the passenger in front of her tried to slam his seat into her lap. She'd suffered such disregard for others on previous flights. She threw her hand up just in time to halt the progress of the seat coming towards her. She held it there firmly until the passenger accepted that his seat would go back no further. With immense satisfaction, she won the wordless power struggle over her right to the small space between each row. She reached for the book in her purse that was sitting on the floor and read the remainder of the flight.

The wheels touched down a few minutes ahead of schedule in Seattle. Katherine followed her fellow passengers towards the escalators that slowly took them down to the baggage claim area. Part way down, she spotted Andrew standing by one of the luggage carrousels talking to a man and women. He was dressed immaculately, wearing a Burberry lined raincoat over a black cashmere sports jacket and gray flannel trousers. Here was a handsome man, dressed to impress. Katherine's reaction would please him.

A buzzer blared and a conveyor belt lurched into motion, carrying a few scattered bags. Andrew looked towards the escalators, smiled, and waved when he saw her coming towards him. He met her half way and kissed her on each cheek. If he regretted that he'd invited her, this exuberant greeting eased Katherine's anxiety that he was sorry she had made the trip.

She let herself be led towards the couple Andrew had been talking with. They waited smiling at her; the man already extending his hand towards her. The introductions. were made with Andrew's inevitable good humor.

"Katherine, these are my friends that I rarely bother to mention, Anne and George St. John. They're members of the Seattle welcoming committee who volunteer their time to stand here and greet passengers from Chicago."

"Special passengers only." Anne St. John hugged Katherine as if they were long lost friends. "Welcome!" Laughing, she stepped back and grinned at Andrew before she cuffed him on his arm. She turned back to Katherine. "Of course, we have been standing here since noon. Andrew didn't want to be late."

George St. John added, "Yes, for God's sake, let's get out of here. They're going to charge us rent if we stand here much longer." He put his arm around Katherine's shoulder and steered her towards the luggage that was by now tumbling along bag after bag. Katherine spotted her suitcase with a yellow piece of yarn tied to the handle. "Here it is," and leaned forward to yank it off the carrousel before it passed by. George took the handle from her after she'd pulled it up and they all headed towards the exit. Katherine glanced back at Andrew following along. She must be off to a good start with these friends because he smiled at her and mouthed, "Thank you." Anne, who was observing them said aloud, "This was worth the wait."

The time change was always a killer for Katherine, who had started her day at eight thirty that morning in Malcolm McDowell's office at Arthur Anderson garnering additional information about the sale of the company. Though it was only nine o'clock in Seattle, it was way past her bedtime in Chicago. They were having dinner at the St. John's home. Unaccustomed to eating late, Katherine would have preferred to stick with the salad Anne set before her, but she dare not offend

George who made a production out of the grilled meat. By the time they said goodnight and drove Andrew's car away from the Seward Park neighborhood, she had overeaten, was tired, and feeling anxious.

Andrew took his hand from the steering wheel and reached over to find hers. "I couldn't tell them no when they insisted on coming with me tonight."

"It was fine, I like them very much. I hope I didn't let you down. With this time change, I'm not at my best." Katherine squeezed his hand and stifled a yawn by covering her mouth with her free hand.

"I was afraid you were going to feel like one of the boys in the fifties that had to sit and chat up the housemother before a date."

"It was rather like that, now that you mention it." She squeezed his hand again. "I loved the fifties. Some things that are never mentioned should be reintroduced into this uncivil society we're living in."

"You mean it wasn't all poodle skirts and saddle shoes back then?" Andrew was grinning.

"Practicing good manners, that was a requirement. Look how well you turned out." Andrew laughed and returned his hand to the wheel.

Katherine rattled on. "While I was in school you wouldn't have dreamed of having your picture taken with a drink in your hand. It wasn't proper."

"No photos in Florida on spring break with band aids for a bathing suit, drunk out of your mind?" Andrew chuckled. "I live for spring break and those photographs."

His humor was like sunshine in a bottle for Katherine; never sure how to take teasing, Katherine enjoyed the way Andrew managed it.

Once home, they didn't dilly-dally, before Andrew led her up the stairs, turning out lights as they went. The master bedroom was at the back of the second floor of the house. Here was a masculine sanctuary with light gray walls and white trim on the woodwork. A queen size bed was centered on a long wall with a small chest of drawers painted in a metallic gray placed next to one side of the bed. A Chinese red lamp and a vase of fresh flowers sat on the chest. On the other side of the bed was a similar version of the chest and lamp, this one stacked with books and a clock radio.

"It's lovely, Andrew, tasteful and elegant. It suits you, and this house."

"You can have the bathroom to yourself. I'll use the one just down the hall." They stood in the middle of the room looking at one another. Andrew stepped forward to give her a real kiss for the first time since she'd arrived. The anticipation, the fear, the unanswered questions, all evaporated temporarily as they found one another again. When Katherine came from the bathroom, Andrew had turned back the bed and was waiting for her. She crawled in beside him and put her head on the pillow beside him just as he had imagined.

"I'm exhausted, Andrew. Do you mind?"

"You're here, that's all that matters." He surprised himself after the anxious moments he'd spent worrying that this was a mistake. Having her here was what mattered. When they awakened the next morning, Andrew looked at the clock. "I can't remember when I've slept past eight o'clock."

It was after 10:00AM by the time Katherine found him in the kitchen fixing coffee. They smiled at one another as if sharing a secret that was amusing. Andrew had vigorously made love to Katherine who responded in kind this time, putting their inhibited Chicago experience behind them.

The phone rang and startled them both. Picking up the receiver, Andrew listened for a moment and then said, "Thank you, but no. We don't want to come and spend the day with you." Smiling at Katherine he listened for a few more moments. "George, don't ever call again." Laughing, he hung up the phone. "They were so taken with you they offered to spend the entire weekend with us."

"We should be thankful he didn't call an hour ago." She walked over and laid her head against Andrew's chest. Showered, he smelled of Old Spice and toothpaste. Andrew put his chin on the top of her head. "Don't move. Just stand here." Katherine felt comforted by Andrew's, reassuring presence. Finally they stepped apart.

"I suppose you expect me to share my newspaper with you over breakfast?" In handing Katherine a section it seemed he was reluctant to let go of.

"Turnabout is fair play. I shared mine when you were in Chicago."

"Oh, all right." He handed her the sports page.

"I'll have the front page, thank you." Katherine swapped sections with him and laughed. Neither of them spoke until Andrew drank the last drop of his coffee. He put the paper down and asked, "Scrambled or over easy?"

Most of the afternoon they spent in the sunroom off the kitchen. It was a comfortable room with a no fuss masculine approach to both the fabrics and objects of art set about on tables. Over the fireplace hung a large oil painting of a garden that Katherine recognized as the front jacket on Andrew's Seattle garden book. He'd commissioned a local artist and the result took pride of place in the room. One wall was lined with bookshelves that appeared to have been arranged by a decorator in anticipation of a feature article in the home section of the newspaper. However long ago, new books now encroached on the symmetry of perfection. There was a door in this room that opened on to a deck and small garden beyond, but an overcast curtain of drizzle prevented Katherine from stepping out to have a closer look.

Andrew sat on the couch next to her reading aloud replies to his inquiries from the owners of the gardens they were considering for the book. Only one reply had turned them away. It was an agreeable letter, how flattered they were to be asked, but at this time the maintenance of the garden was not up to its usual standards citing family illness as the problem. The rest of the gardeners were interested, and asked for more information about the author's intentions. Andrew looked up, "That's the two of us, the authors."

"And, what are our intentions?" Katherine was not clever with innuendoes, but she had a lot to talk about in a very short time. This was as good a place to start as any.

Andrew placed the letters on the coffee table, and topped off the two wine glasses they had hardly touched.

Without preamble, Katherine said, "Robert wants to sell the publishing firm, and I might want to be a part of an employee buyout." She sounded more assured than when she first spoke these same words to Louisa.

"Buy the company? Really?" Andrew looked blindsided. Katherine suspected he hadn't spent much time considering her side of things. She could understand that since trying to figure out what she was capable of giving as well. They were in the same situation thinking that once they each figured out what they wanted for themselves, the other one would want the same thing too.

Katherine reached over and placed her hand on Andrew's cheek. He moved it across his lips and kissed the inside of her hand, holding it there.

"Let me explain. This is in strict confidence, Andrew. There are lawyers and financial people involved, serious stuff. I'm going to Italy the week before Easter to talk in depth with Robert about the meetings I have attended on his behalf."

"Why would he want to sell? It's his inheritance, his parents' life's work, his own successful stewardship that has grown the company. He's making money, I don't understand."

"He wants a lifestyle change and he thinks Italy is the place to do that."

"Running away will help him?" Here were the same words Johanna had used when she accused Katherine of running away from Chapel Hill. Katherine was not to be talked out of her decision, and now she realized, the odds were not good when it came to changing Robert's mind.

Katherine did not explain the options that were available to Robert should he proceed with the sale of the company, but she wanted Andrew to understand that there were several strong possibilities. "There is a larger publishing house in Chicago that has let it be known they would be happy to acquire Davis Publishing, should it become available, which might or might not mean the loss of my job. The thought of closing the books on the company that my parent's best friends started and the loss of my job, are prospects I'd like to keep from happening."

"Will Robert listen to you?" Katherine knew the question Andrew wanted to ask, but could not verbalize, was how this news would affect the two of them.

She also knew that Andrew couldn't see himself living in Chicago, even with her. Nor was he ready to ask, let alone beg, if need be, that she make a life with him in Seattle. Katherine's future with Davis Publishing, though uncertain, was now on the table between them, and it wasn't just location that mattered to her.

Andrew bolted from the couch pulling Katherine along with him. "I'm taking you out for dinner to a quiet, romantic neighborhood cafe, which is more to my liking than the thought of you becoming a part owner at Davis Publishing." He stood looking at her. "I'm embarrassed to say, I hadn't considered that what I wanted wasn't the only deciding factor here."

"It's okay." She kissed him and was glad when he kissed her back in a way that postponed dinner for a while.

❁

It was not an auspicious start to the meal when weather was all they could find to talk about. "Chicago is too damn cold." "Seattle is wet." They laughed and moved to safer ground, the book. Back home, changed into their robes, they watched an old Cary Grant and

Katharine Hepburn movie. They finished off the evening in the kitchen sharing a large bowl of vanilla ice cream with chocolate sauce.

Later, in bed Katherine lay with her head once again on Andrew's shoulder. "Can you hear me purring?" Andrew was rubbing her back.

"If only someone could guarantee that we won't forget the fun stuff like watching a movie under a blanket or licking chocolate sauce off each other's lips. Why do couples stop doing these things?"

Katherine didn't want to answer this question in any serious way. "Hey, you only get a year's guarantee when you buy a plant." She would have taken back what she said if she could. Andrew withdrew his hand from her back and lay looking up at the ceiling. She could do better, even if it was late. She tried again. "Let's enjoy the moment, Andrew. That's all we can do right now, don't you agree?"

Andrew remained still at first, but then by way of reply, he turned towards her. After a moment he found her mouth with a kiss.

The next morning Katherine had yet to call Claire Thompson. They were finishing breakfast. "I didn't let Claire know I was coming, but I want to call her. I didn't know how to tell her there wasn't any time to see her on this trip."

"You were right. I wasn't going to let you out of my sight." Andrew finished spreading jam on an English muffin before he put it on a plate and pushed it towards Katherine. "Have you stayed in touch?"

"It's been wonderful. On the face of it, you wouldn't think we could build a long distance relationship. We're opposites in so many ways."

"I rather thought we were having one of those, a long distance thing." Katherine was getting used to Andrew saying important things while using diversionary tactics like this. He went on. "Am I deceived, and all you want is to co-author a book on English gardens?" He chuckled and handed her a plate of scrambled eggs.

"People at our age having a relationship? That's what you call it then?" She murmured, "Such a revelation, I didn't know." He came around the island and sat beside her. "Tell me more about Claire."

"We talk every few weeks, mostly about the bookstore. She has built a loyal customer base. So many independent bookstores are slowly going out of business either when the original owners reach retirement age or die. Even if the stores are bought the change doesn't seem to work, and over time, the store closes for good."

Andrew put his fork down and looked at Katherine. "I'm glad that isn't the way it works with gardens. New owners, new life, new cultural practices, new plant material that is disease resistant."

"Yes, but you've been in gardens that are run by foundations that do a great job, but the spirit of the gardener is gone. You can feel the difference." Katherine had let her tea grow cold. She got up to pour the dregs down the kitchen sink.

"Here's another idea for a book, Andrew. Why not write one about gardens that have changed hands. What has become of everyone involved?"

"Sounds more up your alley. Write a novel weaving everyone's story." He smiled at her as she turned from the sink to look at him.

"You know, that's not a bad idea." She reached for a sheet of paper from the small kitchen desk built into the kitchen cabinetry. She scribbled a note to herself.

Andrew rose from the bar stool and walked over to the sink where Katherine was fixing a fresh cup of tea. "If Robert does sell his company, why don't you move here and write books with me?"

Katherine remained quiet for a moment not sure how to answer such a question. "We said last night it was best to take things as they come, remember?"

He took the filled teacup from her and set it down on the counter before wrapping his arms around her. He kissed her face and lips. "I just remember this."

191

They stood like this for several minutes. Then Andrew pushed her gently away. "Make your phone call to Claire while I clear up these breakfast things."

She headed towards the family room. "I hope she's home."

Katherine was disappointed when the answering machine kicked on. She identified herself and was starting to speak when Claire picked up. "Here I am. I was running a vacuum and didn't hear the phone."

"I'm in Seattle, Claire. I accepted a last minute invitation from my friend, Andrew Stillman."

"You're kidding? You're here?"

"We have some things to iron out about this book we're working on together." Katherine did not explain that she felt she owed Andrew an explanation about what she was considering.

"I'm not going to get to see you?" The disappointment was obvious in Claire's voice. Can't you come and stay another few days with me?"

"I wish I could, really I do. I've got to get back. I'm leaving soon for Italy to see my boss who's there on sabbatical. I told you about that."

"Italy, wow, lucky you."

"I know. He is giving everyone a full week off before Easter. It's a thank you for holding down the fort while he has been gone. The staff is ecstatic."

"I can image."

The two women talked another fifteen minutes. Claire finally said, "I'm interested in Andrew's role in this visit. Was it something special besides the book?"

With Andrew in the next room, Katherine avoided answering Claire. Had she answered, she would have said Andrew was special; their time together had been lovely. Katherine kept her eyes on the watercolor that hung above the fireplace of the garden she had seen on Bainbridge Island. Her own life was like the long border portrayed in the painting. The color varied by season. Year by year there were

192

changes; things that died back, seedlings sprouting up in unexpected places. There were new plants introduced into the design, yet names she could no longer remember of old plants that had receded into the background. Regardless of where she found herself, the garden border was a perfect metaphor for her life. Whether she was looking out on Lake Michigan, cherishing memories of her parents and friends, or thinking about the girl she once had been. Even sitting here in Andrew Stillman's Queen Anne home, like a garden, there was continuity to her life, an endless border filled with love and dedication, work and prayer. Claire Thompson, on the other end of the telephone, was like a rare plant in this border that required care and friendship to maintain. Katherine was content with this task.

"You must promise that next time you have a few days you will come and work with me in the bookstore. You told me it was one of your un-lived lives. This is your opportunity."

"I promise." Katherine remained seated after she hung up the phone. Andrew recognized the silence and came and sat beside her. They looked up at the painting together.

Katherine flew to Chicago late that afternoon. At the airport it was not an easy parting. Though packaged in a medium size frame, Andrew loomed large. His voice remained energetic like a man in his twenties, but there was a quiet center at the heart of him that made her happy and content. Louisa had been right to ask her if she was sure she wanted to spend more time behind a desk, in charge of anything. It was easy to see herself in that role when she was not standing enfolded in Andrew's arms with his face briefly buried in her hair.

Making her way through security, Katherine was glad she had made the trip, but surprised that it had taken an emotional toll. It was probably a good thing that she had a lot to do in getting ready to leave for Italy. When she boarded the plane and leaned back in her seat, she closed her eyes thinking of what lay ahead. The airplane accelerated down the runway and lifted off. She was sorry to be leaving.

Sitting in his car in the parking garage, Andrew could not bring himself to put the key in the ignition. He'd been anxious over breaking a rule that no one else cared about, and for what? He'd come close to calling Katherine on some trumped up pretext to ask her not to come. The reality of her head on the pillow beside him beat the hell out of a fantasy of her being there. What had been so important about maintaining his independence that had cost him a wife and children? All he had to show for this was a trumped up rule in the place of someone warm beside him.

Flooded with fear, he leaned his head on the steering wheel and took several deep breaths. If he questioned one part of his life, would everything else come a part once he admitted he'd made a mistake with his rules and careful life. Had he become like some politicians in Washington clinging tenaciously to their earliest assumptions, no longer capable of an examined idea? Had it come to this for him?

The blast on the horn from the car he almost hit when he backed out of the parking space set his heart racing. The careful man, the careful driver, a careful life all shifting on a crumbling foundation he'd built with his own hands.

27

At 5:30 Elizabeth stuck her head around the door to Katherine's office. "Unless you need me, I've done all the damage I can do today, I'm saying goodnight."

"Can you come in a minute?" The young woman who strode towards Katherine was almost unrecognizable from the first day they'd met. She wore a short, cropped bronze leather jacket over a cream turtleneck cashmere sweater, and dark brown slacks. A silk scarf was tied around her neck, folded in such a way to take the place of a necklace she might have otherwise worn. Her hair was no longer a bleached and damaged hanging down her back, but a sophisticated style that was cut short to her jaw line. Subtle highlights had been added. Both the length and natural color made her look ten years younger than the harsh look she was wearing when Katherine arrived at Davis Publishing.

Smiling in admiration while Elizabeth eased into the chair in front of the desk, Katherine asked, "What are you going to do with your vacation, or is it a secret?"

"I've met someone." A grin broadcast how pleased she was to make this announcement.

"You can't have my blessing until I meet him." Katherine, grinning, sat back in her chair and began to hum. She stopped after a moment. "Did you jump rope when you were a kid?"

In a tone that asked what this had to do with anything, Elizabeth answered, "Yes." Katherine began to sing, "Elizabeth and a fellow sitting in a tree, K-I-S-S-I-N-G, first comes love, then comes marriage, then comes baby in a baby carriage!" Elizabeth giggled, enjoying Katherine's obvious amusement.

"Sorry," Katherine laughed. "Ever since I've come back to Chicago, the little girl I once was, she pops up and takes over. That was a playground song when we jumped rope." Katherine tried to get serious. "Is this fellow the kind of someone in the song, that leads to marriage?"

"We only see each other on weekends. He's taking a few days off, and we're going to play tourist here in the city, a date everyday with long lunches. I have a few concerns, like a list of movies he wants to rent, which I know I'm not going to like, and I am gearing up to challenge his political assumptions that are all wrong."

"Do you have anything in common?"

"That's what we're going to find out. But I can tell you this, he's gorgeous."

"Oh, well, what more do you need." They both laughed.

Katherine was not worried that Elizabeth would blunder into a relationship that was a 'tried to and couldn't' affair. She was too smart for that. She'd worked hard from the moment Katherine took her under her wing, undergoing the Liza Doolittle transformation that Robert had teased about. The makeover complimented her intelligence, talent, and work ethic. She began her career at Davis Publishing by coming to work in blue jeans and either a black or gray top that always made her look tired. Today she was well on her way to becoming an assistant editor with the people skills to work with an author who either needed hand holding, or a kick in the butt, Robert's words, not Katherine's.

"What about you?" Elizabeth asked. Are you going to stay with your friend in Chapel Hill?"

Katherine hesitated for a moment before answering. "Before I answer that, I would appreciate it if you would consider this a confidential conversation."

Elizabeth sat up straight, put her feet together and her hands in her lap before saying, "Yes, Ma'am." Though teasing, Katherine knew she was, in fact, giving her word.

"I'm going to Italy for the holiday. I have booked my ticket and made a reservation at the Raffaello in Rome. It's within walking distance of the Colosseum and the Roman Forum. I plan on day trips, enjoying the food, and seeing some gardens, though it's a bit early."

"I'm so jealous. Maybe I'll ditch the gorgeous guy for an Italian and let him pinch my bottom." If it had been different circumstances, Katherine would have encouraged Elizabeth to do just that.

"Another time, perhaps." She smiled and felt relieved that she'd decided to disclose enough of her plans so that she would not have to flummox around when she got back.

"You'll meet up with Robert, of course."

There it was, how easy. Elizabeth asked a simple question that only required a simple answer. "Oh yes, I'm sure, if he can spare the time." It had been truthful, plausible and incidental.

Elizabeth rose from the chair. "I'm excited for you, and I hope you are excited for me. Just think, a gorgeous man, full of unexamined ideas that he swallowed whole while at Harvard, and a taste for war movies that use the f-word. Sounds great doesn't it." Elizabeth stopped in the middle of the carpeted expanse between the desk and door. "That was what you wanted to see me about, right, your plans?"

"In fact, I wanted to ask the name of your hairdresser. Who is cutting and coloring your hair? You look divine."

"Thanks to you and the gift certificate you gave me for Christmas from your hair salon. I'm sure the girl I'm seeing is your doing too." She paused before walking through the door. "I'm forever grateful, you know that. I owe you big time."

"Pay it forward, dear girl. I guarantee you that there is a young, talented woman in your future that will need your encouragement. I hope she makes you as proud as you have made me." Elizabeth beamed and whispered, "*Arrivederci.*" Katherine put a finger to her lips in the time-honored gesture of keeping quiet. "*Arrivederci.*"

❁

Katherine deliberately withheld from Robert the exact time and day of her arrival in Rome. She wanted a full day to recover from any jet lag before she tackled him in his tracks over the sale of the business. She booked her flights, and at Robert's suggestion, made a reservation at the Raffaello in Monti. When he called to check on her plans, she raised an objection about his hotel suggestion.

"I hope the neighborhood has changed since ancient times. This *rione* was once the red-light district." She laughed. "Is this is why you like it?"

"Listen to you, a *rione* is it?"

"I looked it up. *Rione* is the name given to a neighborhood in several Italian cities; like a territorial subdivision."

"This *rione*, as you call it, is a gorgeous little neighborhood that people are beginning to notice. The neighborhood is changing, and I want you to see it before it gets too trendy. I meet Antonio and these new friends at a pleasant restaurant on Via San Vito near Maria Maggiore called Trattoria Monti."

Regardless of Robert's high approval rating, a few days later, Katherine was relieved to find an elegantly decorated lobby when she checked in at the hotel. Arriving off the early morning flight she was not surprised that her room was not available. A friendly staff plied her with coffee and rolls while she waited for a room key and a bed that promised oblivion. One of the dark eyed young girls, darting back and forth, came periodically to check on her. "Things are progressing, *Signora.*" When she was finally able to crawl into bed she slept as if someone had knocked her over the head. It was late afternoon by the time she ventured out the door to stand and look around at the signs of the Roman, Medieval, Baroque and Renaissance buildings along the street. It amazed Katherine to think that all it had taken was a plane ride to find herself standing where she was, a place that normally seemed far away. Checking her map, she headed off in the direction of the Basilica of Santa Maria Maggiore to give thanks for her safe travel, and to ask for clarity in these next few days. After her prayers she walked the streets listening to an Italian surround-sound that emanated from a kind of high quality Bose radio. If wagging a cautionary finger in Robert's face ruined the spell these sounds had put him under, she would never forgive herself.

Even after a full night's sleep she was still off kilter the next day. She was glad she'd made the decision to take this day for herself and get her sea legs back under her, as Timothy called them. Over morning coffee, and more rolls, she tried to decide whether to take herself off to Vatican City to spend part of the day, or visit Castel Gandolfo and the Barberini Garden. She read in her guidebook that visitors were accompanied by a multi-lingual guided tour to see the botanical and architectural delights of the pontifical residence. In the end she did both things. She asked the hotel desk clerk to order a taxi to take her to Vatican City. The young woman gave her strict instructions.

"Signora, you must always use an official taxi. They are white, with a "TAXI" sign on the roof and the Rome crest on the doors. Since we have ordered your taxi from the hotel the meter started running when it left a stand where it sits waiting. You will have a few euros on the meter when you get in. It's okay. Here it is customary to round up the fare to a convenient amount like a tip, but not a tip, if you understand me." Katherine thanked her, "*Molte grazie.*" She thought of Johanna's warning that she would be ripped off in Rome by the taxi drivers. Not with the hotel looking out after her like this.

Even the overcast day, with occasional drizzle, could not put a damper on Katherine's spirits when later in the day she walked through the garden. Fleeting thoughts of home accompanied her footsteps. She thought of Louisa and Beatrice and wished she could share this day with them. Had she and Andrew talked about Italy? Further along the path, she wondered how Elizabeth's long lunches were going? It made her chuckle to think of her pretending she liked movies that used the f-word just to impress her date. She hoped she wouldn't do that.

An older couple walked by holding hands, and quietly talking. Katherine's heart lurched. This day was meant for Timothy and her in retirement. Johanna and Douglas would be along nagging them to leave the garden to find a bottle of wine to finish off.

The sun was beginning to burn away the gray skies when Katherine found a bench to sit on where she could rest her feet. She'd enjoyed the tour, and somewhere along the way had been able to let go of Louisa and Beatrice, even Timothy; everyone from home that had been keeping her company. She was glad to let Andrew drift off on his own as well. In this moment she wanted nothing more than to breathe in the scent of the damp vegetation that surrounded her. She would remember this garden long after she had returned to Chicago, revisiting it again in her imagination. Feeling grateful, Katherine never felt more certain of the line in the hymn, (*Jesus loves me this I know*). She had found a healing in this papal garden where other pilgrims had come before her, each leaving a speck of their dust behind, to be walked upon by those who followed after. Being a part of something larger than her own understanding was the gift of this particular moment.

That evening after a bath and nap, Katherine walked along Via San Vito to the restaurant, Trattoria Monti. If meant to be, Robert would already be there. When she arrived, a man in a coat and tie, dressed as a banker might look in the States, held the door of the Trattoria open for her and his companion. She followed the young woman into the restaurant. She too was dressed as if she'd come straight from work, a brief case in one hand and her handbag in the other. Katherine smiled and thanked them. She repeated the word she'd been using all day. "*Grazie.*"

Katherine stood off to the side of the door, and scanned the tables. With his back to the door, it took her a moment to recognize that she was going to be able to pull off her surprise. Robert was sitting with three other men, their wine glasses already half empty. Unrecognized, they paid her no attention until she stopped just behind Robert's shoulder. When they looked up, she smiled at them. *"Sto cercando Robert,* I'm looking for Robert." She placed a hand on his shoulder.

Robert all but upended the table as he jumped to his feet to greet her. "This can't be happening. You aren't arriving until tomorrow." He embraced her, and then threw his head back with a roar. He looked years younger, and in spite of all the food he said he'd been eating, he'd lost some weight. He must not have been wearing a coat and tie when he discovered the fountain of youth here in Italy. Casually dressed, he looked like an understudy for a Ralph Lauren advertisement. Robert had traded his white shirts and vintage sport coats for a green merino wool sweater, and pleated khaki slacks. It was obvious he had shed his troubles for lighter fare.

Robert introduced her around the table. She was sure that *"Piacere di conoscerti"* meant, "Nice to meet you." Still falling over himself, Robert grabbed a chair from the next table while the others scooted around to make room. He kept repeating, "I can't believe this."

By the time Robert walked Katherine back to the Raffaello that night, she might as well have been immersed in a baptismal font filled with red wine. Arising from that font her internal clock was reset, and her inner ear newly attuned to a language whose words sounded musical. She could not resist this religion of gestures and bravado that proclaimed the good news of Italy. Robert had indeed found a perfect priest in his new friend Antonio, whose anointment, albeit with olive oil, had blessed and changed him.

28

The next morning Robert was standing in the lobby waiting when Katherine stepped out of the elevator. "Ready for a walk," he asked? He took her arm, steering her towards the street beyond the front door. They stepped onto a theater stage where the cast of characters were in mid-action already performing their roles. There were businessmen in suits, old women with missing teeth and black scarves tied over their hair, and young children, shrieking with laughter on their way to school. A dog tugged on the end of a leash that pulled an old gentleman forward, while two shop girls ablaze with makeup and hairspray hurried past. No part of the city was exempt from the nuns in their black habits gliding along on invisible feet, or the priests hurrying towards the nearby churches.

Yesterday had been a dress rehearsal for this scene Katherine entered today. With Robert in charge, and through his eyes, it was like the opening street scene in an Italian opera. Katherine murmured with pleasure seeing the costumes and scenery again.

Their ultimate destination was The Hassler Hotel for a late lunch, which gave them the morning to amble along brushing shoulders with the citizens of Rome. Katherine remarked, "It amazes me how generous the Italians are having to jostle with tourists day after day." What astounded Katherine was how exceedingly comfortable Robert was with all of it in just a few months time. A Vespa buzzed by inches away from them on the narrow streets that did not faze him. "I want one of those." He pointed to a bright red scooter that passed by.

"Surely not here in Rome. Coming in from the airport I watched them swerve into oncoming traffic like crazy people. Why aren't there any designated scooter lanes?"

"Any space between two cars will do." Katherine loved the humor of this. They walked on for another ten minutes zigzagging around people who would suddenly come to a stop in the middle of the sidewalk to read their maps. A group of Japanese tourists, each with a camera slung around their necks, and wearing matching tour hats, came out of a hotel and forced them to step into the street.

Back on the sidewalk, Robert said, "This is why I like the Monti area where you're staying. Less crowded. I feel like I blend in and I can pretend I belong in the neighborhood." Robert looked over at Katherine to gauge her mood on the subject.

He continued. "I try to imagine what my life would be like if I stay." They walked on, slowing up to look in shop windows, when other wise not engaged in people watching.

"Ready for some coffee?" Robert asked.

"What, no red wine this early?" She followed him into a small restaurant after agreeing it was still too nippy to sit outside. A matronly woman in a black dress, and shoes reminiscent of the 1930's, took Robert's order. They were laced and clunky. *"Due cappuccini, per favore,"* he said. The woman smiled an encouraging smile at his effort to speak Italian.

Robert held Katherine's chair while she unbuttoned her coat and wiggled out of it. He took it from her and draped it over the back of the chair while she folded a silk scarf from around her neck and put it in her purse.

"I'm amazed, Robert. You've learned to speak a lot of Italian in such a short time, it's impressive." Sitting across from him at the table, she gave him an appraising look. "I haven't told you how great you look, ten years younger for sure. I'd like your formula for that." Robert beamed.

Though they'd agreed to talk business after lunch, Katherine wondered if this warm-up to that conversation would not be equally important, if not more so than the business side of her mission. There was every chance his heart would over-trump his head.

When the woman returned with their cappuccino, Katherine got into the act by smiling up at the woman saying, thank you, *"Grazie."*

She listened while Robert engaged her in conversation, but only understood his question, *"Come stai?"* to which she answered, she was fine. *"Sto bene."* After a few minutes the woman left the table to greet a middle-aged couple that came through the door.

Katherine put her cup down and looked at this man who had run away to Italy to find himself. "Since your call, Robert, I have been thinking how we let the practicalities of life rule the day. I have friends who are considering relocating near adult children, already thinking ahead to the day when they will need their help. Others are going to move to Florida for tax reasons, or to retirement communities for the healthcare amenities. Most will scale back, reduce expenses, sort through things so their children won't have to do it later on. Not one of them, as far as I know, contemplates a move to a place they imagined over the years as their Shangri-La. Seems a shame doesn't it?" Katherine wondered why she had started this conversation from the wrong end of the stick if she hoped to discourage Robert from kicking the traces, and leaving it all behind.

His facial expression changed momentarily, a relaxed look turned serious. "I'm not sure James Hilton did us a favor when he wrote Lost Horizon. We've come to think this permanently happy fictional place, this paradise on earth, is real. It's part of the reason I'm here, hoping to find my Shangri-La."

"Have you found it?" Katherine wasn't sure which she felt more keenly; fear that he might not return to the firm, or his disappointment that there was no paradise to be found here either.

"Too soon to tell, I suppose, but you said I looked ten years younger. In Shangri-La, if you remember, people slowly aged in appearance." Robert glanced at his watch, "Another coffee?" Katherine nodded yes.

"Signora, " he called, and raised two fingers and made a circle with them over their empty cups.

Robert continued. "I know playing the happy tourist is different from making this my home, but I scare myself at times when I realize how much I dread returning to the shuffle between home and the office. I love the work, but my personal life revolves around the edges of other friends' lives that included me in their holidays and family celebrations. I'm still alone, Katherine.

He smiled at the signora that returned to the table with their refills. "*Molte grazie.*" This time he did not encourage her to stay by saying anything further to her.

"I have only myself to blame, Katherine, and you, by the way. You have shown me that moving can have a positive outcome."

That was fine for her, but she didn't want Robert to follow suit. In a pleading voice she asked, "But the firm? You're responsible for it's growth, and the reputation it enjoys today. All of this is important."

Robert raised his hand to stop her from saying more. "I'm eager to read the information you have brought me, and I will, but there is so little time to have you look through the lense I've been using." Katherine reached her hand across the table and waited for him to place his hand in hers. "There is plenty of time," she said. They stood and put on their coats. The woman waved at them, "*Ciao, adopo,*" see you later.

Before climbing the Spanish steps several hours later they mingled with the crowd in the Piazza di Spagna. They stopped to listen to a tour guide. He was gesturing towards the steps. With the noise around them, it only allowed snatches of what he was saying. "Designed by an Italian, paid for by the French, and named for the nearby Spanish Embassy." Robert elbowed Katherine when the guide said something about, "Our love affair with the motorino started when Paiggio debuted the Vespa in 1946. Sales exploded after Audrey Hepburn joined Gregory Peck for a Vespa ride past the Spanish Steps in the movie, Roman Holiday." The movie Katherine had watched a few evenings before leaving for Italy.

By the time they climbed the Steps to the Hassler Hotel, the temperature was warm enough so they could eat their lunch in the Palm Court, the most charming garden restaurant and bar Katherine had ever seen. There were wrought-iron tables and chairs surrounded by pots of flowers and vines growing up the walls of the hotel's inner courtyard.

Katherine tried to read the menu out loud, pronouncing the selections in Italian. With Robert's help, she repeated the choices she liked the sound of. When it came time to place her order, however, she wasn't confident enough to say, *Frittata di carciofi e misticanza.* Instead she said, "I'll have the artichoke omelette with the seasonal salad." She hoped her enthusiasm made up for her inability to say the Italian words correctly.

Robert asked for *Tagliere di salumi e formaggi laziali,* which a glance at the menu told Katherine was a selection of cold cuts and cheeses from Lazio. He added, "I'll have the *Vignarola* as well."

Katherine consulted her menu again. "It says *Vignarola* is a traditional Roman soup."

"*Vignarola* is like a spring vegetable stew. I'll give you a taste." Robert raised his glass of the *Verrazzano Rosso Chianti* towards her. "Here's to the good life in this beautiful place."

Later, with their plates cleared away, and fresh coffee, Katherine drew from her purse the papers the lawyer, Tom Braxton, had given her to deliver. "I don't want to break the spell of this atmosphere, but let's get this out of the way, shall we?" She smiled.

He took the papers from her glancing at them briefly. "I've never given much thought to what I would do with the firm when I left, or for that matter, died. I assumed an outside party would think the business was worth acquiring and buy it. There is a decent living to be made at Davis Publishing."

"The irony in your being away is that Tom said it was a seller's goal to develop a company that can run without them. In testing this out, the owner might take an extended holiday without any contact.

Here you are, already doing that." Katherine took a breath hoping she could deliver her findings without sounding muddled.

"Tom would tell you that when you come back, if the company has a higher value than when you left, the company can probably run without you. I'm not going to tell you that he mentioned a year's absence as an appropriate amount of time for this experiment. Six months is all you get."

Robert nodded his head and grinned. "Has the company increased in value?" Katherine found herself bragging about the good work the editors and staff had done since the New Year.

She handed him several more pages stapled together. "Malcolm McDowell over at Arthur Anderson has good things to say, which I'm sure you're happy to hear."

"I have complete trust in them."

"I can see why, they have been patient and helpful to me, that's for sure. Tom was pretty shook up with the thought of a sale: his father, your father, kind of reaction. He recovered, and hasn't mentioned it since."

"I didn't think about how this was going to hit him, like you and me," he gestured between them, "We grew up together too. He is younger, but our fathers owned a boat together for a while and sailed it out of Belmont Harbor."

"He has your best interests in mind, no doubt about that." Leaning back in her chair, Katherine decided to make a confession.

"I was determined to come here and talk you out of any further thoughts of selling. I had it figured out that you could come back, run the company, but spend part of your time here, holidays and such. I keep thinking about your parents and their dreams. They would not recognize the list you represent today. How proud they would be of the reputation you've garnered, the authors that would have fallen into obscurity. It's a lot to give up." Katherine looked around the Palm court aware of a piano playing quietly in the background. She looked back at him. "I can't do it."

"Do what, talk me out of the idea?"

"I heard a story many years ago about a man who built a boat. It was his dream to finish and sail it. The glorious day came when he unloaded the boat at the water's edge. His wife appears, hands on hips, and says to him, "NO." Imagine being the kind of person who says "NO" to life in others, let alone to themselves." Katherine hesitated before she added, "I can't say no to you." In comfortable silence they finished their coffee.

Katherine changed the subject. She looked across at Robert. "You told me you have seen Mary everywhere you've been; in the churches, along the streets, statues with fresh flowers. You and I have never talked religion, but here is as good a place as any." Robert was sitting forward looking intently at her.

Katherine continued. "It is the yes of Mary that teaches us how to say yes to our own lives. Do you know what I mean? I can't be the one who talks you out of this, if this is what you must do."

Robert handed the papers back. "We will talk some more, of course. I intend to read every word on my own time." He hesitated. "Thank you, Katherine, for this. Meeting with the lawyers and accountants, making the trip, bringing me these papers. Most of all thank you for giving me this time to be away." He pushed back from the table and stood, "Shall we?"

They gathered their coats. Katherine wrapped the silk scarf around her neck once again, and tied it loosely. The Hassler had lived up to its reputation. "Thank you for this experience, Robert. I will never forget it."

"You're most welcome."

29

It would take two and a half hours to drive to Pienza from Rome. Robert's eagerness to return to Pienza was obvious after his three-week stay at the Agriturismo Santa Maria di Pienza. He entertained Katherine on the trip with stories about the people he met while there.

"When we walk through the main gate that's called, Porta al Prato, you will see why I could hardly tear myself away."

"You're not going to chain yourself to a tree and refuse to leave this time are you?"

"I'm rather hoping you will be the one to do that." Katherine was doubtful. She and Timothy had spent their entire visit in Florence years before; it was hard to imagine other places in Italy that could tempt her to stay.

An hour into the trip she felt they had somehow veered off the road into a watercolor painting awash with light that illuminated the vineyards and olive groves they passed. The artist of this painting had included some obligatory cypress trees, and a medieval village thrown in for good measure. She could not take her eyes off the roadside.

It was difficult to turn her attention back to hear Robert say, "Several nights each week the owners hosted a dinner of fresh pasta for the guests. We sat around late into the evening drinking the local wines, and talking about why we had traveled to Italy."

"Did you tell them you were a runaway?"

"Only that I was a publisher visiting for six months."

"Were they impressed with your Italian in this short time?" Robert nodded and grinned. "I think they were. I left out the part about hiring a tutor."

"I didn't mean to sidetrack your story, sorry."

"We drank seriously great wine. Pienza is surrounded by wineries. The wine is often served with their pecorino cheese." Robert sounded dead serious when he said, "Thank God, I'm not an alcoholic. I would have gone off the wagon to drink the Brunello wines of Montalcino."

"Do any of these wineries ship to the States? You'd think with all the Italians in Chicago, you could get the wines you liked at home." He did not comment on this subtle mention of home.

"Some of the guests turned out to be writers. A woman named Cynthia Ford checked in with a small group of clients from Rome, all couples, who filled the remaining rooms. She leads special interest tours to Pienza, and several of the nearby hill towns, Montalcino, San Quirico and Montepulciano. She invited me to join them the day they spent in Pienza. I was fascinated." Robert took his eyes from the road long enough to smile over at Katherine. "I was so jealous of her career that I'm considering becoming a tour guide."

"First it was cooking in an Italian restaurant, and now you're going to be a tour guide when you grow up?"

"Maybe. When I found out Cynthia works as a guide in Rome, contributing to guide books like Time Out Guide to Rome, and Frommer's Italian Islands, I thought, what a job, I could do this too."

"You're not serious, right? Your parents wanted so much more for you." They laughed. Katherine asked, "Have you met anyone working on a travel memoir that Davis Publishing would be interested in? The world is ready for another Dickens and Twain."

"With all the splendid educations people have who move here, you'd think there would be plenty to pick from. I'm starting to lose track of the number of BA in Art History and Architecture I've met since I got here. What a life this Cynthia has. She spends her time between Rome and London, and runs this travel service for tourists who come to Rome. You and I should be so lucky." Robert wondered if Katherine noticed that he'd put an emphasis on the word, 'we?'

She was enjoying herself, and laughed. "No wonder you enjoyed the Agriturismo; with these various females you're talking about." She'd fallen back into her habit of teasing Robert when it came to other women.

"All kidding aside, there is someone that might be a great prospect for us. Rachel Thompson earned her B.A. in History of Art with a focus on Roman art and archaeology. She moved to Rome in 2002, and earned a Master's degree in Italian Gastronomic Culture at the *Università of Roma.* She writes, edits, and contributes to guide books, and *National Geographic.* She offers food tours and wine tastings all over Southern Italy, AND, she's writing a book that is a fictional version of these tours. I like the premise."

"Did you discuss the possibility of her letting us look at the manuscript when she's finished?"

"I did. Couldn't quite manage all play and no work. Lost my head."

"Good for you. Anyone else?"

"You're going to meet one of the most interesting women that is staying in Pienza. Constance Winters has a Master's degree in English and taught at a college back home. When she made Rome her permanent home, she combined her love of cooking and reading mystery stories. She's writing a mystery series set in an Italian culinary cooking school. Her protagonist is an American journalist who teams up with a professor of Italian culinary history to get an inside look at the world of Italian food. She wants to publish the first three in the series within a short time of one another. I read the first book. It's good. She's going to join us for dinner tonight. Hope that's okay?"

"I'm intrigued already."

Upon arrival, they checked into the Relais Chiostro di Pienza, a restored convent in the center of Pienza. Katherine was thrilled with the panoramic view from her window that looked down on a garden she could only imagine, when in a few weeks time, things would be in bloom. Katherine was tempted to pull out her yellow legal pad and pen and stay right where she was. She would begin what all authors aspire to, the great American novel. Instead she freshened up before joining Robert in the lobby for lunch.

"You must see this before we go in." Robert led her to the terrace where they stood in silence. A slight breeze tousled Katherine's hair; she pulled her shawl tighter around her shoulders. They could hear a woman calling in Italian to someone below them, the sound drifting up the hill to where they stood. It was a precious moment, listening in the shadow of this old convent.

Katherine thought, if only I could capture this moment in a snow globe. I could take it home and shake it in the years to come. Finally the chill put an end to their looking at the surrounding landscape. They went inside to have their lunch.

Over coffee Katherine asked, "Robert would you consider selling the business to the employees if you go through with this. If so, I might take a hammer and crack open my piggy bank."

"Would you really?"

"Tom Braxton was not the only one who thought of his father in all this. The long friendship between our parents gave me pause too. When I think of Davis Publishing becoming something else, it's almost as bad as Marshall Field's changing their name to Macy's."

"Before you get your hammer, let me step up my PR campaign I am launching to win you over. I'm going to buy TV spots, and run advertisements in Italian magazines pitching the romance of Italy."

Since her arrival, Robert had neither said, nor done anything that indicated he had made a declaration of love for her over the phone. He'd kept a safe distance between them, giving her time to take the measure of him, as if he acknowledged his love in any way it might precipitate a rush to judgment on her part that he did not want to happen. Katherine decided not to comment about the advertising campaign.

They finished their coffee and Robert signaled for their bill. "This afternoon, I'm going to don my tour guide hat, take you by the hand, and start my campaign in this perfect place." He smiled at her. "I'm already looking forward to the smell of cheese wafting out the doors of the shops we're going to visit. There's one thing more before we go." Katherine, who had started to rise from here seat, sat back down.

"I want to answer your question about selling the business to the employees. I'm not interested in doing that. I can see some rationale for it, because they understand the firm, know its strengths, could keep their jobs, but they can't offer a fair price, let alone top dollar. I don't want to finance the sale. The equity would be at risk until they retired the debt. Better to find an outside party."

"You already have an interested party according to Tom."

"Having the information you have brought me will bring a reality check to this fantasy of a new life here in Italy." Neither of them said anything for a few moments.

"Which is worse, Katherine, the knot I feel in the pit of my stomach when I think about returning, or selling the business?" He started to say more but did not. Again, she sensed he was reluctant to press a vote on joining him regardless of his decision.

Minutes later they stood on Pienza's main street, Corso Rossellino. On the right stood a medieval church, San Francisco. Robert's explanation of the other buildings along the street was impressive. Here was Act Two, another scene, cast and sung, by the local operatic chorus in Pienza. It was utterly charming.

Wandering on, Robert talked less, giving her space to listen and breathe in the Renaissance architecture, the small shops, and the smell of the Pecorino cheese. It was the narrow streets in Pienza, full of medieval nooks and crannies that Katherine loved, taking in the food shops and trattorias, and the interesting artisans' workshops.

Katherine finally commented. "This is unbelievable, no wonder you love it here. Can you picture this as your home?"

"Could you?" He took her hand, and all but jerked her around a corner where laundry hung on lines above them. He kissed her with the sound of a child crying in the background. Holding her, he kissed her again. Katherine turned her face against the Gore-Tex jacket he was wearing and slipped her arms around his waist. In a moment they mutually let go of one another. Katherine smiled up at him. "Kissing runaway boys on street corners, what would my mother say?"

❁

Constance Winters was a plain looking woman in her forties; not exactly frumpy, but wearing clothes that were more out of date than anything. She looked like a page out of an old Talbot's women's catalogue that featured traditional clothing, minus the bright color palate they had evolved over the years.

Constance wore a beige pair of slacks with a matching jacket that was cut like a man's suit jacket. Underneath the jacket was a simple long sleeve cream colored buttoned-down blouse, with collar and cuffs showing. Her light brown hair was tucked behind each ear, a pair of gold hoops the only jewelry she wore. She fit the stereotype of a Bennington elite, East Coast Women's College graduate, covering up any feminine edges that might try to escape. She relied on her intelligence to carry the day. It did.

Robert's enthusiasm to see her again was evident, but he used the occasion to thank Katherine. "I'm able to be here tonight because Katherine is running the company in my absence." He reveled in telling the story of her coming to work for him, and the authors she was now working with. Eventually, they got to the matter at hand, Constance's novels.

When the evening was over, and they stood shaking hands, Katherine said, "After listening to the plot lines of the three books you have finished, it sounds to me like you're poised to have a long successful run like Donna Leon with her mysteries set in Venice."

Constance smiled, "I love her work." Constance handed Katherine a copy of Book One, the only title given to the book at the moment. "I appreciate your commitment to read this. I look forward to your thoughts."

Katherine tucked the manuscript in her bag. Robert was now the middleman on the ground, while finishing his sabbatical. No wonder he was excited to reconnect with this mature woman, who was obviously unafraid of the hard work it takes to create a lasting series. Would Katherine's prayers be answered because this unadorned star had crossed Robert's galaxy at the right moment? She could hope that the pleasure of introducing another author into the successful world of publishing was something he couldn't give up.

It was after midnight when Katherine finally turned off her bedside lamp. A mystery set in an Italian culinary cooking school was a winner.

The next morning they left for Lucca, only a half hour from the Tuscan coast. Katherine remembered it was an easy train ride from Florence, so she knew the direction they were headed. "I'll buy you a gelato, and we can walk the perimeter of the old walls this evening. It's like a park now where people walk and ride bicycles."

From the moment they arrived Katherine was enthralled. Here was a city large enough to engage with, yet small enough to enjoy on an intimate basis. It seemed perfectly located, less crowded. She was surprised when they left the hotel, where they had checked in, when a man loomed up in front of them calling out to Robert as if he were an old friend. "*Come vanno le cose?*" They shook hands vigorously.

"Fine, everything is good." The man shook Katherine's hand as well, and then grabbed her up, kissing her on both cheeks, all the while laughing, and speaking rapidly in Italian. She stood pretending to understand what was being said. Robert was no longer the man she had accompanied to book launching parties; the disengaged, bored, and sometimes, rude man. His reticence had disappeared leaving a smiling, keen, cheerful person. She left them both talking to dart into a store to buy a small Pinocchio.

Robert picked a local favorite in Lucca, Da Francesco's, for dinner that night. "The decor is nothing special, but the food is great. They told me the best of Tuscan food is found here in Lucca, and it must be true, everything is excellent." He looked at the menu, though he'd already announced what he would be ordering as they came through the door.

"The *tortelli lucchese* is the best I have had, and I have eaten this dish all over town. The farro soup with beans is also a classic. The workmen come here and eat the simple roasted meats. I ordered a plate of baby lamb that had a piece of leg, breast and loin, all lightly seasoned with salt, pepper, thyme, garlic and olive oil; it was delicious."

"Trying to keep up with you on this trip, walking miles, I have figured out how you are eating all this extraordinary food and haven't put on any weight. It better work for me." Robert patted his stomach and grinned.

The friendly staff came and went from their table. When Katherine tried her broken Italian on them, they spoke to her in English, and explained the dishes on the menu. Every meal was like a birthday celebration, surrounded by good and friendly people, drinking delicious regional wine, in no hurry to have the evening come to an end.

After their meal, Katherine handed Robert a small wrapped box. "Here, I have something for you."

He took the gift and shook it several times next to his ear. "When did you buy this, I haven't let you out of my sight?" He pulled the ribbon from the box. "What's this?" He unwrapped the tissue paper from around a five-inch ornament of Pinocchio. Laughing, he looked across at her and sang, ("*I've got no strings so I have fun, I'm not tied up to anyone, once I did, but now I'm free, I've got no strings on me.*")

Katherine finished, ("*Hi ho Pinocchio, nothing ever bothers me.*) Wonderful Geppetto fashioning Pinocchio out of a walking stick." She smiled. "I need a truthful answer from you. I thought if I gave you your own Pinocchio, your nose would grow if you tried to tell me a fib."

"I wish there were time to take you to Collodi near here; the villa and Baroque gardens where Carlo Lorenzini spent his childhood. He

216

used the pseudonym Carlo Collodi to write the book." Robert nodded, "*Grazie.*" to the server who brought their coffee. "You will come back so I can take you, tell me that you will."

"I believe you just answered my question; you're going to stay aren't you?" She watched him set his cup down. For a moment he looked at her without a word. He put two fingers on his nose as if to pinch it. "Just checking." Katherine appreciated his sense of humor, even knowing that this answer was going to change her future too.

"I am going to stay, Katherine. I will come home, of course, as I promised. I hope the buyer that came trolling to Tom Braxton is for real. It is a reputable Chicago company and chances are they'd keep the editorial staff. I know it's drastic, but there you have it."

"What will you do? Will you live in Rome?"

"I thought that would depend on you." He put a hand up to stop her when she started to answer.

"A new friend recommended that I spend time in Pienza and Lucca. At first I wanted to continue doing what I was doing in Rome with Antonio and his friends, a young academic couple I met in a bookstore, and an artist, all who took me under their wing. They were like a maintenance drug that a good diagnostician prescribed after I got here. When I was able to tear myself away, and spend time at the Agriturismo Santa Maria di Pienza, I felt I was entering a rehab program. By the time I got to Lucca my recovery seemed certain. I began to think of leaving it all behind, as they say, and moving permanently, which leaves me with a question for you." He looked quite serious. "You're not going to fall in love with me are you?"

It was true. "You are a different person, you're right about that. I told you how great you look, years younger, and who can resist this place." She gestured around the restaurant with the smell of Italian food hanging in the air, laughter that encircled them from nearby tables where Italian couples dined.

"I'm happy for you, Robert. Devastated that you're going to sell Davis Publishing, miserable that my Chicago life will be so drastically changed with you gone, amazed at your bravery and transformation, but no, I think we both knew when we kissed on the street corner that it is not meant to be."

"I thought when you came back into my life, the work we share, how amazing you are, that this was how the story was supposed to end, a cosmic intervention in my life that I do not deserve."

"There is a part of me that will return to Chicago hoping you will still change your mind, but we talked earlier about people that are starting over for practical reasons; Lucca seems like a Shangri-La to me. After I get over myself about this, I will rejoice in your decision to live your life in this new way."

Robert reached across the table and took the hand she offered. He expected to feel disheartened knowing that what he imagined possible, was not possible, after all. As if on cue, the couple sitting next to them rose from their seats and wished them goodnight, "*Buonasera,*" they called as they walked past. Robert's face lit up, "*Ciao, Arriverderci.*"

30

The next morning, Robert stood with Katherine in the main terminal at the airport waiting to check her bag. "I will see you the end of June unless Tom Braxton needs me sooner." He handed Katherine one of his 3x5 cards with the name and number of a Limo Service written on it. "They have your flight number and arrival time and should meet you at baggage."

Katherine was genuinely grateful; anticipating how worn out she would be at the end of the flight home. "This is kind, Robert, thank you. It's been a remarkable few days. I intend to nominate you for the tour guide of the year award." She reached up and kissed him on his cheek. "While here, I tried to look at everything through your eyes. I understand why you don't want to leave. I feel quite desolate myself that I'm headed back so soon."

"This is what I want for the rest of my life. Everyone says it is a frustrating place when it comes to doing business, buying property, but they learn to live with it because the positive things outweigh the negatives."

"Will you stay in Rome with Antonio and the others for the rest of your sabbatical?"

"You remember the man we met on the street when we first arrived in Lucca?" Katherine nodded, "Of course."

"He is a real estate agent and has found several apartments to show me. I'm driving back tomorrow to meet him." He smiled his new Ralph Lauren man of leisure and panache smile.

"Will you do me a favor?" Katherine asked.

"Of course, anything." Reaching the head of the line, an attendant tagged Katherine's bags and hefted them on a conveyor belt. She thought once again that it was a technological marvel that luggage made it on to the right airplane.

They stood aside to finish these last thoughts. "Would you consider making me a condition of the sale, I want to stay on a few more years?"

Robert smiled. "Here at the last moment, you aren't going to change your mind, and tell me to buy an apartment for two?"

"Ridiculous, isn't it? Turning down a chance like this." She gestured around her before reaching her hand up as if to brush something from his jacket. He looked puzzled. Katherine explained. "There is a bit of ash left on your shoulder." She flicked some invisible particle with her fingers from the other shoulder. "You told me you felt like a Phoenix reborn from its own ashes." Robert registered that he understood.

Katherine turned to go. "When someone makes reference to the Phoenix, I will no longer think of it as a myth. Now I believe it is a possibility."

"Thanks, Katherine." He'd never meant a thank you more than he did now. He caught her hand, "I'll do what I can to see that you and the sale of the business are one in the same." Robert watched her meld into the color and movement of people heading away from him to some other place. He was relieved that he was not one of these departing souls. He turned and retraced his steps towards the parking garage. Working his way through the crush of people he noticed an airport cafe where he could order a cappuccino in exchange for a place to sit down. He needed to collect himself before tackling the traffic back into Rome.

Seated with coffee, he glanced at his watch. Katherine would be checked in at her boarding gate by now. Flooded with gratitude for her, with little doubt of his love, he realized it was the kind of love you feel for the person who finds you lost and disoriented in a dark woods and saves your life. When she came to work for him it was as if she'd brought bright flood lamps like those seen around a crime scene. He had been plodding along where everything looked the same until the illumination from her lamps revealed a clearly marked trail he could follow out of the darkness. He was no longer lost, but found, as the old hymn said.

Finished with his coffee, he was hesitant to leave the airport knowing Katherine was still waiting for her plane. He would miss her company. In inviting her to Italy he wanted to prove that he was a man worth loving. Maria put that notion in his head for which he was grateful. Katherine acknowledged that the transformation he'd come looking for had found him. He blew her a mental kiss as he had seen her do so often.

Opening his rental car door he could smell a trace of Katherine's Chanel perfume, but the greatest gift she'd left behind was when she brushed the supposed ash from his jacket acknowledging that he was indeed, reborn.

Headed for Monti, Robert hoped Antonio was free for lunch. Regardless, he would ask to spend the night before driving to Lucca in the morning.

❋

The gate area was filling fast. Katherine sat with her carry-on bag at her feet, grateful to have a seat to wait out the hour. The weeklong pace had taken its toll. She would miss the world Robert had shared with her, appreciating Italy as she never had before. On the one hand, she was relieved to have their relationship clarified, but deeply unhappy that Robert's decision would change her life, and the future of Davis Publishing. These last weeks had been a long rollercoaster ride, so it came as no surprise that she was coming down with a cold. Now, ready to fly home, she felt emotionally spent. She wasn't looking forward to the hours that stretched before her until she could crawl into her own bed. Off kilter, she grew irritated as she watched the passengers around her that looked like they had fallen out of a ragbag. It seemed there was no longer a proper dress code while traveling. It made her want to shout, "What's the matter with you people?"

Could the travelers that were wearing baggy sweat pants have come straight from a last minute workout at the gym? She spotted a short, plump woman, old enough to know better, wearing gray leggings that accentuated her ample size thighs under a short shirt. The Doc Marten shoes were the final insult.

Katherine watched a young mother sitting opposite her on a bank of chairs, as she began to nurse her baldheaded baby. She did not bother to cover her ample breast with a blanket or diaper while she helped the baby find her nipple. Evidently, there was no longer a degree of modesty called for in this public place either. What was the world coming to with its apparent disregard for propriety, a word she hadn't heard or used in a long time?

Katherine knew her appraisal of everyone around her was based on quick assumptions, a hairstyle, the words printed on a tee shirt, the shoes they were wearing. Louisa would tell her that it said more about how old she was than the improprieties she was noticing.

In the midst of people watching, Katherine made up her mind to actually suggest to several authors she was working with that they head to the nearest boarding gate area. Everyone seemed to vibrate with instant messages that said, I work out, I am an earth mother, I am retired, and will never wear a shirt and tie again. There were the GQ (Gentleman's Quarterly magazine) type guys with all their toys hanging from their ears, and at their fingertips. Katherine liked the older couples, holding hands, still friends, on their way some place together. Think of the stories they could tell.

With imagination, the woman sitting down the way between a schoolboy and his look alike dad could walk onto the pages of a best seller. Unadorned, the woman wore a pair of tennis shoes that contributed to the collection of restless feet dancing on the floor where people sat. She was wearing a man's oversized white tee shirt that hung out over her blue jeans, another popular choice of pants to travel in. With no makeup or jewelry, except a plain gold wedding band, was she deliberately seeking anonymity? Was this a family fleeing to

America to enter a witness protection program? Was her haircut, looking like an eight dollar barber chair special, all she had time for before catching this plane to get home to see a dying father? The possibilities were endless.

Katherine felt guilty when she decided this plain Jane was a perfect candidate for a makeover TV show that would insist she give up her 'look' in exchange for a softer feminine style, starting with the addition of color around her face. The truth of all this speculation probably boiled down to simple economics that drove the choice of her wardrobe or lack thereof. Unlike Elizabeth, she had no one in her life to give her a gift certificate to an upscale beauty salon in Chicago, who catered to women her age, and kept them looking beautiful.

The woman must have felt Katherine staring at her. It was too late to glance away. She looked across the space between them and smiled at Katherine, who hoped she wasn't clairvoyant. To make up for these uncharitable thoughts, Katherine smiled her most winning smile in return. She then looked down at the book unopened in her hand, and hoped the woman would look elsewhere too.

With only minutes left before the flight would be called, Katherine took up with a strawberry blond boy, who with his family grabbed the seats next to her the moment the previous occupants took one more bathroom opportunity, or a quick food run. The little guy was about eight, and none too pleased when told to sit still or incur a dire punishment that made no impression on him. "We won't be able to fly to see your Granny if you can't behave." It was obvious that this idle threat from the School of Discipline got what it deserved; the fidgeting only worsened. A tennis shoe began to brush back and forth against Katherine's leg; a marker that came with a coloring book the boy had been bribed with, had been turned into a sword. Katherine was glad she was wearing a black pants suit in case the child decided to run her through.

The on time flight was announced, and people began to board the plane by sections. Standing in line behind the little boy, and his family,

Katherine noticed a grass green stripe down the father's extra large Mickey Mouse shirtsleeve. This sweet brown-eyed boy shyly waved goodbye to her when they entered the cabin of the plane. Junior was surely going to jiggle someone all the way to New York.

31

Katherine was grateful that Robert had arranged for a limousine
service to meet her at O'Hare upon arrival. She willingly turned herself
over to the driver who pulled her bag from the carousel and led her
to a waiting car at curbside. With her head resting back against the
luxurious leather seat, she closed her eyes as the limo cleared the
airport. Robert was now a world away, his embrace in the early
morning Roman light now a memory. The week away had been indeed
another kind of baptism, submerged briefly in the sights and sounds of
Italy. She wanted to hang on to every moment of this trip, even the
pasta sauce she'd spilled on her coat that had gone unnoticed at the
time. It represented the numerous meals she'd enjoyed.

  She wasn't ready to resume her responsibilities the next day at the
office. She wanted one more stroll through the Monti neighborhood to
the restaurant where she'd surprised Robert and his friends. She
wanted to follow the nuns back to the church to pray, and light another
candle. Though she had not accomplished what she set out to do in
luring Robert back to his life at Davis Publishing, he'd promised to
make the sale contingent on keeping her job. It was a selfish request,
and one she would not expect the buyers to seriously honor, but
thinking it was possible would give her time to sort out what was
coming. Would she continue the work she loved or no longer call
herself an editor, but a writer. What about Andrew who had been left
behind while she relished her Italian adventure?

  The hum of the limousine wheels on the pavement increased as
they sped up. Without opening her eyes Katherine knew where she
was, driving beneath the aluminum light standards that lined the
Kennedy Expressway into the city. Physically she'd made it home, yet
her emotions lagged behind. Who knew how long it would take before
she let go of Pienza and Lucca, captivated by the history and charm of
both places where she'd listened to prayers proclaiming the Good

News in Italian. Robert had been partially successful with his supposed ad campaign; she had at least fallen in love in Italy.

Katherine would think of him now as a renewed man having wriggled out of his cautious and methodical skin. He now appeared vigorous, quite sexy in fact, and joyful. Maybe he was the luckiest person she had ever known. He'd gone in search of Shangri la and was convinced he'd found it. Katherine would no longer look for obstacles to place in his way by wishing it were different; she would do all she could to help him secure what he had found.

❀

There was no problem getting into the office early the next morning having awakened at 4:00AM and dressed by 5:00AM. She drank a pot of tea and started her laundry before it was time to head to the office. Arriving, she waited outside her office door, greeting everyone who began arriving from their vacation. The elevator doors opened revealing a smiling and rested batch of employees. Greeting them she made an announcement, "Editors and assistants, conference room in half an hour." She walked among the secretaries' desks that were spread across the large partitioned floor speaking to each of them. The invigorated women gave her a quick recap of their unexpected paid vacation. Robert would be pleased to hear what the week off had allowed these energized workers to enjoy. "Slept and read." "Painted my entire apartment." "Went home to my family for the first time in over a year." "Went out every night and slept in each morning." It was Elizabeth she motioned into her office for a fuller report.

"What's the verdict? Did this young man survive the week?" Elizabeth grinned.

"He did. I like him. He is a considerate," she almost said lover, but knew instinctively it was inappropriate information for her mentor. "Considerate, interesting guy."

"How so?" Katherine was now seated behind her desk and motioned Elizabeth to sit in one of the chairs drawn up on the other side. "You were going to start with lunch dates."

"Which turned into afternoons going to museums and listening to his architectural lectures as we walked a different part of downtown each day. He has an engineering degree, but is going to school at night to become an architect."

"Ambitious, I like that." Elizabeth was beaming. They say pregnant women have a glow; but Katherine recognized a different glow that she suspected had to do with the word considerate. Here was another example of how things were a changing. The clothes people now traveled in, nursing babies in plain sight, and sleeping with a man before marriage. Katherine mentioned none of this, but said, "Go slow, that's all I ask. And be careful."

Elizabeth ducked her head as if overcome with shyness. Was there nothing she could get past this woman? Hoping to hide her embarrassment, she made it worse. "We never got around to the war movies, thank goodness."

"Not to worry. You each have a TV set and if it becomes necessary, he can watch his violent films in another room. That's how Timothy and I worked it out." She held Elizabeth's gaze and marveled that here was another happy face.

"What about your trip?" Elizabeth wanted to redirect the conversation for fear Katherine had already guessed about the late afternoon vigorous bedroom exercise that had taken place.

"I have caught a cold, but it's worth it." She coughed and wiped her nose with a Kleenex to demonstrate she was telling the truth. "I forget how simple it is to get on a plane, step off hours later into a world that seems so far away. The only other time I traveled to Italy was with Timothy to Florence years ago. Though this trip was far shorter, it is more wonderful than I realized." She reached into the tote that was sitting under her desk and pulled out a package to hand across her desk.

227

"Oh, wow, for me?" Elizabeth pulled the string, and with a quick flourish snatched the brown paper off, letting both fall in her lap. She unfolded a large silk scarf with a black border that had a central floral motif. "It's beautiful. I love it."

"Lest you think I am spoiling you, Rome is full of street vendors selling scarves at prices tourists can't resist. I'm glad you like it, I got myself one as well." She watched Elizabeth drape the scarf over her shoulders and admired the results.

Katherine glanced at her watch. "It's time to gather the troops." She rose from her chair. "I'll tell you more later." Elizabeth came around the desk and hugged her while Katherine patted her on the back. "See you in a few minutes."

"Thank you again, for everything." Elizabeth started for the door. "It was a good week for both of us." She turned back, "I hear your caution about this guy, but I think he's promising."

"What's his name?"

"Timothy O'Brian." Elizabeth said, with an Irish lilt in her voice.

"Oh my, I knew a Timothy once. We courted, and fell in love."

"Yeah, well, maybe I will get lucky and this Timothy will be my forever-after." She closed the door and left Katherine holding on to her desk with both hands. In her case, forever after, hadn't been long enough. Katherine remembered a quote she'd seen in a friend's powder room. "Don't cry because it's over, smile because it happened." Overtired, Katherine slumped back into her chair and wept. Thinking of Timothy, and rejoicing with Elizabeth, all at the same time.

❀

Katherine had been asleep for two hours when the phone rang. She had been dead on her feet by the time she left the office at five. It would take a good night's sleep to get her internal clock back on Central Standard Time. She was in bed by seven. She'd fallen asleep with her reading glasses on, and a book resting on her stomach. Her bedside lamp was still on. The ring of the telephone jolted her awake. Confused, she hesitated before picking up the phone.

"Are you home safe and sound?" Andrew's voice greeted her.

"Part of me has made it to Chicago, the rest I got separated from in Pienza, or maybe Rome." Katherine put the book and her glasses on the nightstand.

"You sound like you have a cold."

"That too. I don't know how you can avoid catching one closed up in a plane for hours. I turned off the air that blows on you, but I guess it didn't help." Katherine was now sitting on the side of her bed.

"I'm sorry you're sick. I wanted to reach you before you were off to bed. Did you talk Robert into changing his mind about selling the company?"

"I have come back resigned to the sale."

"I am surprised. Quite a momentous decision for everyone." He paused. "What will you do?" It was not the question he wanted to ask, but something in Katherine's voice, her cold, or jet lag, did not sound like she'd missed him. He, on the other hand, had been looking at the clock every hour waiting until he could call her at home after work.

Moving to the kitchen, Katherine put water on for tea. She needed a strong cup and two Advil as long as she was up. Still muddled, she tried to concentrate on their conversation. "How are you, Andrew? The writing coming along?"

"I have missed you, that's how I am. You have ruined my life in case you haven't noticed. I was once a self-satisfied man, living a life I have carefully constructed. Now I'm lonely and ornery, and realize I have been stupid."

Katherine got no further than putting a couple of tea bags into her porcelain pot. She stood listening to Andrew with her mouth open. She'd never heard him rant about anything. This was about her, the two of them, their lives separated not only by distance, but also by a narrative that excluded one another.

"I want you to get on a plane, pack your cold if you must, crawl into my bed and we willl figure it all out. I have no idea what you want because it has been all about me. I was worried about my world here. Now I realize you have your own world there that makes you happy. What's going to happen to us?"

Katherine grabbed a Kleenex to wipe her dripping nose. Tears glistened in her eyes as well. She wanted to talk, but she was sick, and in need of sleep. She leaned against the counter top and pictured Andrew standing in the kitchen in his Queen Anne District house. "Listen to me, Andrew. I can't have this conversation now with this cold and lack of sleep, but we're going to have it. If it were possible, I would crawl in beside you now and ask you to whisper sweet nothings in my ear until I could fall asleep. At this moment I don't know what's going to happen to us, but it sounds to me like you have made up your mind that you want to figure it out. Give me a few days to catch up with myself. The minute I'm on my feet we will meet half way somewhere. Neutral ground as they say. Okay?"

Relief in his voice Andrew said, "Okay."

Katherine finished her cup of tea while looking out into the darkness over the lake. She needed some Advil with the hope of feeling better by the morning. It wasn't just a cold that had her discombobulated; the certainties in her life were once again threatened. Would she have a job after the sale of the company? Should she consider Seattle as her possible Shangri-la after all? She set the empty cup down on the coffee table, and walked back to her bedroom, this time turning off her bedside lamp. Falling into bed, she sought oblivion from her worries.

32

Katherine left from home for an appointment with Tom Braxton. She was feeling better after a few nights of good sleep in her own bed. She'd stuffed her purse with a wad of Kleenex and several lemon and honey cough drops, just in case. It felt good to walk along Lake Shore Drive. The temperatures all week had hovered in the low 60's, putting a smile on the weary faces of Chicagoans. Katherine was more than ready for the long slog of mid-west cold weather to end. It looked like April was going to provide a timely spring for a change.

"Did you enjoy your time in Italy?" Katherine sat facing Tom Braxton. He was dressed once again as the affluent, yet conservative, lawyer that he was. His hair, perfectly trimmed, and his suit with a thin stripe, conveyed the message that here was a man capable of handling your legal matters with brilliant efficiency. His smile saved him from appearing so rigid as to be boring. Katherine noticed he had the habit of running his hand down his tie, this one a navy blue and silver stripe.

"It was wonderful, and best of all, I no longer question Robert's sanity. The change in him is startling. I doubt he has ever been as happy in his entire life as he is now." Katherine laughed, "I thought about staying myself."

"He's not going to change his mind is he?"

"Have you been to Italy, Tom?"

"Never had time. Is it worth giving up a family business for?"

"In Robert's case, I guess it is."

"I confirmed with him that he has a buyer."

"Review Press?"

"I told you they are also a client of ours. My instructions were to get back to them if Davis Publishing ever became available. There are things to work out, of course, but they're seriously interested. This acquisition is compatible with their company mission."

Katherine reached for the cup of coffee the attorney had poured her. "They have a fine reputation. Quite something for a mid-west publisher."

Tom was flipping through the single file that lay out on his desk. He paused. "They have 900 titles in print and publish about 60 new titles a year." Katherine already knew this because she'd done some homework herself.

Katherine said, "There are at least five imprints. Review Press, Hill Books, Sphere Publishing, Wind Publishing and Academy Press. Impressive, yes?" Tom nodded in agreement.

"I assured Robert that they have the financial where with all to buy Davis Publishing, but the devil is always in the details, as they say."

"I presumed on our old friendship by asking him if he would make me a contingency in the final sale of Davis Publishing. He said he would try. Is something like that even possible?"

"We'll find out, won't we." There was a quiet knock on the door before it opened. Tom Braxton looked up and waved a man into the room. "Katherine, I'd like you to meet one of our senior partners. I asked him to join us."

Katherine swiveled in her leather chair to watch a tall gentleman walk towards her with chalky white wavy hair, rather on the long side. With piercing blue eyes, a nose that was narrow and slightly hooked, Katherine wondered if he was on loan from a Hollywood movie company. Not because he was grand, but because he was a slim combination of Robert Mitchum and Kurt Douglas. He was definitely the strong, silent type that commanded attention, even without his friendly smile. He extended his hand to her. "Lovely to meet you Katherine, I'm David Middleton." He took the chair beside her and then reached across Tom Braxton's desk and shook his hand.

"David recently retired as the Dean of the University of Chicago's law school, and has returned on retainer to Braxton and Braxton where he began his law career with my father."

Turning towards Katherine, David said, "Retired, but happy to keep my oar in the water. They have even found a desk for me." David Middleton presented himself as a man who was comfortable with the stage in his life he now found himself. He appeared relaxed and amiable. Though militarily erect, and impeccably dressed, he came across as self-effacing. He made no effort to expand on his credentials.

Tom Braxton went on to explain why he had asked David to join them. "David will be representing Review Press in the sale of Davis Publishing. There are some conflict of interest issues, that he and I will address, but there should be no problem."

For another fifteen minutes Katherine listened to the two men discuss the legal ramifications of representing both clients. She understood very little of what they said, but was content to sit and act as if she did. In spirit, she receded further back into the large leather chair she occupied, and took a quick glance around at the wood paneling and artwork that was tastefully displayed on the walls. By Katherine's reckoning, the paintings were by Chicago artists. A six-armed brass chandelier, with jade green shades, hung from a ceiling medallion, which highlighted the decor of this intentionally masculine sanctuary. The office plants, predictable and utilitarian, added nothing to the richness of the room. She was sure the plants were in need of fertilizer. She knew very little about the sale of a business, but she knew plants. She would keep to herself that in her own milieu she was as competent as either of these men. She had regained that certainty. It was 11:30AM when they all stood to shake hands once again. Tom Braxton walked with Katherine across the expanse of his office, and David held open the door. "Thanks for your help with this, Katherine. We will be in touch, of course."

"I'm happy to facilitate anything you need at our end of things." She hoped her tone didn't gave away either her concern for the employees of Davis Publishing or for herself.

As if an afterthought, Tom said, "Robert has given me his information in Lucca should we need to reach him. He mentioned that

233

he would cut his sabbatical short if need be. I tried to reassure him he could leave things to us for now."

Katherine remained just inside the office door looking at both men. "After a short visit to Lucca, I understand how he can entertain this idea of taking up a new life. His father would be appalled, but after seeing him, I find myself cheering him on." Tom Braxton said goodbye to Katherine and David Middleton who accompanied her to the elevators.

Expecting to say goodbye, Katherine was caught off guard with David's spontaneous invitation. "Let me take you to lunch, Katherine. I'd be honored if you have time." It didn't seem much of a risk to have lunch with this man in his late sixties or early seventies, courtly manners and all.

"You must understand," he added, "This is not a business luncheon. I'm retired in a great city that has a Greek neighborhood with a restaurant I'm crazy about. This lunch is about making a new friend." He smiled at her before he reached over and pushed the down button for the elevator. Katherine glanced at her watch. "I'd be delighted, David, and you're absolutely right, it is a great city."

She stopped and called Elizabeth before leaving the building while David stepped out to hail a cab. Katherine said, "It's me, checking in. I have been invited out to lunch in Greek Town before I come back to the office."

"Lucky you, some place good, I imagine." Elizabeth slipped her nail file in the top drawer of her desk as if Katherine could see what she was doing. "I wish I was invited, I need a break."

"What? Lost momentary interest in the enthralling manuscript on your computer screen?"

Elizabeth didn't bother to confirm Katherine was right. "I imagine it is the Greek Isles Restaurant if you're going to Greektown. Order the Chicken Greek Salad. It's the best." She refrained from asking who had done the inviting.

"See you when I see you. Hold down the fort." She rang off. Elizabeth turned her attention back to the next chapter in Jessica Lovejoy's book.

David gave the cab driver an address on South Halsted Street between Adams and Quincy West of the Loop, the neighborhood where the Greek community had established itself decades before.

"I should have asked if you like Greek food. This is okay, isn't it?"

"I love gyros." It had been years since Katherine had eaten this Greek dish of meat roasted on a spit and served on pita bread with tomato, onion and tzatziki sauce.

"The first time I had it I'd brought my daughter home to see my parents; they took us to Greek Town to eat. It might have been 1968. Everyone but Louisa loved this new food.

"I don't know if you knew this, but gyros became so popular that it brought attention to the Greek community in a way they had not enjoyed before. People began to flock there to eat. The popularity emboldened the Greeks to celebrate their heritage with less apology and more vigor."

"It's still the most popular destination, right?"

At 2:00PM Katherine and David were still talking. Their luncheon plates had been cleared and they were drinking strong coffee. "You must come and visit me in Hyde Park, Katherine. I live near the University of Chicago's campus."

"I have only visited the campus once, but I still remember the beautiful architecture."

David went on talking about the Law School. " John D. Rockefeller and a coalition of donors started it in 1908. I'm proud to say it has gone on to become one of the highest rated law schools in the United States."

"You left Braxton's law firm to teach at the law school?"

"I've spent most of my adult life teaching there and eventually became the Dean. I loved every minute of it, but am reveling in my release from the responsibility of the day to day operation of the place."

"Do you like to travel, Katherine? It has become my number one reason to retire. I just returned from a two-week visit with a friend who left Chicago upon his retirement and headed to Charleston, South Carolina. He told me he never intended to be cold again."

"Does that appeal to you?" Katherine asked.

"What appeals to me is visiting friends who have scurried off to wonderful destinations. Leave Chicago? It would be a shame to give away all my wool topcoats and down vests to Goodwill."

"I hadn't thought about it that way. Next winter I'll remind myself that I have gone to a great deal of expense to buy the right warm clothes. I actually like them."

They left the restaurant at 3:00PM. The cab dropped Katherine off first. David stood on the pavement saying goodbye. "I have enjoyed myself immensely, Katherine. You were generous to let me take up so much of your time."

"It was a treat. Thank you." David brushed a kiss on each side of her cheeks in gallant European fashion.

She watched him get back in the cab looking like a ladder that folds up in sections. Before he pulled the door after him, he called back to her, "I'll call you soon to plan your visit to my neck of the woods."

"I look forward to it." Katherine waved goodbye as the cab pulled away.

❁

Andrew had worked all morning and was late for his lunch date with the St. Johns at Quincy's Chargrilled Burgers, a place they liked for a beer and a good hamburger. He saw them waving at him when he came in the door.

"Sorry, I lost track of time." He leaned down and kissed Anne St. John on her forehead, and shook hands with George, before pulling out the metal chair beside him. It had been several weeks since he'd last seen them, which was unusual in the long history of their friendship. Andrew had turned down an invitation to a movie, and another to an exhibit of one of their friends at an art gallery. Today, he had finally grown tired of his own company. "He beamed at them. "I'm glad to see you." He meant it.

"How's the writing coming?" Ann St. John expected to hear a glowing report regardless of the truth of Andrew's answer. "You've either been hiding from us or getting a lot accomplished."

Andrew took a sip from the glass of beer the waitress plunked down in front of him, which George had ordered for him. He licked the foam off his lips and grinned at Anne. "If you'd send Georgie-boy here packing, we would never be parted again."

"Yeah, right," scoffed George. What happened to what's her name?" He smiled at Andrew.

"What's her name is never going to move to Seattle, and I'm never going to move to Chicago. I'm heartbroken is what's happening."

"I knew this was a bad idea right from the start." George thumped his hand on the table. Anne looked at her husband in disbelief. "You loved her from the first moment you met her."

"Never, she isn't right for him."

"So, you didn't mean it when you said she was the best thing that had ever happened to him?"

Turning towards Andrew, George said, "Pay her no attention, she's referring to some pillow talk when I was trying to have my way with her." George smiled at his wife, a smile Andrew had seen pass between them a million times over the years, one of deep contentment and appreciation for each other. Andrew had observed many times the silent message that passed between them, their signal for what lay ahead behind closed doors. Andrew would have to look away, embarrassed that he could read their minds so easily.

At times, like this, Andrew envied their relationship. It was obvious George never missed a chance to take his wife to bed. On trips with other friends, they would all have to wait for the St. Johns. As late as they might be for breakfast, they often joined cocktail hour when it was well underway. By Andrew's calculations, they'd been making love for forty years.

Andrew appreciated George's round about way of support. "You're one lucky, SOB, my friend, that's all I can say."

The restaurant was crowded, the service slow, which meant another round of beer while they waited for their food. They'd long ago agreed that the delay was intentional so they could sell more drinks. It was always worth the wait, nonetheless.

George got serious. "What are you going to do about Katherine?"

"I thought we were writing a book together and going to England to interview the gardeners we agreed upon. Now I'm not sure this will happen."

"Why not?" Anne thought of the women in Andrew's past that he'd grown tired of while trying to please them. In time, he would always scuttle home, free to live his life as he pleased.

"Because Chicago isn't in the cards, and Katherine isn't ready to leave a job she loves for me."

"She's told you that."

"Not yet."

"And, you? Would you give up this life to be with her?" George tried to keep the disappointment out of his voice. He'd been sure that this lovely woman was what his friend had always been looking for.

"I have been holed up at home trying to imagine my life if I left Seattle, my home, my friends." Andrew looked at the St. Johns and shook his head. "I doubt I could survive away from the life I have created here."

George slipped his arm around Andrew's shoulder. "Now you're talking. There will be another bus along shortly, you can catch that one." Andrew appreciated what the St. Johns were trying to do. He needed bolstering, which their constant good humor, and support did.

Anne reached across the table and took his hand. "I'm sorry, Andrew. Really, I feel terrible for both of you. I know you're in love with her. This isn't the same as the others."

"No, it isn't, but what is the same is that I can't make the changes I would need to make if I were to pursue Katherine to the ends of the earth, which is shorthand for Chicago. It's damn cold there in January." They managed a laugh while the waitress put a hamburger and fries in front of each of them.

In between mouthfuls George asked, "You're going to talk about all this with her?"

"She has a lousy cold and is just back from Italy. She will call when she recovers. I don't expect she'll surprise me by telling me she wants nothing more in life than to live with me in my Queen Anne house. I do think I've tempted her, and I haven't given up hope that this could happen, but I am practicing the notion of getting on with my life without her." Andrew ate the rest of his meal in silence listening to his friends as they kibitzed back and forth making merry for him. This is what dear friends do for an old fart, he thought, they humor him.

Hugging goodbye out in front of Quincy's, Andrew never appreciated the St Johns more. "I can tell you one thing I have learned out of this." He hesitated before adding what he could hardly admit to himself. "I'm rethinking my rules and regulations, except for a new Rule One."

"Which is?" George was amused that Andrew admitted he had rules.

"In the future, if I should be lucky enough to find anyone half as wonderful as Katherine, she must live in Seattle. After that, there are no more rules."

George called over his shoulder as he and Anne turned to go. "Johnny, We'll Hardly Know Ye."

33

Katherine knew Elizabeth was glad to see the back of her, and her cold, by the time they left work together at the end of the day. She'd been coughing in earnest since returning to the office from her lunch with David Middleton.

"This weekend, you better stay close to home with that cold." The two women rode the crowded elevator to the ground floor of the building. Katherine all but choked trying not to cough on the others. Out on the sidewalk, she couldn't hold back any longer and covered her mouth with her hand. When she'd finished, she said, "This sounds worse than I feel."

Elizabeth eyed her with sympathy. "You could have stayed home, you know."

"Believe me, I thought about it, but after the time off, I couldn't face the office newspaper opinion page."

"We haven't got a newspaper." Katherine shrugged as if that made no difference.

"What about you, what have you planned?" Katherine stepped back from Elizabeth when she leaned in to hug her goodbye. "Better not."

Elizabeth was ready to tell Katherine the state of things. "I'm having a houseguest for the weekend. Gorgeous-man is bringing pizza tonight, several movies, and wine." She paused, "And whatever he does or does not sleep in."

"I see," though Katherine had guessed as much already.

"I figured you already knew, so I might as well come clean.

"Easy does it." Katherine wagged a cautionary finger.

A slight breeze stirred a whirl of city debris from the pavement. Katherine burrowed her head into the sleeve of her lightweight coat and coughed again. Recovering, she said, "I have got to get home."

"Me too, I'm off to Ravenswood, home sweet Chicago."

"You don't need to tell me these things, Elizabeth, but are you asking for my permission?"

"When I was growing up, in the end, I was always glad when my mother didn't let me do some of the things the other kids were doing. She provided the excuse I needed."

"I trust your good judgment to make the right decision for yourself."

"That's a lot of responsibility, making good decisions." She waved goodbye.

❁

Katherine changed out of her clothes and into her gown and robe for the evening. With luck, she would be asleep by 8:00PM. She'd waited all week for this night; Friday couldn't come soon enough. She was relieved to be sitting in her kitchen drinking hot tea and eating an English muffin. The ringing telephone made her jump.

"Hi, Mom, it's me." Katherine had not talked to her daughter all week except to let her know she'd returned safely from Italy. She was glad to hear Louisa's voice.

"How's my little girl?" They both laughed. Years before when Katherine had actually been asking about her toddler granddaughter, Louisa had answered, "I'm fine." Katherine learned the lesson that no matter how old Louisa would become, it was she, not Beatrice, who would remain Katherine's little girl.

"I've heard from Beatrice, and have some exciting news for you." Katherine's heart sank. Was this the phone call she dreaded that would tell her Beatrice was marrying her Greek god?

"How would you like to fly to New York next weekend and welcome her home from Greece?"

"Are you serious? How marvelous. Why not here to Chicago?"

"She will be living in New York again, and needs to find a place;

I told her we would fly out and help her look."

"She's coming home for good?" Katherine covered the phone while she coughed. She took a sip of tea that was rapidly cooling down.

"Home until the next opportunity comes along to go abroad or some exotic place."

This evening Katherine felt she could hardly make it down the long hall to her bedroom, but in another week, she would surely be fit to travel. "Book my ticket, I'm coming with you. This is stupendous."

"It is indeed. I've known the job in New York was in the works, but I didn't want you to get your hopes up if they changed their minds."

"What about the young man she is in love with?"

"His parents made it abundantly clear they did not want their only son marrying an American, even if she could speak their language fluently."

"I'm eternally grateful to them for raising an obedient son."

"Can you fly out Thursday evening, Mom?

"I can leave from work. Can't wait." Several more coughing episodes ended the conversation. Katherine turned out the lights as she made her way back to bed. She checked to be sure her alarm was turned off, and settled into her bed for what she hoped would be a restorative night's sleep.

❀

They caught the 7:00 PM plane to New York. Both women agreed to leave all work behind and enjoy the occasion. They dubbed the trip, the Three Musketeers Reunion. Beatrice was waiting for them when they arrived in the lobby of the hotel. A healthy bronze glow enveloped her. She looked slim and fit, a combination of healthy Mediterranean food and plenty of walking. They sat in the bar off the lobby and enjoyed a glass of wine. It had been too long a day for Beatrice to linger. Mother and grandmother hugged their little girl goodnight outside her door, finding their own room further down the hall.

"She looks beautiful, Louisa. No worse for the wear I'd say."

"Not a bit. I'm relieved she's back. I can get to New York, and so can you. She'd kept in touch with the friends she made when she first came to work for the bank here, and we know she is adaptable. She'll settle back into a New York state of mind, as the song says. I'll hold out hope that she will come back to Chicago one day."

Katherine was happy to pull the covers back on her bed and crawl in. "I will make you a small wager that she does come back. I give her two years out here, before she asks for a transfer. You'll see."

"I wish I knew for certain. I can't make up my mind what to do about the house. I love it so much. Beatrice is the fourth generation in that house."

"It has nineteen rooms." Katherine was working hard to see the house through Louisa's perspective.

Louisa leaned back against her own pillows and sighed. "They're building some lovely new apartments on Green Bay Road in Winnetka. I have seen a model. It's a quick walk to the train, and everything I need is close by. It's tempting."

"I have said it before, to have you and your precious family living on Asbury is a dream come true. I have relived so many memories about growing up there, but I have learned at least one thing since your Dad died. We must go on reinventing ourselves throughout the years. What worked for us once, may no longer serve us any more, and should be pruned away. The house worked for a long time, now things have changed. The Winnetka apartments sound perfect. Do it, Louisa. Even if Beatrice comes back to Chicago, chances are slim to nothing that she would live with you in that big house. She will want to be downtown, living in Lincoln Park, or one of the neighborhoods where the young people gravitate."

"Which would be close to you."

Katherine laughed and scooted down under the sheets. "We could all live together, how about that?"

"You'd be an unreliable landlord. No telling what you'll be doing in a few years time. Running Davis Publishing, living in Robert's house in Kenilworth, caring for his dog because he can't sell, or enjoying various men who try to lure you into their life. No, I better find a place of my own, and so should Beatrice." Louisa reached over and turned out both sides of the lamp between their beds. "Goodnight, Mom, sleep fast." Katherine made no attempt to answer.

They spent all Saturday looking at small rental apartments that were exorbitantly priced. Last on their list was a visit with a young woman who also worked for the bank in their loan department. She was looking for a new roommate. Louisa and Katherine left the two girls in the apartment, sizing one another up, while they explored the possibility of sharing.

Waiting in a coffee shop around the corner, Katherine broached the subject of a trip she wanted Louisa to make with her. "How about coming with me to Seattle to see Claire Thompson over the long Memorial Day weekend?"

"You haven't mentioned her lately."

"We talk on Sunday evenings like we were kids calling home from college. It's been wonderful. It's difficult for her to leave her business and come to Chicago. I told her I would come there and hope you would be interested in going too. We actually won't see that much of her because we're needed to run the bookstore."

"Where will she be? I thought that was the point." The waiter refilled their coffee cups. Looking at her watch, Katherine was surprised that it had been over an hour since leaving Beatrice.

"Claire is having surgery on a foot. She has several friends that are going to help her out. One will stay at home with her, and the other is taking vacation from her job to keep the store open. Going out will give both of them a break." Katherine grinned at her daughter. "One of my unlived lives is owning a bookstore. I can't wait to play store owner for a few days."

"I'm not sure, Mom. I want to get to know Claire, but if I get serious about this move, I need to catch the last of the spring market. It's not like I have to shovel out or anything." Katherine was never sure how her daughter managed to work, and take care of the big house. She'd become a time management specialist, and a neatness freak, all in one. She was so good at it, she started giving the gift of reorganizing her friends' closets as a birthday present. This included buying the white plastic hangers that she used to hang their clothes by color.

"I want to talk to Beatrice about the house over dinner, if that's okay."

"You two girls go out. I'd enjoy dinner in the room. We can talk when you get back." Though mildly disappointed that Louisa didn't have the time to go with her to Seattle, it might be less complicated going on her own. The predicament was Andrew. She was relieved Louisa hadn't thought to ask about him.

Katherine had not spoken to Andrew other than their brief conversation when she returned from Italy. She'd been thinking a lot about him as she tried to imagine what life would be like if she left Chicago to be with him. He had been like the great physician to her, a pleasant and contented man that ministered peace and certainty. His life was settled, which Katherine admired. He was the perfect leading man for any actress placed in the role of the accomplished woman who nonetheless, needed, and wanted, a love life. He'd proved to her that she was not through with being needed, as she imagined. He made her laugh, and she knew the value of that. Their shared interest in a myriad of things, including gardening, added to their compatibility. The writing of a book together on English Gardens was a perfect fit. She would be sorry if continuing their project together was impossible because of an uncertain future.

The question was, did she love him enough to upend her world for his. She'd read a line in a novel years ago, *the only way you can live with a man is if you can't live without him.* There was a great deal of truth in that statement.

Between working at the store and spending the nights with Claire, where she could also be of some help, she would see very little of Andrew on this visit. If she were not sitting here in this coffee shop in New York City, Katherine would bury her face in her hands and boohoo. The fact that neither of them could live together in the same city was a deal breaker. She'd been right all along when she'd told Louisa. "Having a love life in two different time zones is difficult."

Katherine didn't want to share her sorrow with Louisa. She had enough on her own plate to contend with. She managed to sound cheery when she said, "We'll have other opportunities to go and visit Claire. Sell the house, get your new arrangements in hand. Beatrice will cry, we'll all cry, but you need to do this for yourself. It will turn out to be a blessing, just as my move has been to me since moving to Chicago."

It was two hours before Beatrice came though the door of the coffee shop. She looked elated when she joined them. "I think I've got something worked out."

"This gal was the ticket?" her mother asked.

"Sorry it took so long." She nodded at the waiter who offered coffee. "Have you been drinking coffee all this time? You must be wired."

"Not a problem, there was time for dessert too." Louisa was quick to add, "We split it."

"I'm sure you noticed, but Linda, the girl you met, is still basically living out of boxes. She hasn't begun to create a home for herself. She's waiting."

Katherine asked, "On what?"

246

"On a man. The two of us are in different places in our lives. She suggested that we walk down a block and visit her friend, Rosemary Watkins. Rosemary's roommate has moved to Minneapolis, and she'd like a roommate. She has her masters in international business too. We got on right away. She travels extensively, loves the city and her job, and has definitely created a life."

"You're certain this is right for you, Honey?" Louisa had never been as good at making quick decisions as her daughter.

"We agreed to try one another on for a month. I'm going to stay in the bank's corporate apartment they have offered. Rosemary and I will do things together, if she's okay with it, and it works for me, I'll move in the first of next month. I have a feeling this is going to be great."

They paid their bill, and said goodbye to the man who'd plied them with fresh coffee and pastry. By the time Louisa and Beatrice returned from their dinner, Katherine was propped up in bed reading. She looked up when the two of them came through the door.

"Have a good catch up?" Katherine asked. Beatrice crawled in beside her and stretched out. "Wonder how long it's going to take me to adjust to the time here. I've been awake since 4:00AM." Still in her clothes she turned on her side and did not move.

"Katherine lowered her voice, "Everything okay?"

"We both cried. You would have fit right in." She smiled at Katherine. "She's tired," pointing at Beatrice, "Nothing is quite sinking in."

"Shall we let her stay here?"

"It's up to you, but I think she's out for the night."

Louisa got ready for bed, kissed her mother on the forehead before she turned out the lights. This time Katherine whispered, "Goodnight, Love."

34

Andrew was once again waiting for her in the baggage claim area. By telephone, before making the trip, they'd been as honest with one another as they could be, finally tackling the problem of leaving their lives for one another. They didn't rule out the possibility of working something out, but when the conversation ended, they both knew they had only postponed the inevitable.

Their plan was to drive straight to Andrew's so Katherine could add her input to the neat piles of book notes he had waiting for her. When they reached the house Katherine's suitcase remained in the car. Once inside the door, Andrew grasped Katherine's hand and pulled her to him. The two hours they were going to work on the book turned out differently.

"This is not going to help either of us you know." Katherine lay with her head on Andrew's shoulder.

"What are you talking about? It helped me." They both laughed. This laughter was the crux of their problem. They enjoyed one another, shared the same notions of right and wrong, had been raised with similar values. No matter how content they were with one another in Andrew's bed, and with all the plusses between them, they both knew that leaving their lives for one another was proving to be insurmountable.

"I have missed you." Andrew pressed his lips against Katherine's temple.

She had missed him too, even though there was a lot on her plate that needed attention. Top of the list was her future at Davis Publishing. She had yet to tell Andrew that when she recognized how desperately she hoped to keep her job, that this was the final answer concerning their future. At this stage in their lives, she thought love and companionship would outweigh other considerations, but moving for either of them was turning out to be the most important consideration of all.

With his head resting against Katherine's he began to talk to her in a quiet reflective voice. "In a screwy sort of way, my life here has become more valuable. When I realized how hard it would be to give it up, I started to notice things again. All along, my friends have been my family. I see how lucky I am to have this house and garden. I know having you here with me would make all of it even greater, but the sadness of not having you here has been an awakening in and of itself. Maybe life isn't over as I was beginning to think."

They stayed in bed for another hour, sometimes talking. When it was time to leave for Claire's, they both agreed that far from hurting each other by their intimacy, it had validated them both.

❀

Katherine arrived at Claire's condo later than expected, but she felt relieved. The time she had alone with Andrew helped them rethink their future. They agreed to continue their work together on The English Garden book, and if Katherine could join him in England, she would. Katherine wasn't sure she believed any of it, but it was a comfortable place to leave things. It was certainly less painful than an abrupt goodbye.

Katherine pressed the intercom on Claire Thompson's building. When Claire answered, Katherine hollered at her as if that was the only way her voice could reach the top of the building, "I'm here, Claire."

"Great, come on up. The door is unlocked for you." The buzzer rang to let Katherine enter where she then headed to the elevator. When Katherine came in, Claire was by herself, sitting with her foot propped up. Katherine leaned over her and gave her a hug. "Poor thing."

"I am a poor thing. You just missed my babysitter. She'll be back in the morning. You are her new best friend, giving her a break like this."

"What a good friend she is to you. How's your foot?" Katherine nodded towards the glass of water and small brown container of pills next to Claire's chair.

"The pain's better already. Just knowing I've got these standing by helps."

"I'm worried you will send me straight back to Chicago if I don't sell any books?"

Claire laughed. "Don't give them away because you can't work the credit card machine." The two women settled into a comfortable conversation that lasted for several more hours. By the time Katherine helped Claire to bed, and later turned out the light in the guest room that she would occupy for the next few days, she was looking forward to launching her career at the bookstore.

McCoy's opened at 9:30AM the next morning. Katherine was there by 9:00AM and managed to turn off the security system without setting off the alarm. She was still amused over Claire's parting admonition. "No reading on the job," which was a part of Katherine's fantasy of running a bookstore in the first place.

The first customer in the door was startled to see a stranger standing behind the counter. Katherine smiled at the woman who was about her own age. She had a list in her hand. "Good morning. How can I help you?"

""I need books for three daughters who have birthdays coming up." The women stuck out her hand. "I'm Patricia Mahan, and you are new."

"Katherine White, stand in for Claire who has had surgery on a foot; she has to keep it elevated for a few days. She has entrusted me to sell you books for your daughters. Are they addicted readers?"

"They are. It makes it easy to give them gifts. What would you recommend?" The woman followed Katherine over to the fiction section of the store.

"Are they local by any chance?" The woman nodded, yes. "They're welcome to exchange their book if I steer you wrong." A half hour later, following a pleasant exchange between book lovers, Katherine rang up Ian McEwan's, *Atonement*, Gail Godwin's, *Father Melancholy's Daughter,* and Rosamunde Pilcher's, *The Shell Seekers;* three novels that had stood the test of time, and were personal favorites of Katherine's. When Patricia turned to leave with her three wrapped books in the cloth carryall bag she's pulled from her purse, the next customers were coming in the door. They all greeted each other by name. Katherine wondered if everyone that came to buy books at McCoy's eventually became friends. As Patricia Mahan left the store she said, "Katherine, will take good care of you." The bell on the door tingled her departure.

It was 11:45AM when Andrew walked in the door surprising Katherine with a bag from the restaurant down the street. "I've brought the book lady some lunch." Katherine, who was enjoying herself, was surprised how quickly the morning had passed. She proudly announced, "I have sold eight books."

"Keep it up, and Claire will beg you to stay." They cleared off a small table by setting a few books on the counter. Andrew pulled from the bag two carryout containers filled with Caesar salad. He also set out two lidded paper cups holding ice tea. "I asked for sweet tea and they looked at me like I was nuts."

"You're amazing. I hadn't thought about how I would manage lunch." Just as they sat down to eat, more customers arrived. They all seemed to be on a mission, hastily picking up a book and out the door to their next errand.

Katherine, ringing up sales, watched as Andrew interacted with the customers, exchanging book recommendations and information on other nearby restaurants for lunch. They tried once more to sit down to eat.

Between mouthfuls, Katherine said, "You were having fun. You may have missed your calling, a born book salesman."

"There's something about people who love books, right?" They finished their salads before the bell rang on the door once more. Andrew cleared off their mess taking it to the back where a large waste can stood. Katherine was in the non-fiction section when he blew her a kiss behind the backs of the two men she was waiting on. He heard her say, "If you haven't read Doris Kearns Goodwin's, A *Team of Rivals,* you might consider it."

It was only four days, but a lot of standing. At her age, Katherine had a new appreciation for a job sitting behind a desk. The book sales proved Claire right in keeping the store open. Andrew continued to bring lunch, which was the only time they saw each other since each evening Katherine returned to Claire. At some point after their dinner, they huddled together to look at photograph albums and share stories about their mothers.

When it was time to return to Chicago, Katherine was concerned for Claire. "I don't know how you are going to go back to work next week." Katherine was assured that with the help of a few more friends, it would all work out.

She leaned down to hug Claire goodbye. ""I have loved being with you."

"I owe you big time. Thank you for all your help. The one thing we did not talk about was your friend, Andrew. I rather hoped he would lure you out here permanently."

"Not in the cards." Katherine left it at that. "I may have misread him, but here is a thought for you. Andrew was a natural at the store. A great reader, he pretended his mission was bringing my lunch, but I think, like me, he has a yen to own a bookstore. Why don't you ask him to come and give you a hand, as a favor, while you're curtailed? See what comes of it."

"Now there's something to think about." She lifted an imaginary glass, "Here's to Madeline and Evelyn."

"And, to us."

Katherine didn't have long to wait on the sidewalk out front of Claire's building before Andrew pulled up. He lowered the window, sounding like a cab driver, he yelled, "The airport or my bedroom, lady?"

"I'm afraid it's the airport. Got a plane to catch." She slid in and fastened her seat belt before kissing two of her fingers to reach over to brush Andrew's check with them.

Somehow she manufactured cheerful banter, though she knew neither one of them was happy. Katherine wanted to tell Andrew how much he meant to her, in spite of the contradiction of staying in Chicago.

As if Andrew had read her mind, he said, "There's a lot I want to say, but it won't be enough."

Katherine smiled. "I know, me too."

On the curb at the airport, Katherine put her arms around Andrew. "Thank you."

He kissed her check. "Be well, Katherine. I'll be in touch." She watched him get back in his car. Neither of them had been able to say what they would have liked, their shared sadness would have to suffice.

35

Robert stood blowing cigarette smoke out the bedroom window. He'd
given in to this old habit, telling himself that the stress of finding the
right place to live was temporary, and so was smoking. The lights were
on in the apartment across the narrow street where a young couple
lived, fought often, and made up in leisure; with an equal amount of
rumpus. It amused him, this Italian gusto. Robert was now listening for
the young man's return each afternoon. Calling up to the open window
for his wife, she would appear, shouting down, gesturing and
excited. This Italian exuberance was invigorating.

The close proximity of the apartments along his street formed an
enclave where the inhabitants had become a distinct congregation unto
themselves. At the end of the day, it was as if the residents duly noted
whether all were present and accounted for. In time, Robert hoped his
neighbors would account for him. He already loved the sights and
sounds of the tapered street, the smell of cooking, and the laughter and
vitality that lingered after all was dark and quiet. The combination of
these things served as a tonic Robert intended to imbibe daily.

Behind him, Maria lay asleep in his bed, her breathing mute and
comforting. Yesterday she had driven from Rome to put her seal of
approval on his new home. Thinking about her turned him from the
window, and back into bed, where he could touch her as he liked. She
made herself clear. "I will never leave Rome, but for you I will drive to
one of my favorite places in Italy, and take you to bed. You won't get a
better offer." For now, it was a perfect arrangement.

Robert began to nuzzle this undemanding woman of humor, with
her artistic temperament that routinely disregarded any rules. He
succeeded in awakening her. She smiled over at him. "For a reason

I cannot fathom, Maria, tell me why you want my company?" She answered with a long kiss. Irresistible, and on her terms, Robert could not ask for more, and did not need to.

The next morning Maria drove Robert to Rome where she dropped him at the airport. She stood on the curbside at Departures with her arms wrapped around his neck, pressing her generous body to him. He was delighted to star in what felt like a scene from a movie. Blowing kisses, she returned to her car calling out the window as she pulled away. "*Ciao, Arriverderci,* Come back."

Robert remained where he stood, reluctant to go into the terminal. It was not only Maria that he would miss, but this city where he now had a few friends. He was making progress with the language, understanding and being understood, which added to his sense of belonging. He loved the food, and, of all things, the places that compelled him to pray. Lucca was the answer to this new life; and when he returned, he would settle in for good.

❀

Robert turned the key in the lock of his front door in Kenilworth. He could smell the lake on the breeze that stirred the trees in the parkway. This familiar aroma, the magnitude of what he'd set in motion, on the heels of a long flight, and little sleep, rendered him as emotionally spent as he could remember. When Davis jumped into his arms, his caretakers having delivered him to the house for this homecoming, Robert slid to the floor, dog in his arms, and let him lick his face. Tears of joy in seeing the animal again welled in his eyes. He sat rubbing his ears, pouring into the dog his genuine happiness at their reunion. The young family that had been dog-sitting had not usurped the dog's heart after all. In a few minutes Robert disentangled himself, picked up his suitcase, and headed upstairs. Everything was immaculate. Baird and

Warner, the real estate company, had staged the house, after removing all photographs and memorabilia that made a house a home. He could never understand why this was required, but he had given his permission to do whatever they felt necessary to sell the house. One month after the listing, a couple with a young family made an offer that required little dickering. Robert was happy to lower the price rather than bother with paint and carpeting.

Today was Sunday, June 30th, and he would close on the house tomorrow. His plan all formulated, he wanted to arrive at the office ahead of Katherine. This would honor the date they'd agreed upon. The house closing was scheduled for the afternoon. What he wanted now was to get into his bed, but first, he found a leash to walk an eager Davis up Sheridan Road.

They reached Kenilworth Avenue, and turned left walking towards Holy Comforter Episcopal Church. He wanted to visit his parents buried in the columbarium. Walking briskly, Robert wondered if there was a prize for a person like himself when having a late mid-life crisis of gigantic proportion. If so, he should consider filling out an application. He'd stack up the magnitude of his decisions against anyone.

The dog pulled him forward, happy to retrace the steps he'd been making since a puppy. Robert could see himself as the boy he once was, walking other dogs in this same direction. He remembered himself as a teenager, who carefully drove the New Trier High School Drivers Education car down the Kenilworth streets that surrounded the high school. Now here he was as the grown man who'd sold his home on Raleigh Road, not far from where he'd been raised. He couldn't see that his six-month absence had made any discernible impact on the village. The Kenilworth of yesterday, today and tomorrow, for all intent and purposes, seemed the same.

Sitting on the bench in the columbarium garden, the dog at his feet, he began the inner conversation he wanted to have with his father. "I've sold Davis Publishing, Dad. I'm sorry to disappoint you like this.

I want you and Mom to know how grateful I am for raising me in this beautiful suburb, for the protection this place gave me from the larger world while I grew up. I am grateful for everything including Davis Publishing. It has provided an enviable lifestyle."

When Robert added his million dollar home sale, a sizable gain on his investment, to the sale of the company, moving to Italy was easily done. "I'll be back, I promise."

When he died, the plan was to join his parents here in this garden where their urns were interred. They would face eternity together, from this Kenilworth zip code.

Robert rose from the bench and wept in front of his parent's niche, something he had not been able to do at the time of their deaths. He backed away, leaving the church garden with the heart of a boy who was leaving home for the first time. Retracing his steps in a heightened state of awareness, he tried to notice everything about the houses, where once he'd known the names of all that occupied them. Every yard and porch he passed added weight to his steps. It felt like each of the houses he passed were calling him on the carpet. "Explain yourself, young man! Why are you leaving home?"

A few doors from his home, the two young boys who had been caring for Davis called out to the dog who tore the leash from Robert's hand to rush to meet them. He wiggled, licked, and was happy to see them. Robert was stunned with the identical greeting the two boys received. He watched them throw a ball that laid in the grass, which the dog went to fetch, the leash bouncing along behind him. Perhaps it wasn't the best idea to take the dog from these boys, and sentence Davis to a life in an apartment. The people who hand out the prize for best late mid-life crisis would surely want it back, if a dog was the deal breaker on this whole mad scheme.

❄

No one questioned any of Katherine's efforts while she prepared for Robert's return. She cleared the last of her things from his office on Saturday morning. In moving back to her own office it seemed to have shrunk in size, making her sorry to abdicate Robert's office after all. The big question was whether she was going to have any office at all when the sale was finalized?

Robert probably would not notice, but Katherine was sure the office clearers wouldn't do a proper job to suit her so she took an extra hour to clean herself. She removed books from shelves and wiped them off, and then concentrated on the accumulated dust that clung to Robert's memorabilia. By the time she finished, she felt all was ready.

On Monday morning Robert was sitting at his desk when she appeared at his office door. Her relief to find him there on the appointed date was evident as she opened her arms wide to greet him. "I must insist you speak English, *Signore,* my Italian is limited." They met by his desk, and Robert held her tight.

"I kept my bargain, but only for you." They sat down in the two chairs in front of the desk.

"You came home because you had no choice."

Robert got up and closed his door. "I'm going to say hello to everyone when we're done here. It will take the rest of the morning."

"Will you tell them?" Katherine dreaded this moment when the sale of the publishing firm would become common knowledge. She knew the staff would join her in worrying about what the future held for everyone at Davis Publishing.

"I will meet with the editorial staff at 9:00AM in the conference room. Best to tell them all together. I'm concerned the news will be evident when they return to their offices so I'll speak with everyone else right afterward. I'd like you to sit in on both meetings"

"The next few hours aren't going to be easy."

When it was all over, Robert looked completely drained. He'd been succinct when he explained the business side of the sale, but surprised everyone when he told them about the emotional state he'd been in when he left for Italy. Though this was serious news, which shocked everyone, they all noticed the miraculous change in Robert.

One of the senior editors said to Katherine, "I've never seem him as effusive, energized, and in no apparent hurry to end the meeting. He stayed as long as people had questions."

A secretary told Katherine, "He is usually restrained. I've never known Robert to greet everyone as he did. He didn't bother to hide his affection or gratitude for all of us carrying on while he was away."

Katherine marveled at how reassuring Robert sounded when he answered the question that was paramount on the employees' minds. "I have already asked that each of you be allowed to retain your jobs if that's what you'd like. There are no guarantees, but I have their assurance that they will assess their needs and speak with each of you. In the meantime, I ask that you continue with your duties. You will have six months to pursue other options, or settle with the new owners the details of retaining your positions. If you can see your way to stay through December, each of you will have a bonus check commensurate with your salary. Do not hesitate to take time from your job to follow through on interviews or related job search necessities. I know you won't take advantage of this courtesy."

Robert was a few minutes late to the closing that afternoon. If he could manage the next hour, he would have survived the day that was changing his life, and the lives of many others. Sitting with the new owners, and the realtors involved, papers were signed, keys given over to the new owners. He would pay them rent for the month of July, and vacate the premises August 1. Tomorrow morning, he would book his return flight to Rome.

36

While Robert worked at home, Katherine continued in her capacity as stand in boss. She spent a great deal of her time answering phone calls from authors who'd been notified of the sale who were checking on their contractual arrangements. The reputation of the buyers seemed to reassure everyone. When Jessica Lovejoy called, she jumped right in. "You'll remain my editor, right?"

"How are you Jessica? How's your tennis?" Katherine could tease her now about her work habits. "You know, if you would give up tennis, you could write a book in half the time."

Jessica ignored the comment. "The sale isn't going to affect the release date for the new book is it?" Some things would never change about this self-absorbed woman. Katherine noted that she made no inquiry about Robert, or the staff of Davis Publishing. Only as an after thought did she say, "I can understand wanting to leave Chicago, terrible weather, but Italy?"

Katherine would have the answer to Jessica's questions after Labor Day. She hoped she was still her editor. Until then she was trying to hide her apprehension about the future. Everybody was worried about the same thing.

"If you keep your job, Katherine, will I be able to keep mine?" She was having lunch with Elizabeth.

"I told them I needed you. But, you don't need me to plead your case." She looked across the table at Elizabeth's worried face. "Now that I think about it, they might keep you, and let me go."

"You're trying to make me feel better." She smiled at Katherine. "Keep it up." They laughed.

"Are you looking into anything else?" Katherine was concerned that Elizabeth might rush into a marriage with her young man if she lost her job. He'd proposed, insisting on her answer soon.

"Are you going to say yes to your Irishman?"

"Yes, if I have a job, not yet, if I don't. I don't want to start a marriage living in either of our small places living cheek to jowl. We've each got some money saved. We could find something in the Lincoln Square area on two salaries."

"Keep praying, Elizabeth, that's what I'm doing. I'm hoping that having looked after things while Robert's been gone will add to my value. Six months ought to count for something." They each had their own thoughts when they started on the salads that were set before them. Neither of them talked. Finally Katherine said, "Early September can't come soon enough for all of us." She took a few more bites of her food. "I know your interview went well, you will be a great asset to them."

"They were complimentary when it was over. They seemed to appreciate the work experience I've received under your tutelage. I resisted saying that I could show them a before and after photograph of the improved version they'd be getting."

"You mean the college graduate that looked like she was late to class?"

"It was that bad?"

"I'm proud of you."

"I'm proud of me too. Thank you."

❀

Katherine helped Robert where she could, while he packed and made arrangements to ship the household goods and furniture he was keeping. On this Saturday morning she drove out to spend the day and lend a hand. They were sitting on the back patio taking a break. "The expense must be astronomical, Robert."

"The family that bought the house made an offer on some of the things I can't take like this patio furniture. Since there are no family members to pass the antiques onto, I decided that the sentimental value outweighs the cost. I've made that mistake several times before. The family treasures are destined for an Italian revival."

"How so?"

When I'm gone, some high-spirited Italian will acquire my things, and a new family will tell stories around the dining room table. I have no doubt that my English pine table will wind up with cigarette burns, and wine glass rings. I shudder to think of it."

Later, they began to pack the china that was in the kitchen cabinets. "You know you won't be able to resist acquiring pieces of Italian pottery."

"In the mean time, I'll go on using the family china and silver."

"What about your art work?"

"There is adequate wall space in the Lucca apartment to accommodate what I have. My pieces aren't as interesting as a painting a new friend has given me as a house-warming gift. I liked it the first day I saw it. It's propped up against a wall in my bedroom."

Katherine knew that Robert's apartment was bare of everything except a bed, and something to sit on, and eat off of. There was no doubt in her mind that the space would benefit from his good taste, and the possessions of several generations of his family who had lived on the North Shore of Chicago, influenced by their times and economic progress.

The final few days, Katherine accompanied Robert to a series of recognition and farewell parties. The Chicago publishing community wined and dined him. His parents were remembered in their farewell speeches. Friends and colleagues toasted the future of Davis Publishing, soon to be known as Review Press. The office party was the only occasion that proved uncomfortable, though the staff made a gallant attempt to wish Robert well. With their jobs in limbo, they were not
at their best. No one appeared happier when the event was over than Robert.

At the end of July, the housekeeping details of the move were settled. Literally, the floors had been swept and the oven cleaned. Robert walked through the empty rooms, checking one last time in closets and opening kitchen cabinet doors. With his Oriental rugs rolled, and on their way to Lucca, his footsteps on the wooden floors echoed in the high ceiling rooms. He told Katherine, "The young family that bought the house must be willing to eat hot dogs and baked bean for years to come to pay the taxes."

"Willing to sacrifice to get their kids into the school system."

"My life might have been different if I'd been willing to move from this large house when I first divorced. Kenilworth has always been a family centered village, of which I have none."

"I can't blame you though, this house is an architectural gem, in spite of the old tile in the bathrooms, and the outdated kitchen,"

"I agreed to a final sale price that took those things into consideration."

"You know what the realtors say, "Location, location, location."

"The worst part of this whole thing has been deciding to leave Davis with the two boys down the street. It was awful. I handed the leash to the older boy and didn't dare lean down to touch him again. I turned and made a hasty retreat towards home. When I glanced back, Davis was watching me, but his tail wasn't wagging. It was the final blow to a heart-wrenching scene. I'm just thankful he didn't understand that this parting is different." Robert couldn't speak of the dog's sad eyes that gave evidence to the contrary.

"You know Kermit the frog says, 'It isn't easy being green.'"

Robert answered, "It certainly is not!"

In the taxi to the airport, he looked out the window and saw an airplane's contrail in the bright sunlit sky that looked like a direction arrow. If not an arrow, perhaps it was like Jacob's ladder where any moment he could expect to see angels ascending and descending. The direction arrow was pointed to Rome, his next stop. If a ladder, he was on the second rung. By the time he reached Lucca, he would be in Shangri-La.

✿

Waiting for the buyers to finalize their plans had given Katherine time to think about what retirement might look like, if there was no job offer. Top of her list was to stop pushing her own writing off to the side. She wanted to stay in Chicago, but her short time in Italy confirmed her desire to do more traveling. She could count on a free guest room in Italy. The most important discovery while waiting, was clarifying why she wanted to go on working.

Louisa had been the one who kept pressing the question. "Does it really matter if they don't hire you?"

Katherine and Louisa were having lunch. This time when the question was asked, Katherine had an answer. "Yes, it matters. It has to do with your grandparents, and Robert's parents too. They would all be pleased if I could stay and help the new owners get off to a good start. It would constitute as payback to all four of them."

Louisa nodded she understood. "They would be surprised, that's for sure, at what's taken place."

"You've heard me say before, I feel I wound up with the best of each of my parents, my father's energy, and extroverted tendencies, and my mother's capacity for introspection. These attributes have more than equipped me for the years I've lived beyond them. I can't ever thank them enough, really."

"Robert's parents were obviously amazing people."

"I hope the new owners will continue to build on the firms fine reputation."

✿

A few days later, Katherine stood facing east looking out her bedroom window. The sun was rising imperceptibly out of the lake from its blue and lavender spectrum. She offered up her prayers of thanksgiving for the new day and for the future.

The anticipated decisions from Review Press had been announced the day before. Elizabeth burst through Katherine's office door. "I got the job! They offered me a raise and additional responsibilities."

"I'm pleased for you." Katherine came around her desk and shook Elizabeth's hand before giving her a bear hug. "Does this mean you'll soon be living in Lincoln Square?"

"I think it does." Elizabeth drew back from her. "Have you heard from them? Can you tell me anything?"

"I signed a contract at the end of the day yesterday. I'll be part of a senior management team for the next two years. We'll see to the day to day operations for the owners' newest publishing acquisition." Katherine was grinning.

"What about everyone else?"

"Those who work through the end of the year will have their bonus check to ease the pain of change."

Elizabeth headed for the door. "I've got to call the gorgeous man and tell him the good news."

"I knew Review Press recognized a good thing when they saw it."

"It was my haircut and color that did it." Grinning back at Katherine, Elizabeth closed the door behind her.

When Louisa heard the news she insisted on driving downtown to take Katherine to dinner to celebrate. Raising a glass of wine, she said, "You landed on your feet again, Mom. Quite a dismount when you stop to think about it."

"Not bad for an editor with prospects." Katherine reached over and took Louisa's hand. "Last week I saw a green, rectangular sign on the roadside that said, *Cook County*. I got to thinking, would it be helpful if people were given a series of life signs on their personal journey?"

Louisa laughed. You mean, *Heads Up: You're Beginning A New Phase Of Your Life, or You're Headed For Trouble, Slow Down?"*

"You can't pass your driver's test if you don't know what the color and shape of the road signs mean."

"You think people would welcome a sign that tells them how many miles they had left before reaching their final destination?"

"You're probably right there." Katherine laughed.

Over their poached salmon salads, Katherine asked, "Do you remember when we talked about Beatrice's *best guess* spelling as a child? I never dreamed it would have such broad implications."

Louisa pulled the white napkin back that covered the bread selection. After taking a hard crust roll, she offered Katherine a peek, who declined a choice. "What do you mean, Mom?"

"I made a *best guess* when I moved to Chicago. Robert's departure for Italy, has been his *best guess.* Together, Andrew and I have made *a best guess.* You are in the midst of making yours. Beatrice has come back to New York in making hers. Each of us have been willing to risk a *best guess,* and in that risk, come to find out, are the possibilities of life."

"I like the Buddhist proverb that says, *If you are facing in the right direction, all you have to do is keep on walking."*

Katherine exclaimed, "Exactly, I love it. I took a risk and facing East has been the right direction for me."

"It certainly seems that way. I'm glad for you."

"Since moving back to Chicago, the memories of my childhood, your grandparents, the ETHS crowd that remains connected, have all felt like interchangeable lenses stored in a camera bag." Katherine offered her wine glass so Louisa could top it off.

"I've adopted the Ken Burns effect when it comes to thinking about the past."

"I didn't know you knew who Ken Burns was."

"I didn't, but when you watch a documentary, his name comes up.

I have been able to focus on a distant experience, gradually drawing closer to the memory, remembering the details, before I run out of time and have to let the memory fade away until another time. When I pan across the years, the Burns effect allows me to see that nothing in my life has been wasted. Both the good and the bad have been necessary in becoming who I am."

"Here's an idea, Mom. Why not call your memoir, The Ken Burns Effect."

"I just might do that."

Still at her bedroom window, the sunrise Katherine was watching promised a beautiful fall day. A glance at the clock said it was time to pull away from the view, or be late to the office. From her clothes closet, she chose carefully what she would wear; mindful of the dinner invitation she'd accepted from David Middleton after work. There was plenty of news to tell him this time. In perfect copperplate script, a post card from him was propped up on the dresser. It touched her every time she reread the message. He had written a James Joyce line from Ulysses. "Still to us at twilight comes love's old sweet song."

Acknowledgements

A book takes a long time to research and write. For the second time, my husband, Bob, covered for me so I could keep my head down and keep going. He answered telephones, took messages, paid for take out food for dinner when needed. He left me alone to write. I am grateful to him for these kindnesses. He also played an important new role in the writing of *Facing East*. Because he commuted to Leo Burnett Advertising in Chicago throughout his career, it placed him in a unique position to point out errors. "Don't you mean Outer Drive here? You wrote Lake Shore Drive." Throw in commas, discussions about what I thought I was saying, but hadn't, and you have a great right hand man. I thank him for this assistance. I'm grateful to Barbara Clare, who designed both my novel covers. She is a creative, gifted, designer. I hope people will judge my books by their covers.

I love the research, the writing, even the endless process of rewriting. I knew I'd finished *Facing East* when in editing I began to write again what I'd already taken out. A writer lives in two worlds, the one they are creating, and the one where they forget appointments and people's birthdays. It can't be helped. I already miss Katherine's world, especially the little girl and her parents that showed up on these pages. It allowed Stepheny, Madeline and Norman to be together again. (*Now my consolation is in the stardust of a song.*)

269

About the Author

Stepheny was born in Chicago, Illinois and raised in Evanston. She graduated from Evanston Township High School and the University of Kentucky. She lives in North Carolina with her husband where she writes and gardens. Her first novel, *Greening of a Heart* is set in the Cotswold village of Burford. Visit her at stephenyhoughtlin.com She will be waiting by the garden gate for you.